PRAISE

TAKING A SHOT

"[Jaci Burton] delivers the passionate, inventive, sexually explicit love scenes that fans expect . . . However, *Taking a Shot* isn't just about hot sex. Burton offers plenty of emotion and conflict in a memorable relationship-driven story."   —*USA Today*

"Ms. Burton has a way of writing intense scenes that are both sensual and raw . . . Plenty of romance, sexy men, hot steamy loving, and humor."   —*Smexy Books Romance Reviews*

"For this third Play-by-Play entry, there's no shortage of volatile, steamy sex, but the story development is the key to this thoughtful tale. While the heroine figures her life out, the reader will enjoy the smokin'-hot sex that draws the protagonists together—over and over again."   —*RT Book Reviews*

"Jenna and Ty's story far surpassed my expectations. This one is hot enough to melt the ice off the hockey rink on which its hero plays."   —*Romance Novel News*

"A very spicy read. Jenna and Ty had great chemistry."
    —*Book Binge*

continued . . . CALGARY PUBLIC LIBRARY

OCT   2012

CHANGING THE GAME

"This book is wonderful from beginning to end, even for those who are not baseball fans."
—*RT Book Reviews*

"*Changing the Game* is an extraordinary novel—a definite home run!"
—*Joyfully Reviewed*

"A strong plot, complex characters, sexy athletes, and nonstop passion make this book a must-read."
—*Fresh Fiction*

THE PERFECT PLAY

"The characters are incredible. They are human and complex and real and perfect."
—*Night Owl Reviews*

"Holy smokes! I am pretty sure I saw steam rising from every page."
—*Fresh Fiction*

"This book delivers."
—*Dear Author*

"A beautiful romance that is smooth as silk . . . One hell of a good time, a romance to remember . . . leaves us begging for more."
—*Joyfully Reviewed*

"Hot, hot, hot! . . . Romance at its best! Highly recommended! Very steamy."
—*Coffee Table Reviews*

"The romance sparkles as the sex sizzles."
—*RT Book Reviews*

CALGARY PUBLIC LIBRARY

OCT   2012

FURTHER PRAISE FOR THE WORK OF

JACI BURTON

"Realistic dialogue, spicy bedroom scenes, and a spitfire heroine make this one to pick up and savor." —*Publishers Weekly*

"Jaci Burton delivers."
—Cherry Adair, *New York Times* bestselling author

"Lively and funny . . . intense and loving." —*The Road to Romance*

"An invitation to every woman's wildest fantasies."
—*Romance Junkies*

"As always, Jaci Burton delivers a hot read." —*Fresh Fiction*

"Burton is a master at sexual tension!" —*RT Book Reviews*

Titles by Jaci Burton

RIDING WILD
RIDING TEMPTATION
RIDING ON INSTINCT
RIDING THE NIGHT

WILD, WICKED, & WANTON
BOUND, BRANDED, & BRAZEN

THE PERFECT PLAY
CHANGING THE GAME
TAKING A SHOT
PLAYING TO WIN

Anthologies

UNLACED
(with Jasmine Haynes, Joey W. Hill, and Denise Rossetti)

EXCLUSIVE
(with Eden Bradley and Lisa Renee Jones)

LACED WITH DESIRE
(with Jasmine Haynes, Joey W. Hill, and Denise Rossetti)

NAUTI AND WILD
(with Lora Leigh)

PLAYING
to
WIN

JACI BURTON

HEAT | NEW YORK

THE BERKLEY PUBLISHING GROUP
Published by the Penguin Group
Penguin Group (USA) Inc.
375 Hudson Street, New York, New York 10014, USA
Penguin Group (Canada), 90 Eglinton Avenue East, Suite 700, Toronto, Ontario M4P 2Y3, Canada
(a division of Pearson Penguin Canada Inc.) • Penguin Books Ltd., 80 Strand, London WC2R 0RL,
England • Penguin Group Ireland, 25 St. Stephen's Green, Dublin 2, Ireland (a division of Penguin
Books Ltd.) • Penguin Group (Australia), 250 Camberwell Road, Camberwell, Victoria 3124, Australia
(a division of Pearson Australia Group Pty. Ltd.) • Penguin Books India Pvt. Ltd., 11 Community
Centre, Panchsheel Park, New Delhi—110 017, India • Penguin Group (NZ), 67 Apollo Drive,
Rosedale, Auckland 0632, New Zealand (a division of Pearson New Zealand Ltd.) • Penguin Books
(South Africa) (Pty.) Ltd., 24 Sturdee Avenue, Rosebank, Johannesburg 2196, South Africa

Penguin Books Ltd., Registered Offices: 80 Strand, London WC2R 0RL, England

This book is an original publication of The Berkley Publishing Group.

This is a work of fiction. Names, characters, places, and incidents either are the product of the author's
imagination or are used fictitiously, and any resemblance to actual persons, living or dead, business
establishments, events, or locales is entirely coincidental. The publisher does not have any control over
and does not assume any responsibility for author or third-party websites or their content.

Copyright © 2012 by Jaci Burton.
Excerpt from *Thrown by a Curve* copyright © 2012 by Jaci Burton.
Cover photograph by Claudio Marinesco.
Cover art direction and design by Rita Frangie.
Text design by Kristin del Rosario.

All rights reserved.
No part of this book may be reproduced, scanned, or distributed in any printed or
electronic form without permission. Please do not participate in or encourage piracy of
copyrighted materials in violation of the author's rights. Purchase only authorized editions.
HEAT and the HEAT design are trademarks of Penguin Group (USA) Inc.

PUBLISHING HISTORY
Heat trade paperback edition / September 2012

Library of Congress Cataloging-in-Publication Data

Burton, Jaci.
Playing to win / Jaci Burton.—Heat trade paperback ed.
p.   cm.
ISBN 978-0-425-24783-9
1. Man-woman relationships—Fiction.   I. Title.
PS3602.U776P56   2012
813'.6—dc23
2012011830

PRINTED IN THE UNITED STATES OF AMERICA

10 9 8 7 6 5 4 3 2 1

To Charlie.

When it's fun and when it's not so fun,
I know I can always reach for you and you'll be there.

Love you.

ACKNOWLEDGMENTS

Thanks to Maya Banks, for the lengthy phone calls that always inspire me, make me laugh, and renew me. And to Shannon Stacey, for always being there, for always being my friend.

ONE

COLE RILEY HAD BUILT HIS REPUTATION ON BEING tough, especially on the football field. He didn't yield, and when he had the ball in his hands, there was only one thing on his mind— the end zone. He was hardheaded and single-minded, and he liked to win.

Same thing with women—once he had a target in mind, he went for her until he scored.

So even though tonight's team party was a target-rich environ-ment, and more than a handful of the sexy women who'd come tonight were giving him the once-over, he hadn't set his mind on anyone during the few hours he'd been here.

Which was unusual for him. He liked the ladies. The ladies liked him. No ego on his part; he just enjoyed women, and he loved being around them. They were sweet, fun to be with, smelled great, and made him feel good. There was nothing bad about that. In return, he showed them a good time, spent money on them, and never lied to them or tried to be anything other than who he was.

He'd learned a long time ago that women liked honest men. His mother would slap him sideways if he ever lied to a woman. He might be a little wild and reckless, but he wasn't dishonest. He never promised a woman anything he wasn't willing to deliver.

Which meant steering clear of women looking to hook a boyfriend, a husband, or any kind of commitment. He gravitated toward the party girls, like the hot redhead and the statuesque brunette who'd been hovering near his radar all night. Those were the women who wanted to have the same kind of no-strings-attached fun he did. It was only a matter of time before he went in for the kill. After all, the hunt was part of the fun. All the circling, eyeing, and flirting was a game. He did love the game—and he played the game to win.

Trying to figure out a woman's angle was the fun part. They each had an angle, an ulterior motive. Some wanted nothing more than an autograph or a picture they could post on some social media site so they could show their friends they'd partied with football player Cole Riley. Others wanted to hook up for the night, hoping to share his bed so they'd have more permanent memories. If they wanted a good time, he was more than willing to show them one.

The redhead and the brunette were definitely good-time girls. He could tell by the body language and the looks they gave him. They wanted a lot more than an autograph or a picture.

Easy score, right?

So why did his focus keep drifting to the cool blonde sitting by herself at a table in the corner? She wasn't his type at all. She wasn't wearing a skintight dress that showed ample amounts of tits and ass. She wore a simple, black short-sleeved dress that fell to her knees. Though she did have killer legs—legs he'd like to see a lot more of. She just wasn't showing off her assets.

She was beautiful, sure, with a face that would stop traffic. And the way she was put together screamed money or high society. Her hair was twisted up behind her head, she wore a pearl necklace that didn't look cheap or fake, and he'd been with enough women to know that little designer purse sitting on the table in front of her cost a lot of money.

Maybe she was related to the team owner. But he hadn't seen anyone come within ten feet of the table in the past two hours. She was no wallflower, but she wasn't giving off vibes that said, *Come talk to me.*

Wasn't his problem. He didn't know her and he intended to have fun tonight. Team parties were always a blast, and even better, this one was media free. He could down a few drinks, chill with the ladies, and have a good time.

There were plenty of women here to have the kind of fun he was looking for, and the blonde wasn't the right type. He could tell from the rigid set of her shoulders and the stick-up-her-ass way she sat that she wasn't a partier. She surveyed the room and gave off definite "keep the fuck away from me" signals, which was likely why no one approached her.

Still, his gaze kept gravitating back to her. He hated seeing anyone sitting alone. He went up to the bar and nudged Grant Cassidy, the Traders quarterback.

Grant turned, then nodded. "Hey, Riley. What's up?"

"Do you have any idea who that blonde is sitting by herself over in the corner?"

Grant followed the motion of Cole's head, then frowned. "No. Who is she?"

"No idea. I figured you know everyone on the team. Is she related to the owner?"

Grant shook his head. "Ted Miller's daughter is a brunette. And she isn't here tonight. I have no idea who the blonde is. She looks mean."

Cole laughed. "That's what I thought, too."

He should ignore her and concentrate on the two other women. But for some reason she kept grabbing his attention and wouldn't let go.

Maybe it was because she kept staring at him. Not in the way other women looked at him—the take-me-home-with-you-tonight plea. Her gaze was cool and assessing. An occasional brief glance and then she'd look away, like she wasn't at all interested in him.

Oh, she was interested all right. They all were.

So maybe she was a game player after all, and this was a new kind of game.

He pushed off the bar and headed her way. She could throw off all the stay-away signals she wanted, but he was curious now. Someone that beautiful was alone for a reason.

He stopped at her table and her gaze lifted, slowly assessing him. She didn't smile, but she didn't frown, either.

"You here alone?" he asked.

"As you can see, I am."

Southern accent. It fit her. She was all peaches-and-cream complexion, full lips, and the prettiest eyes—the color of his favorite whiskey.

He slid his hand out. "I'm Cole Riley, wide receiver with the Traders."

She slipped her hand in his and finally gave him a smile—the kind of smile that made a man glad to be a man.

"Hello, Cole. I'm Savannah Brooks. Won't you sit down?"

Bingo.

LORD HAVE MERCY, BUT COLE RILEY'S PHOTOS AND videos did not do the man justice.

In person he made a woman go weak in the knees. Savannah was glad she was sitting down, because now she understood the mystique she'd read about in the tabloids and all the articles about him as a lady-killer.

Sure, she'd seen all the photos, and he was certainly pretty. Great body, beautiful dark hair. She could see how some women might be attracted to him, but she hadn't understood why he was such a hot commodity.

But in person? Oh, yes, definitely. He had charisma, a way of looking at a woman that would make her drop her panties faster than he could flash those unusual eyes in her direction.

She'd felt the heart palpitations when he slid his very large hand in hers and graced her with one look of his drop-dead—what color were his eyes anyway? They were gray, tinged with blue, like a sky coloring up for a storm.

Amazing. When he looked at her it was as if everyone else in the room fell away and she was the only woman on earth. Which she knew wasn't true, because she'd studied him all night long, and there were at least twenty women focused on him as if they were a starving pack of wolves and he was meat.

He wasn't meaty at all. He was perfect and absolutely delicious. About six foot one and 215 pounds of sex on a stick would be her guess.

If she were out scouting for a man—which she wasn't—she'd pick him out of a crowd. With his inky black hair and gorgeous, well-toned and muscular body, he stood out, even if he did wear his hair a little long and shaggy. There was a certain presence to him. Arrogance, maybe. She'd read his file, and so she was surprised when she hadn't found him commanding the room or involved in a brawl or wrapped around two or three women in a dark corner.

Maybe the media had blown his off-the-field antics out of proportion. Maybe his reputation was more hype than anything.

But she'd reserve judgment until she got to know him better.

"So, Savannah Brooks. Why are you sitting here all alone?"

"I'm observing."

He cocked a brow, his defenses obviously up, as he leaned forward on the edge of the chair like he was ready to take flight. "You're not a reporter, are you?"

She smiled at him. "No. I'm not a reporter."

He relaxed and leaned back against the chair, stretching his long legs out in front of him. "Okay, then."

"I take it you don't like reporters."

"Nope."

"And why is that?"

"They lie."

"About you."

"All the damn time."

"What kind of lies have they told about you?"

"I don't want to talk about me. Let's talk about you. You have a beautiful Southern accent, Savannah. Where are you from?"

Not at all what she'd read about him. That he was an egomaniac, that every conversation centered on him, his stats, his prowess in the bedroom, that he hit on women as a second career, pressuring them to go home with him.

Maybe the media did have it wrong.

"I'm originally from Atlanta."

"But you don't live there now."

"No."

He smiled when she didn't offer any more information. He had an amazing, off-kilter smile that made her stomach flutter. She had to stop being such a girl about him. He might be flirting but she was here on business.

"Do you want me to guess?" he asked.

"Not at all. I live in St. Louis right now."

"Right now. Are you moving soon?"

"No. My job's keeping me here for the moment."

"A lady of mystery. I like that. But this hardly seems the city for a Georgia peach like you."

"Really. And what kind of city should I be living in?"

"You seem perfectly bred for the south, obviously. All Southern-refined, laid-back beauty. Not here."

He was certainly a smooth talker. "St. Louis is charming."

"Agreed. It definitely has its charms. Does your job move you around a lot?"

He listened. A good quality. "It does."

"And what do you do for a living, Savannah?"

"I'm a consultant."

"Broad concept. What kind of consultant?"

"An image consultant."

He frowned. "What does an image consultant do?"

"I assist clients who need help either boosting their image or changing it."

"That must be an interesting job."

"I love my work. To have a positive impact on people's lives is very rewarding."

He grinned. "Good for you."

"And what about your job, Cole?"

"I've played football since I was a kid. To be able to do this for a living is a dream come true. I'm very grateful."

He was poised, confident, and polite. Why didn't he come across like this in interviews? Why was he portrayed in such a negative light? There was more to Cole Riley than what she'd read about in his file.

"Would you like a drink, Savannah?"

"No, I'm fine with the sparkling water, thank you."

"Okay. You still haven't told me what you're doing at this shindig."

"I'm meeting a new client."

"You work in sports?"

"I work in all fields, but lately I've been concentrating a lot on sports figures."

He cocked his head to the side and studied her. "Yeah? About to redo someone's image?"

"As a matter of fact, I am."

"Huh. I wonder who screwed up and needs a makeover." He looked around the room, studying all the players in attendance. "Couldn't be our star quarterback. Cassidy eats, drinks, and pisses charm."

She resisted the laugh. It wouldn't be appropriate.

He looked at her, then around again, zeroing in on a group of players clustered in the middle of the room. "It's Moose Clements, isn't it? That guy couldn't give a decent interview if you gave him a personality implant. Or maybe Jim Highland, the Traders' defensive end. You want to talk attitude issues? That guy has serious problems. He's your new client, isn't he?"

She stood, smoothed out her dress. "Unfortunately, it's time for me to go. It was very nice meeting you, Cole."

"You're leaving?"

"I'm afraid so."

He grabbed her hand. "Wait."

She paused.

"I want to see you again."

"Oh, you will." She smiled as she walked out of the room. This was going to be very interesting.

COLE WATCHED SAVANNAH WALK AWAY, STRUCK BY her elegant beauty.

He was wrong. Definitely no stick up her ass. She walked with a slight sway to her hips—nothing obvious or attention grabbing about her, but she was all woman.

And dammit, he'd just stood there like a tongue-tied teenager and let her get away.

He should have gotten her number, or asked her out. Instead, he'd acted brain-dead.

That wasn't his style. Probably because he never had to go after a woman. They always came to him.

He moved to go after her, but a hand on his arm stopped him. He turned to see his agent, Elizabeth Darnell, looking up at him.

He frowned. "Liz. What are you doing here?"

"We need to talk, remember?"

He frowned, recalling somewhere in the back of his mind he'd agreed to have a quick sit-down with her tonight. But right now his attention was on the door, where Savannah had disappeared. "Not now."

"Definitely now. Did you forget the meeting we agreed to?"

He more than likely ignored Liz's edict that they had some important business to talk about tonight. Since he'd signed with her a few months ago, there'd been a lot of orders. He didn't like being given orders.

He tried for one of his patient, charming smiles. "Come on, Liz. We're at a party."

She raised her gaze to his in a look of disbelief. "Really? You're going to try that smokin'-hot charm on me? I'm immune, you know." She flashed her engagement ring at him.

"I wasn't flirting with you, honest. Gavin would kick my ass."

"You're damn right, he would."

"I was just trying to get back to the party. There's this woman . . ."

Liz rolled her eyes. "You have plenty of time to party. And I'm sure about twenty women to choose from, if not more. I just need a few minutes of your time. And we had an agreement when I signed you," she said, giving him that steely-eyed gaze. "Remember?"

"Yeah, yeah. I remember."

"Good. Then let's go."

"We're leaving?"

"Just across the hall. There's someone we need to meet with. When we're finished you can get back to the party. And your women. And whatever it is that you want to do with them."

Hopefully it wouldn't take long. Maybe Savannah was still around somewhere and he could hook up with her again.

Elizabeth led him to a room across the hall. It was a small meeting room with rows of tables.

"Have a seat."

"I'd rather stand."

She gave him the look, the one that meant she was going to argue until she won. He was just as stubborn, but time was important right now, so he grabbed a chair, spun it around, and straddled it.

"What did I do now?"

"Tonight? Nothing so far. But I want to remind you about your attitude."

He rolled his eyes. "That's what you wanted to meet about tonight? We've already had this discussion."

"I know. And we're going to talk about it again. The hometown crowd likes a winner. They also like someone who isn't constantly in the tabloids for an overindulgence of partying, for treading on his fellow players like they're the shit beneath his Nikes, for accumulating more speeding tickets than the national debt, and for throwing the very expensive cameras of the paparazzi into a fountain. And if that wasn't bad enough, following it up with a punch to the guy's jaw."

"Hey, he shoved the fucking camera in my face. Not just close to my face, but *in* my face. What was I supposed to do—say cheese and smile for him?"

"Yes. That's exactly what you were supposed to do. Or turn around and walk away. You need to learn to control your temper and be taught how to behave in public. You need some lessons on how to interact with the media."

Cole snorted. "I think I know how to handle myself just fine."

Liz tapped her foot, though how she managed to stand upright on those five-inch heels was beyond him.

"And if you recall, when I agreed to sign you on as a client— mainly because no other agent wanted to be within five miles of you—and I managed to somehow get you signed with St. Louis, you agreed to do anything I asked of you."

He thought that meant the slightly painful salary cut he'd had to take. At least Liz was savvy enough to put performance bonuses in the contract. He'd show them he wasn't washed up. He was still an ass-kicker and this season would prove it. "I did what you asked, didn't I?"

"Oh, the salary cut was just the beginning, Cole. Your image is toast. You know it, I know it, and Coach Tallarino knows it. If the coach wasn't such a good friend of your cousin Mick—and if he didn't owe me a few dozen favors—I guarantee you wouldn't have this job."

Cole wasn't buying it. The Traders signed him because he had the talent and plenty of it. Agents liked to make threats to keep their players in line. He knew how this game was played. All he had to do was sit here and listen to Liz's spiel for a few minutes, then he'd be outta here.

"The clock is ticking. It's only a matter of time before no one will touch you, no matter how good you are on the field. You're a PR nightmare."

He stood and faced Liz, doing exactly what she said he wasn't capable of. He took a deep breath and tried to keep his temper under control. "I'm a damn good wide receiver."

"That might be true, but until you stop the nonsense off the field and prove to the coach, your team, the media, and the general public that you've grown up and your bad-boy days are over, it doesn't matter if you score ten touchdowns a game. Reputation is everything in football."

He blew out a sigh. Why couldn't his stats be enough? What difference did it make what he did during his off hours? So he liked to party a little. So what? His bad rep was the media's fault anyway. He was at the top of his game. After six years in the NFL, he'd damn well earned the right to relax and enjoy life.

But yeah. PR. He understood. And if he had to toe the line for a while until he got in the good graces of the fans and the coach, that's what he'd do.

"What do you want me to do?"

"I'm bringing in someone to help you."

He frowned. "Who?"

"Just hang on a second." She sent a text message, and a minute later the door opened.

He was shocked when Savannah walked in.

Relieved to see her, Cole grinned, glad he hadn't lost the opportunity to spend more time with her.

"Hey. I was wondering where you'd wandered off to," he said.

"You two know each other?" Liz asked.

"Yeah. We met earlier." Cole turned to Liz. "You know Savannah?"

Liz's lips lifted. "As a matter of fact, I do. And you're going to get to know her a lot better. Savannah is your new image consultant."

He pivoted and looked at Savannah, who gave him a serene smile.

The pieces fell into place. He'd been screwed by the pretty blonde. The game player had been played.

"*My* image consultant? What the fuck?"

TWO

COLE NARROWED HIS GAZE AT SAVANNAH. "YOU played me."

"I did not."

"You didn't tell me who you were."

"As a matter of fact, I told you exactly who I was and what I did for a living."

"That's bullshit. You told me you were there to observe. You didn't say you were there to watch *me*. Were you looking for me to make an ass of myself?"

"I was hoping you wouldn't. And you didn't. Until now."

"Well, this is fun," Liz said, stepping between Cole and Savannah. She turned to Cole. "Look, I have no idea what went on between the two of you, but the team has hired Savannah to work with you, so like it or not, she's yours."

Cole glared at Savannah. "I don't like it. She isn't mine, and I don't want her."

"Tough shit. She's the best in her field, and you'll do what she says."

Great. Someone else to tell him what to do. An image consultant? He didn't need anyone to change him. "And if I don't?"

"Then you'll have to answer to the team owner, and as I mentioned earlier, you're out of options."

He took a deep breath and let it out. He'd make this work. Peaches there seemed like a pussycat, and he could be pleasant if he wanted to be. He'd just wrap her around his finger and then go about his business, and still make the owner, his coach, and Liz happy.

It was a win-win for everyone. "Fine."

Liz smiled. "Good. I'm out of here. I've got wedding plans to finalize."

"I'm so excited for you, Elizabeth," Savannah said, turning her attention to Liz. "How are the wedding preparations going?"

"Everything's moving right along, thanks to my future sister-in-law, Tara, who's the best wedding planner ever. If it weren't for her and Gavin's sister, Jenna, I'd have slit my wrists by now."

Savannah laughed, and the sound shot right to Cole's dick. She had a throaty laugh, the kind you'd expect to hear in a smoky strip joint, not from Miss Image Makeover.

Savannah put her hand over Liz's. "I'm sure you'll be a beautiful bride."

"Thank you." Liz turned to Cole and gave him a glare. "You behave yourself. And please cooperate. This is the only chance you're going to get."

"I promise to be on my best behavior."

"Why does that worry me so much?" She rolled her eyes and walked out the door, leaving him alone with Savannah.

He turned to face her. "Did you enjoy that?"

She gave him a benign look. "Enjoy what?"

"Leading me on. Letting me think you were some stranger

alone at the party, when the whole time you'd been watching me and you knew who I was."

"I can't help what you thought, Cole. But you behaved like a gentleman. Not at all like the tabloids portray you."

"I told you the media lies."

"We'll see."

He'd wanted something different between them. His body wanted something more than what his mind wanted. He was still attracted to her, and now he had to work with her. This sucked. "Now what?" he asked.

"Now you can go back to your party. We'll get started tomorrow morning."

"Can't. I work out with my trainer in the mornings."

"Where, and what time?"

He told her.

"Fine. I'll meet you there."

He arched a brow. "You going to work out?"

"I might. But we'll do our work after you're finished."

"Whatever."

Her lips lifted. "I promise, these lessons won't hurt at all."

"Lessons? What lessons?"

"You'll see. Good night, Cole."

For the second time that night, she walked out on him.

SAVANNAH LAID HER PURSE DOWN ON THE GLASS table in her living room, kicked off her shoes, and headed into the bedroom, reaching for the zipper of her dress. She pulled the dress off and hung it up, then stopped in front of the bathroom mirror to stare at herself.

She'd worn her La Perla bra and panties tonight. They were so pretty, a blush pink, with lace and silk. Sexy, provocative.

Unfortunately, the only person admiring the ensemble was her.

She inhaled and let out a long sigh, removing the clip and pins holding her hair up. She ran her fingers through her hair, pulling it forward.

She wasn't bad-looking. Average breasts, her body a little on the curvy side. She liked to eat and she could easily slip into the overweight category if she wasn't so active. She had a lot of restless energy, so she burned a lot of calories that way, which kept her metabolism rolling at a pretty high rate. But she had great legs. She worked out regularly so she could maintain her stamina at the level required to keep up with her clients.

Like her new client, Cole Riley, who'd hit all her hot buttons tonight. Actually, he'd been the first client she'd been assigned to who'd turned her head and made her think of him as something other than just a client.

That man had testosterone stamped on every inch of him. He was hard to ignore. The way he looked at her, pursued her, made her wish he wasn't her client.

But he was. Starting tomorrow.

Tonight, though, she could think about what might have happened had she been able to indulge in the attraction that had been so obvious between them.

She'd always gone for the bad boys, the kind her mother warned her against, which made her want them all the more. And the one thing her mother had told her was that you could never change a bad boy.

But that's what she did now, and she did a damn good job of it.

Too bad she was going to have to change Cole Riley. He was bad boy personified, and one look at him tonight had revved all her engines.

She rubbed her thumbs over her nipples, sucking in a breath at the sensitivity she felt even through her bra.

She moved to the bedroom and stretched out on her bed. The bed she'd be sleeping alone in tonight, just like every night. She dug in her heels and pushed backward until she lay in the center of the bed, then spread her legs, letting the ceiling fan bathe her body with cool air.

Cole Riley was interesting. If he hadn't been her assigned client, what might have happened between them tonight?

She undid the clasp on her bra and freed her breasts, allowing her hands to wander. Not at all the same as a man's hands—a man's very large hands that would cover her breasts, rolling her nipples between his fingers.

She gasped as the sensation sparked between her legs. She clamped her thighs together, her pussy pulsing with the need to be touched. She brushed her thumb over her nipple while snaking her hand down her stomach, closing her eyes as the image of what she and Cole could do together flashed into her mind.

Cole shouldn't be in her fantasies. He was her new client, and thinking about him as she slid her hand inside her panties was a monumentally bad idea. But she couldn't get him out of her head. He was who she wanted touching her. His hands would be calloused and strong, not feminine and soft as she stroked the silken folds of her sex. She wanted someone who'd demand her response, who'd know what to do with a woman's body.

She gasped as she slid her fingers down, teasing the folds of her pussy with the light drag of her fingernails. Would Cole be gentle with her, or would he be rough as he dipped two fingers inside her, using the heel of his hand against her clit.

She arched against the sensation, closing her eyes and imagining him next to her, his lips closing over her nipple, drawing it into the wet heat of his mouth. She'd reach out and hold him there—her nipples were so sensitive. She'd want it harder, would need more of that delicious pain.

Moisture coated her fingers, spasms tightening around them as she pulled them out, then thrust them inside her again, fucking herself.

"Yes," she whispered, digging her heels against the mattress as she lifted against the spiral of need that raged inside her. She needed to come. She needed it hard and deep. "Fuck me, Cole."

He'd remove his fingers and take off his clothes, leaving her throbbing and wet and pulsing with anticipation, his cock hard and ready. And when he plunged inside her, she'd cry out. It had been so long. She'd wrap her legs around him as he filled her, so ready to climax that he'd shove her over the edge in only a couple thrusts.

"Oh, god, I'm going to come," she whispered to the empty room as she rubbed her clit, her mind whirling with the imagined act. Cole was buried deep in her imagination, as hard as she imagined him buried inside her. She shoved her fingers deeper inside her pussy, using her other hand to strum her clit until she exploded, whimpering at the wash of incredible orgasm that sent wave after wave over her until she relaxed, limp on the bed, her legs splayed out while she caught her breath.

Mercy. She tried to swallow, but her throat had gone dry. She got up and went into the kitchen to grab some ice and a glass of water, her legs still quaking with the aftereffects of her climax. She headed back into the bathroom, stopping to stare at herself in the mirror.

A totally different picture now. Naked from the waist up, her hair was mussed from thrashing about on the bed. She wore only her panties and a decided blush on her cheeks.

Good Southern girls didn't think about new clients the way she'd just done, and certainly didn't masturbate thinking about them. Then again, she wasn't a good Southern girl, was she? She had naughty thoughts and wicked desires and a need for a man to bring it all out of her. Too bad she didn't have the time—or the right guy.

Of course, Cole Riley might have been the right guy, given the right circumstances. Tomorrow she was going to have to work with him, and she'd just had very dirty thoughts about him. That was wrong on so many levels.

She'd been tense lately, that was all. And had gone a very long time without a release. Cole had merely been—convenient. And attractive. And loaded with sex appeal. It had been natural for him to pop into her fantasies. But that was a one-time occasion, and it wasn't going to happen again.

She was going to have to wipe this event from her thoughts.

Cole Riley was a client and not fantasy fodder.

THREE

"ONE MORE REP."

On the bench press, Cole looked up at his trainer, Mario, at the moment wishing he could kick his ass. But since he currently held two hundred pounds of weight balancing precariously over his chest, he'd have to put a hold on that ass-kicking. He held the bar in his hands, sweat pouring off his brow, his arms shaking like a goddamned first-timer at the gym.

"Come on, you pussy, three more reps."

He pushed, hoping like hell Mario would be there to catch the bar in case it came crashing down on his chest.

"That's it, Cole. You've got it. You're almost there."

"Eat. Shit. And." He racked the bar, sat up, and leaned over, feeling like he was going to puke. He swung his legs over the side of the bench and glared at Mario. "Die."

Mario patted Cole on the back. "I knew you could do it."

"Fuck you."

"See, I've always suspected you had the hots for me. But you're not my type."

"Bullshit. I'm totally your type. Tall, well-built, and athletic."

Mario laughed. "Exactly. Just like my boyfriend. But if you're interested, I could set you up with a few really hot guys."

Cole rolled his eyes at Mario, pushed off the bench and stood. "No, thanks. I have enough trouble dealing with women." He looked at the front door, where Savannah was coming in. "Speaking of, here comes my newest problem."

Mario followed Cole's gaze. "Wow. She's a stunner."

Admittedly, Mario was right. In a conservative, short-sleeved red dress that clung to her curves and high heels that showcased her long legs, Savannah commanded attention.

She was beautiful. And irritating. And untrustworthy.

She walked through the doors into the gym, smiling when she saw him. She headed toward them, and Cole was struck again by her walk. And her legs. Damn her legs, anyway. He needed to remember the untrustworthy part.

"Good morning, Cole," she said, then turned to Mario and held out her hand. "I'm Savannah Brooks."

Mario shook her hand. "Mario Genino. I'm Cole's trainer."

She gave Cole the once-over. "You do a fine job of it, Mario."

Mario laughed. "Thanks. I work him over pretty good. What do you do for Cole, Savannah?"

Oh, shit. The last thing he needed was for Mario—or anyone—to find out the team had hired a fucking image consultant for him. "She's—"

"I'm doing some consulting work for him. Someone with Cole's talent and vast portfolio needs expert assistance, as you can probably imagine."

Mario nodded. "Hell, yeah. Have to protect his assets."

Savannah smiled. "Indeed, we do."

Mario glanced up at the clock. "I hate to greet and run, but my next client will be coming in soon. Nice to meet you, Savannah. Cole, I'll abuse you again tomorrow."

"Of course. I wouldn't want to keep you. Nice meeting you, Mario," Savannah said.

"Yeah, see you, Mario." Cole waited until Mario left, then turned to her. "You lied. Again."

She lifted her chin. "I did not."

"You didn't tell him what you were really hired to do."

"I don't think it's anyone's business. And I merely altered the truth a bit, while not lying."

He crossed his arms. "Whatever. What's on the agenda for today?"

"Your workout is finished?"

"Yeah."

"What are your plans after this?"

"Lunch. I need to load up on some protein after I work out."

"Fine. We'll have lunch, and I'll go over the plans."

"Okay. I need to shower."

"I'll wait for you in the lobby."

She was being accommodating. Nice. He didn't want her to be nice. He wanted to argue with her. He wanted her to be a bitch. Anything so he wouldn't like her.

He showered and dressed, and when he went out to the lobby, she was talking to a couple of the guys from the team who'd come to work out. Single and a few years younger than him, Jamarcus Davis and Lon Fields were offensive stars on the Traders. Both had reputations for being lady-killers, and rightly so. Solidly built, damn good-looking, and friendly with women, they were loaded with charm, and even worse, neither of them had shitty reputations like he did.

Looked like they were charming Savannah, too. She had a smile on her face when he got close. She was even laughing—that damn laugh that made his balls quiver.

She caught his eye as he approached. "Oh, there you are."

Jamarcus and Lon turned, too, and their smiles died.

"You're with Riley?" Jamarcus asked, surprise on his face.

"Yes, I am. Are you ready to go, Cole?"

"Yup." He took Savannah's arm and led her to the door, winking at Jamarcus and Lon. "See you later, guys."

"Yeah, later, Cole," Lon said with obvious disappointment.

"We can take your car if that's all right with you," Savannah said, sliding her sunglasses on as they stepped outside. "You can just drop me off after we're finished."

"That's fine."

"Let me grab my briefcase first." She stopped at one of those hybrid tree-hugger cars, grabbed a leather bag, then joined him at his gas-guzzler SUV.

"Sorry," he said as she climbed in, hiking her dress up. "I didn't know you'd be getting in with me or I'd have brought the car."

"It's no trouble."

Especially no trouble for him since he got a glimpse of her spectacular thighs. Jesus, he'd have to focus on something else so he wouldn't sprout a hard-on. Now that really would be unprofessional.

He started up the SUV and turned to her. "What do you like to eat?"

"I'm not fussy. Wherever you want to go is fine with me."

"Okay." He headed out, deciding that, instead of his favorite hamburger joint, they'd go to an actual restaurant, something that served a selection of stuff, since he had no idea what she liked. Though why that mattered to him, he had no idea. She was an imposition. He should make her eat big, fat, greasy burgers.

"You didn't tell them I was your client."

"Excuse me?" she asked, turning away from the window to look at him.

"Jamarcus and Lon. You know they thought you were my date."

"Did they? I guess that's their mistake then, isn't it?" She returned to staring out the window.

He smiled, shook his head, and pondered the mystery that was

Savannah Brooks. It was hard not to like her, even though he was opposed to working with her. Though he guessed it was the idea of an image consultant he didn't like. He liked her just fine. Or maybe he was just attracted to her legs and her gorgeous face.

Since it was unlikely she was going to date him, it didn't matter what he thought about her personally, so they might as well get this over with. He pulled into the restaurant parking lot.

"This place?" she asked.

"What about this place?"

"I don't know. It's charming. A little Italian restaurant named Carmen's? You seem like a burger or steak kind of guy."

"I come here a lot. Great food."

He came around to her side and assisted her in getting out of his SUV.

"Thank you," she said, smoothing her dress down over her legs as she stepped onto the parking lot. She grabbed her bag and they went inside, where Carmen was working as hostess today.

"Cole," she said, kissing both his cheeks. "So nice to see you here." She looked over at Savannah and a gleam sparked in her eyes. "Oh, you have a new girl."

To Carmen, who was nearly eighty, every woman was a "girl."

"Carmen, this is Savannah Brooks."

Carmen enveloped Savannah in her ample frame. "Honey, you're beautiful."

"Thank you. Your restaurant is lovely."

Carmen looped her arm in Savannah's. "Thank you. My father opened this restaurant. It's very special to our family. Cole's parents come here a lot. I've known this kid since he was five years old. He used to throw spaghetti on the floor."

Savannah laughed. "Is that right?"

"You bet. He and his sister would come in here with their parents every Friday for dinner."

"That's fascinating," Savannah said.

Carmen threw Cole a look over her shoulder. "Come along, sonny."

Maybe he shouldn't have brought Savannah here.

Cole followed as Carmen showed them to their table. He shook his head when Carmen led them to the one in the corner. The dark corner. He could tell Carmen they weren't on a date, but what would be the point?

"I'll be sure to tell Mike not to bother you two so much during lunch, okay?" She kissed Cole on the cheek and left.

"Carmen's sweet. Misguided, but sweet," Cole said as he held the chair out for Savannah.

"Thank you. And yes, she's very nice. Obviously, she's practically family. You've been coming here this long?"

He shrugged. "I told you. I like the food."

Savannah looked around. "It's a great place. Very atmospheric. I love the dark tables, the cheery red-and-white curtains." She inspected the olive oil and balsamic vinegar bottles. "So, your parents come here a lot?"

He knew what she was doing—trying to get to know him better. He should have hit the steak house.

Fortunately, Mike, their waiter, came over and took their order and brought their bread and drinks.

Cole took a drink of his water and looked at Savannah. "I guess you can tell me what I have to look forward to."

"Are you sure you wouldn't rather eat first?" Savannah asked with a smile.

"It's that bad?"

She laughed. "I don't think it's bad at all. At first I'll be shadowing you for a while, mainly to figure out your routine and watch your interactions. Then I'll have some suggestions."

"Shadowing me? You mean to monitor my behavior."

"No. To get a feel for your routine." She reached into her bag and pulled out a file.

Cole cocked a brow. "You have a file on me?"

"The team provided media reports, analysis of your on-field behavior from prior teams, and altercations you've had in the past, all contributing to a profile I've put together on you."

They waited while Mike put their lunch in front of them. Since Cole was hungry, he dug into his chicken Parmesan while Savannah ate her chicken salad. All the while, he stared at the folder she'd pushed off to the side.

"So what's your conclusion?" he asked.

"This is just a preliminary analysis, but my belief is that you have anger management issues."

He let out a snort. "I do not."

She speared a leaf of lettuce, and didn't argue with him.

"Seriously. I don't have anger management issues. Or any other kind of issues. I told you last night, the media lies. They blow everything out of proportion."

"What about your issues with the teams you've been on?"

He shrugged. "Personality clashes. I've just been on the wrong teams."

"I see. And you think it'll be different with the Traders."

"Yeah. I've already connected with them. This is a good fit for me."

"So assuming this team is, in fact, a good fit for you and you have no skirmishes with anyone on your team, from players to management, what about your personal life?"

"What about it? I told you it's not me, it's the media."

She laid her fork down and dabbed at the corners of her mouth with the napkin. "To some extent, you're likely correct. The media has a tendency to overdramatize and exaggerate. But if you don't give them anything to work with, they have nothing to report. You give them plenty, so even if what's there is minor, they have the opportunity to blow it up."

"That's bullshit." He pushed his empty plate to the side and finished his glass of water. Mike was right there to refill it, then blended into the darkness of the restaurant again. "I don't give them anything. They make shit up."

"You also have an issue of not being able to accept blame for your actions."

"If I'm wrong, I'll accept blame."

She raised her fork, then paused, her lips lifting in a hint of a smile. "Let me guess. You're never wrong?"

Irritation spiked. He pushed it down, refusing to get into an argument with her here. "I didn't say that. And you're baiting me."

"I'm not baiting you, Cole. We're having a conversation. Your anger is quick to spark. Once it does, you don't back down. That's why you get into trouble so easily. And so often."

He sucked in a breath, trying to keep control. "So is this an exercise to see how fast you can piss me off?"

"No." She looked down at her plate, then back up at him. "It's lunch."

"You think this is funny."

"I wasn't making a joke. I'm trying to get you to understand that you're angry for no reason. We're having a conversation. A conversation that you've turned into what you think is me attacking you." She pushed her plate to the side and drew the file folder in front of her, opened it up and pulled out photos and articles. "If you'd like, you can explain these photos and altercations. Give me an understanding of you, of what was happening during these events."

He took the photos. "This one was at a club. I was kicking back with some friends, and suddenly there are ten cameras in my face. Lights are popping, they're pushing the woman I was with just to get closer to me. What the hell was I supposed to do? I shoved them out of the way so I could get my date out of there. She was freaked out."

He pulled out an article, this one from some tabloid rag that said he'd been drunk and passed out in a club. He snorted. "Paparazzi tripped me while I was trying to get away from them. So they take this photo of me lying facedown in a club and then print that I'm drunk and passed out."

At her dubious look, he shot her a glare. "I don't drink during the season. It affects my performance. Look at the date." He handed the article back to her.

"October fifteenth."

"Exactly. Deep in the middle of the season. No alcohol. You can go to the club owners and ask them."

She filed the article away. "I don't think that's necessary."

"This one, I was out with my parents. My parents. That's news? It was their anniversary and I wanted to take them out to dinner. Someplace nice and quiet, and the goddamned media shows up. I'm not an actor. I'm not Hollywood. I'm just a jock. Taking my parents out to dinner isn't newsworthy. Yet they stalked me and hounded my parents, blinding them with their cameras."

"Did you bring a date that night?"

He frowned. "What?"

"When you took your parents out to dinner for their anniversary. Did you bring a date?"

"Yeah."

"That's why you had the media stalking you. You're a hot commodity, Cole. You've had big endorsement deals, you've done commercials, and you've been known to date high-profile women. That makes you attractive to the media. Next time you want to take your parents out for a quiet dinner, don't bring a date."

"It shouldn't matter whether I bring a date or not. The media should leave me alone."

She smiled at him. "What you want and what you're going to get are two different things. You've been in the NFL for six years now, and you were hot even when you played college ball. If you don't want this life, then maybe you should consider retiring."

He was about ready to let Peaches hoof it back to her car. "That's a bullshit suggestion."

"And you're a whiner. You have a great career, you make more money than most of the people in this country will ever dream of. You have a ton of perks, you can retire before you're forty and live a life of luxury—provided you're financially astute and haven't pissed it all away. Yet you've cornered yourself into a terrible reputation and your career is hanging by a thread. What? Fame, money, and success aren't enough for you? Are you unhappy?"

He pushed his chair back, pulled a wad of bills out of his wallet, and threw them on the table, then tossed some extra at her. "You can take a cab back to your car, Peaches. We're done here."

He walked out.

NOW *THAT* WAS THE COLE RILEY SHE'D RESEARCHED. Savannah took a deep breath and reached for her glass of iced tea to take a sip.

Carmen came over. "Are you all right, dear?"

She smiled up at the woman. "I'm just fine. Thank you for asking. I believe Cole left more than enough money to cover the bill."

She clasped her hands together. "He always does. He's very generous."

Yeah, he was generous, all right. She left the money he'd thrown at her, figuring Mike could use it. She pushed back her chair and stood. "The meal was wonderful, Carmen. Thank you so much."

"It's so unlike Cole to be so, to be such a . . ."

Jerk? Asshole? Prick? Baby? Seemed to her he'd acted just as she'd expected. Exactly as the profile had indicated. She laid her hand on Carmen's arm. "It's quite all right, Carmen."

"Men. They're difficult to understand sometimes. My Fred. Most of the time he's so warm and loving. And then sometimes I'd like to bash him upside the head with my cast-iron skillet. Of course they'd arrest me if I killed him, so I call him names instead."

She couldn't imagine a mean word coming out of the tiny woman, but Savannah laughed. "Well, yes, killing them is illegal."

Carmen linked her arm with Savannah's. "They're all a pain in the ass every now and then and require a lot of patience. But the great sex is worth it."

Savannah blinked. "I'm sure it is. Thank you again for lunch, Carmen. I'll just call a taxi."

"You wait in here, then. It's hot outside." Carmen wandered off and Savannah stared after her.

Clearly Savannah had a lot to learn about men and women and relationships. Right now she was happy to be single.

She pulled out her phone when she walked outside, surprised to see Cole parked at the front door. He was leaning against the passenger-side door, his arms crossed in front of him.

"So maybe I do have a temper."

She slipped her phone in her purse and walked toward him.

"And maybe I can be an asshole."

She put on her sunglasses and tilted her head back.

"I'm sorry," he said. "But not everything in your super secret file there is true."

"Then start proving me wrong instead of proving everything in it is right."

He clenched his jaw, but then he gave her a quick nod. He moved away and opened the door for her, helped her up, then climbed in on his side.

"Where to now?" he asked.

"I'm yours to command. Take me wherever you're going."

He relaxed his shoulders, shot her a grin, and started the car.

At least he didn't stay angry long. Point in his favor.

FOUR

COLE DROVE SAVANNAH BACK TO HER CAR FIRST AND told her she'd need a change of clothes for later.

Since she intended to shadow him to determine his routine, she told him he might as well follow her to her place, then they could go in one car.

He'd expected her to live in a condo like he did, so he was surprised when she pulled into the driveway of a single-story home. The lawn was well maintained, with a huge tree in the front and a nice porch where two chairs and a table sat. Hanging pottery made it seem . . . homey.

"Wow. Nice digs. Team footing the bill for this?"

She didn't answer and instead went to the door and opened it. He followed her inside, where it was also nice. It wasn't a new home, but it was decorated nicely—all warm colors with overstuffed sofas and pillows and wood tables and flooring.

She laid her briefcase on the table. "Would you like something to drink?"

"Water is good."

"Help yourself in the kitchen." She headed toward her bedroom, then stopped at the doorway and turned to face him. "What kind of clothes will I need?"

"Got a party dress?"

"Define party dress."

"Night club."

"Yes."

"Bring that. You can change at my place."

"All right." Savannah went to her closet and selected a black and white cocktail dress and a pair of shoes, bagged her makeup and some jewelry, and came back into the kitchen.

Cole had a bottled water in his hand and was standing at her back door, looking out at the lake.

She'd bought the house for the lake view. She liked having the unfenced property, didn't want the obstruction to mar the beauty of the lake. She liked sitting out back and watching kids play and parents walking them along the path. Occasionally, ducks would frolic in the water. It gave her a sense of peace and allowed her mind to settle.

Her mind was definitely not settled now, not with a stunningly attractive man standing in her kitchen. He'd struck a casual pose and hadn't yet noticed her, so he was relaxed and unguarded, just peering out at the water.

In profile, he was magnificent, his shoulders wide, his waist lean, and his face photogenic. No wonder the media ate him up. He had the longest eyelashes she'd ever seen on a man, and the way his hair curled at the nape of his neck made her itch to slide her fingers into the tendrils and see if it felt as soft and thick as it looked.

He finally spotted her, turned his head and smiled.

He took her breath away.

He was a client, not a date. Not a man she was going to sleep with, so everything on her body that was throbbing could just stop.

"I'm ready."

"Let me take those." He grabbed her garment bag and the small bag she'd placed her other things in. She opened the door and they went out and climbed into his SUV.

She watched his hands on the steering wheel as he drove. Strong, confident. He even drove the speed limit, though she wondered if he was on his best behavior because she was with him. She'd read his file—he'd gotten so many speeding tickets she was surprised he still had a driver's license.

Which made her wonder just where one of those strong, confident hands would be if she were his date, not his image consultant.

Maybe she should have had two orgasms last night instead of just one. She'd been on the road a lot lately, and had nearly doubled her clientele in the past six months. Good for business, bad for her tension level. And none of those clients were of the sexy, fantasy-inducing quality like Cole Riley. He might have issues, but she wanted to devour him like her favorite homemade biscuits, all slathered in butter and honey.

Which got her to thinking about licking honey off Cole's naked chest, her tongue dipping into the hollow of his oh-so-spectacular naked abs. Then she'd move lower . . .

"You're quiet."

Her gaze shot to his, her body in flames as she pushed the wicked fantasy to the back of her mind. She'd get back to it later. "Just taking in the view."

He frowned. "We're on the highway, Savannah. Not much to see but a lot of shopping centers and a blur of lights."

"True. But I'm always driving. It's nice to be a passenger for a change and get to take in the sights."

He shrugged. "Whatever rocks your world."

Cole, apparently, was rocking her world. In a most inappropriate way. She needed to get her mind back on track. It helped when Cole exited the highway and she had more to look at than the aforementioned shopping centers and lights.

"So, you haven't bought a house?" she asked after he drove a few miles and pulled into a condominium complex and parked.

He got out and grabbed her stuff, then helped her out of the car.

"No. I'm single, have no pets, and who knows if I'll end up being traded again. No sense in putting down money on property right now until I see if it works out with the Traders."

She followed him to his front door and waited while he unlocked it. "That makes sense. Though with your income, I would imagine you'd need some tax breaks."

He looked at her and smiled. "I have investments."

"Good to know."

He opened the door and turned on the lights. She stepped into a place she hadn't expected. Definitely a bachelor pad, decorated with a lot of black and chrome, with a huge flat-screen television mounted on the wall, along with multiple game equipment. But it was neat and tidy, with leather couches and stellar décor, from lamps to tables and even a few throw pillows and accent rugs.

"This is very nice. You decorate it yourself?"

"Thanks. And no, I don't have decorating talent. But I do have a sister. She did it for me."

She followed him down the hall and into one of the bedrooms—she counted three. The master was huge, with a king-size bed, two dressers, and an enviable closet. This place might have more square footage than her house.

The bed had a light brown comforter and about nine pillows, which made her want to dive in and make herself at home.

"I'll just lay this stuff on the bed. You can change before we go out."

"That'll be fine. Thanks."

He led her into the living room, then turned. "Would you like a drink?"

"Sparkling water if you have it. If not, plain water is fine."

"Sparkling it is."

She took a seat on the sofa. "You keep your bar well stocked?"

"Yeah. For all those wild parties I throw."

She cocked a brow, trying to determine if he was serious or not. "Seems to me you do plenty of public partying."

He brought her the glass. "I don't throw wild parties here. The last thing I want is to have a bunch of people at my place trashing it."

"So you were joking."

He sat on the loveseat across from the sofa. "You need to work on your sense of humor, Savannah."

She bristled. "I have a sense of humor."

"Do you?" He smiled behind his glass.

She decided at that moment that he was mean and she'd no longer have fantasies about him. She was cured.

"So, now what do you do with the rest of your day?"

"Since it's before the season starts, I might play some video games until it's time to go out."

She grabbed her phone. "Too early to go out. So you'll just hang out and play games?"

He reached over and took a binder from the coffee table. "No. Since I'm with a new team this year I have to learn the playbook. I need to study."

She gave him a critical look. "Really."

"Yeah, really. You don't walk onto the field knowing every play. But if you'd rather play some games . . ."

"No, by all means. Do whatever it is you do. I have work of my own to do. I won't get in your way."

He opened the binder and started reading. She got out her phone and checked her email. After answering several, she pulled out her laptop, typed up some reports and made a few notes. She looked up occasionally to find Cole's brows furrowed in concentration. He didn't deviate as he went over page after page of the playbook. Not once, but three times.

She gave him credit for being thorough.

"How long does it take to learn the playbook?" she asked.

He didn't look up at her. "A while. I need to know every play."

"And there are a lot."

He finally glanced up at her. "Yeah."

She laid her work down next to her. "You work hard at your job."

"Yes."

"You want to be appreciated for what you do."

"On the field. Not off."

"Then why is so much attention paid to what you do off the field?"

He laid the book down and focused on her. "Wish I knew the answer to that."

Interesting. She sensed the frustration in his voice. Maybe there was more to Cole than she thought. But that remained to be seen. They were only in the beginning stages. He was charming, no doubt. Polite enough, but he obviously had serious issues with his temper. She'd glimpsed that earlier, and she barely knew him.

But she knew enough that she wanted to know more. For the time being, she left him alone so he could do his work. She dug into her briefcase and did her own, and a few hours passed before Cole rose and told her it was time to get dressed.

"I figured we'd get something to eat before we went out. It could be a long night."

He gave her use of his bedroom to change and freshen up her makeup, grabbing his clothes to change in one of the other rooms.

When she came out, he was waiting for her in the living room. Her breath caught. Dressed in black slacks and a black button-down shirt, he looked sexy. Compelling. And utterly dangerous to her already fragile libido.

He smiled at her. "You look sexy, Peaches."

She couldn't help the tingle at the nickname. "You should call me Savannah. I'm not your date or your girlfriend."

"It annoys you."

"It doesn't annoy me. It's just unprofessional."

"Okay. Savannah. Or should I refer to you as Ms. Brooks? Or Miss Brooks? Or is it Mrs. Brooks?"

She rolled her eyes. "Now you're being annoying."

He laughed. "Let's roll, Sa-van-nah."

He'd enunciated every syllable of her name. Slowly. She might prefer the nickname after all.

They went outside and Cole led her to his Lexus. Mid-range, not the cheapest, but not top-of-the-line, either.

"This car is nice," she said after he climbed inside. "But for some reason I expected you to be driving . . . I don't know. A Lamborghini or Ferrari."

He laughed as he put the car in gear and drove away. "I don't piss away my money on frivolous shit like cars. I'm on the road half the year anyway, so what's the point in having an expensive car I don't have time to drive?"

And again he surprised her.

They stopped for a nice dinner and then drove to the club. Though she wasn't sure what she'd been expecting—something high-end, in the downtown area, maybe? This wasn't it. The club was in a nondescript tan brick building. It looked more like an office building than a nightclub, and if it wasn't for the ostentatious blinking sign proclaiming it Club Caress, she'd never have known it was a hot spot for the twenty- and thirty-something crowd.

And a hot spot it must have been, because the parking lot was full.

Cole pulled up out front and grinned at the valet.

"Hey, Mark," he said, tossing his keys as he rounded the vehicle.

"What's up, Cole?"

He held out his arm for her, and they went inside.

It was pitch-black, except for all the crazy lights, and the noise was earsplitting. She felt the heavy beat of the music in her chest as they made their way through the crowd, and it didn't take long for Savannah to realize that Cole knew everyone here. People waved and called out his name, and women shot evil looks in her direction.

Clearly, he was a popular guy.

He slipped his hand in hers when the crowd swelled around them. Cole led her through the mix of people standing in their way. Fortunately, he was like Moses and the oglers were like the Red Sea, because they parted to let them through to the bar.

The bar was something to behold. Sleek and a shiny, polished black, it had to be fifty feet long. Colorful, neon backlit bottles glowed in rows as high as the ceiling. It was a true work of art.

"Take a seat," he said, and she shifted onto one of the cushioned bar stools.

"What would you like to drink?" he asked.

"Sparkling water would be fine for me."

He lifted two fingers and a female bartender with short red hair and beautiful, full lips came over.

"Riley. What's up?"

"Not much, Kara. How's it going tonight?"

"Busier than a one-armed paper hanger. What can I get for you?"

"I'll have a double shot of Patron Silver. The lady wants sparkling water."

She nodded. "You got it."

Kara served up Cole's shot and poured Savannah's drink into a glass, leaving her the bottle.

"Thank you," Savannah said.

"You're welcome, honey."

"You gonna run a tab?"

Cole nodded and slid Kara his credit card. He downed his drink in one swallow. She poured him another shot, then went on her way, but not before another bartender, this one a brunette with cleavage that made Savannah jealous, came by.

"Hey, babe. Haven't seen you for a few days," she said.

"I've been busy."

She reached across the bar and squeezed his hand. "Don't be so busy. Miss you around here."

The woman cut a glare to Savannah, then sauntered off.

"One of your many girlfriends?" Savannah asked.

Cole downed his shot, which was replaced right away by a tall glass of what she assumed was ice water. That Kara was efficient.

He smiled at Savannah. "Lulu is a friend."

"She doesn't like me being here."

"She's protective. I get a lot of women hanging on me, trying to get something from me. Lulu watches out for me."

"So, she's like your bodyguard."

"Not exactly. But I've helped her out in the past. She thinks she owes me the same."

Savannah had no idea what that meant. Helped her out how? Financially? Or did he beat up an ex-boyfriend for her? It was none of her business, really, she was just curious, especially since Lulu kept shooting scathing looks her way, and it was the kind of look a woman gave another woman when said first woman was trying to move in on the other's boyfriend.

Maybe Cole was unaware of how Lulu felt about him.

And maybe Savannah needed to watch her back tonight, especially considering Lulu wasn't the only one giving her looks that might kill. Cole was obviously a regular here, and several women stopped by to hug him or kiss him on the cheek. They lingered only long enough to say hello once they saw Savannah, but they glanced contemptuously at Savannah as they walked away.

"I'm not very popular here," she said as he hugged one of his many admirers and took his seat next to her.

He frowned. "What?"

"Your female friends are shooting daggers at me."

He scanned the crowd. "No, they're not."

She shook her head and turned around to face the bar. "From your friend Lulu to every woman who's come up to greet you. Every single one of them has given me a look that would drop me dead to the floor if it had a weapon attached to it. Obviously you're very sought after."

"Nah. They're just my friends."

"Maybe from your perspective. Not theirs. Open your eyes, Cole. These women are in love with you."

He snorted.

"Okay, fine. They're at least in seriously heavy lust. And they don't appreciate that you're not here solo tonight."

Cole had no idea where Savannah was getting her ideas. These were his party friends, his drinking buddies, and his dance partners. None of them were girlfriends. While it was true he never brought a date here, he never made any promises to any of these women that would give them hope of being exclusive. So why would they be pissed that he brought Savannah?

But as he sat and talked to Savannah, he kept his gaze on the women hovering around them.

She was right. They weren't happy. Whenever he happened to glance at them, they were all smiles. But as soon as he turned away, they folded their arms and gave Savannah the death glare.

Huh. Who knew? He tried to be honest with them and let them know how the game was played.

Maybe they hadn't been listening.

"Let's dance," he said to Savannah.

Her eyes widened. "I don't think that's a good idea."

"It's a great idea." He held out his hand.

She shook her head. "Remember what I told you about this not being a date? I'm merely here to observe."

"Good." He took her by the waist and lifted her off the bar stool, then grabbed her hand. "You can observe me on the dance floor."

She narrowed her gaze at him. "Do you ever take no for an answer?"

"Absolutely. I'm not that kind of guy, Savannah."

She sighed and moved in closer to him on the crowded dance floor. The music was loud, the beat gyrating, and Cole got into watching Savannah dance.

She had moves, and once she relaxed and got into the music, she could shake her hips just right.

His objective in getting her on the dance floor was to shake loose some of his groupies. Now that he knew they were getting possessive, he wanted to put an end to it, let them know that when he was here with a lady, they needed to go about their business and find their own fun. It was one thing when he came to the club as a single. Then it was a free-for-all and he didn't mind choosing one woman after another to dance and party with.

But them claiming ownership of him at the club? His life didn't work that way. He was a free agent and no woman was going to put a claim on him. If he wanted to bring a date—even though Savannah wasn't really a date—then he'd damn well do that.

Except he wasn't checking out the other women to see if they'd found other amusement. He was concentrating on Savannah, on the skintight dress she wore and the way it hiked up on her legs whenever she raised her arms over her head and swiveled around in a fast circle. She got his blood pumping, and when the next song slowed things down, he couldn't resist sliding his arm around her and drawing her close.

She narrowed her gaze at him and gave him a wary look, but he figured she must like dancing because she didn't walk away. Instead, she flung an arm around his neck and slid close, but still kept her distance. It made him want to grab her and feel her body touching his.

"You are dangerous, Peaches."

"We're just dancing here, Cole. Don't read anything into it."

"Not reading anything. This is just business."

"Of course it is."

They were both lying. She shifted her hips, her body inches from his crotch.

Tempting. Oh so tempting. And his dick was getting hard.

Savannah was a smart woman. She had to notice, so he put his hands on her hips and swung her out, this time making sure when he pulled her back, he tugged her close.

She immediately pulled away, creating that inch or so of space between them.

It didn't help, because she knew how to move, and when she turned her back to him and swayed her hips to the music, he broke into a sweat.

She might not be grinding against him, but he still felt her.

Christ. Maybe she was deliberately torturing him, or maybe this was her way of telling all his friends to fuck off by the way she danced with him. Either way, he was hard as steel and his balls were throbbing.

If they were alone he'd know exactly what to do. He'd wrap his arm around her waist and pull her against him, then slide his hands up to her sweet, full breasts, cup them until her nipples hardened, pull the top of her dress down, then turn her around so he could taste her sweet mouth. When he had his fill of kissing her, he'd move down and suck on her nipples until she moaned. He'd strip her down and lay her on his bed so he could lick her pussy and make her come. And then—

Yeah. The direction of his thoughts wasn't helping his erection. Fortunately, the song ended and another one started up.

"Mind if I take over?"

One of his club friends—Sheila—stepped in front of Savannah.

Savannah half turned and met Cole's gaze for a fraction of a second before she turned to Sheila and smiled. "He's all yours. I need a breather anyway."

"Hey, wait," Cole said. But Savannah had already disappeared into the crowd.

So maybe the signals he'd gotten had been all in his head, because she'd sure walked away easily enough.

SAVANNAH WATCHED THE WOMEN SQUEAL WITH JOY AS Cole was swallowed up by sequins, spandex, miles of legs, and a lot of hair.

She could tell from the look on his face when she'd walked away that he'd been confused, then angry. With her. She wasn't sure what she'd done wrong. She'd told him from the outset that she wanted to observe and nothing more, but he'd acted affronted when she'd wandered off to sit and watch instead of interacting with him.

It wasn't her fault she didn't want to act like his date. She wasn't his date.

He'd wanted to dance. She'd danced. And maybe the dance might have gotten a little hot—maybe she'd been more than affected by being so close to him, but she'd kept her distance.

And okay, that whole distance thing had been difficult, especially when he'd tugged her against him, and she'd felt how hard he was—everywhere. It had been tempting to stay there, to run her hands over his broad shoulders, to test his abs and see if they were as real as the photos she'd seen.

But she'd been good. She'd walked away. And when another woman had wanted to cut in, it had been fine with her. She wasn't the least bit interested in Cole Riley. That other girl could have him.

So could those other six women with skinny bodies and big boobs. And from the way they were all playing grab-ass on the dance floor, they certainly all wanted him. He hadn't even bothered to look back at her. For all he knew, she could have left by now.

Not that she was jealous. She was here to watch his behavior—to do her job.

Yeah, you did a fine job ogling his erection on the dance floor, Savannah.

Ignoring her thoughts, she watched Cole in the middle of the half-dozen-girl sandwich. Really, were some of them even old enough to be in this club? Cole was . . . hmm . . . close to thirty? If that brassy redhead was twenty-one, then Savannah was a Yankee. And even if the girl was twenty-one—barely—he was still too old for her.

Me-ow, Savannah.

Oh, shut up. She was merely making an observation.

"You'll never have him."

Savannah dragged her gaze away from the dance floor. Lulu stood next to her, arms folded, a smug smile on her face.

"Excuse me?"

Lulu nodded toward the dance floor. "Cole. You'll never have him."

"Oh, honey. I don't want him."

Lulu seemed at a loss for words for a few seconds. "Then what are you doing here with him?"

Savannah gave her a sweet smile. "None of your business."

The woman leaned in. "Everything about Cole is my business."

"Apparently not, or he would have told you what I was doing here with him."

Lulu's lips tightened. She stared back at Cole like a jealous lover.

Another one Cole was clueless about. He needed to pay attention to his women.

"You're in love with him?"

Lulu shot her a glare. "I am not."

"Sweetie, you need to do a better job of disguising your feelings. It's written all over your face."

"I don't know what you're talking about. He's just my friend and I hate that these girls throw themselves at him."

"When you'd rather he throw himself at you?"

"No. *No.* He's nice to them. Too nice. He doesn't see that they're using him. I just want to protect him."

Savannah swiveled on the bar stool. Lulu's cheeks were stained a dark pink.

Maybe she'd been wrong. Lulu wasn't in love with Cole. It wasn't jealousy she saw on Lulu's face; it was something else. Anger? Frustration? So maybe it was more of a little-sister-worship kind of thing. She really was trying to be protective.

"I don't think he needs protecting. He's a big boy and capable of making his own decisions."

"You don't understand. He tries to please everyone. He doesn't want to hurt anyone's feelings."

That wasn't what the media reports said. The file she had indicated Cole was all about pleasing himself. And yet he seemed to have a lot of friends. Not all of them were women, either. After the dance he extricated himself from his harem and stopped along the way to jaw with a few men who had tables near the dance floor. He stopped, sat, and the waitress brought him drinks—water, she noticed—and he laughed with them. Talking football, no doubt. A crowd would gather, guys again.

So not only did women find him desirable, but men wanted to hang out with him, too. Not surprising. Cole had that charisma thing going for him. He was open and approachable and didn't walk into a club like this acting like a celebrity, even though they treated him like one. He was relaxed and friendly and very charming.

And yet he had this terrible image as a troublemaker. Wherever he was, fights broke out and he was typically painted as the instigator. He had a rep for having a bad attitude, for acting like a jerk.

Where was that guy? Because so far tonight she hadn't seen him. After he finished talking to the men, a couple of the girls pulled him onto the dance floor. He went willingly, seeming to give enough attention to both women to keep them happy.

"Shit." Lulu scanned a couple men who'd entered through the front door.

"What's wrong?" Savannah asked.

"Trouble." Lulu brushed past her and headed toward Cole, insinuated herself into the middle of the dance party to whisper in his ear. He looked where Lulu motioned and frowned, said something to the girls, who nodded and walked away.

Then he came toward her.

"Let's go," he said.

"Is something wrong?"

"Yeah. The media showed up."

She turned around and scanned the club. "Really? I don't see anyone."

"That's the idea. They don't want you to notice them. But Lulu can spot them. They sneak in, hide their cameras and audio recording equipment. She's smarter than they are, though. She knows all their faces."

He took her hand and led her toward the back of the club, down a narrow hallway toward the restrooms. He made a left into the manager's office.

"We'll head out the back door through the alley," Cole said.

"Why not just go out the front door?"

He stopped, turned to her. "You want your picture spread across the sports blogs and in the tabloids next week as my latest girlfriend?"

"No, thank you." That would not be good for her business.

"Then let me do it my way."

She tugged on his hand. "Wait. Won't they just follow us?"

He grinned. "Peaches, I've been at this awhile. I might get caught now and then, but I'm getting smarter at beating them at their own game."

The manager's door opened and one of the front door bouncers walked in. Similar in height to Cole, with the same dark hair, he nodded. "You ready?"

"Yeah. Thanks, Dave."

"No problem. Kasey's bringing your car around. I'll meet you at IHOP in thirty." Dave handed a set of keys to Cole, who gave his to Dave.

"Try not to break any speed limits."

Dave laughed. "No guarantees." He opened the door and dashed out. Savannah caught a glimpse of Cole's Lexus parked right at the door. Dave dove in and took off in a hurry.

Savannah followed Dave's exit. "The paparazzi will follow Dave, thinking that's you in the car."

"Yup."

She turned to face him, realizing he still had hold of her hand. Jerking it away would be rude. "So now what?"

"We'll wait here for a few, make sure they took the bait, then we'll head out in Dave's car."

"You've done this before."

He smiled down at her and her stomach fluttered. There was something about the intensity of his eyes.

"A few times."

"Makes me wonder what you were escaping from."

"Was I doing anything bad out there? Drunk and disorderly? Roughing up any women? Getting into fights?"

"No."

He left it at that. Maybe he was right, and she was looking for something that wasn't there in the first place.

"You're good to go, Cole. They're gone."

She turned to see Lulu peeking her head in the door.

He let go of her hand and went over to Lulu. "Thanks for the heads-up, Lou."

Lulu hugged him. "You know I always have your back. Dave's truck is in the back of the lot."

He opened the door for Savannah. "We'll go out this way and around the side."

Savannah smiled at Lulu, who gave her a nod, and Cole shut the door behind them.

Dave drove a beat-up truck on lifts, so Cole had to pick her up to put her into the seat. The engine roared to life with the dual-exhaust pipes choking out a rumble of noise. Savannah looked around, expecting someone to notice them.

No one did.

"Dave does drag racing on the weekends," Cole explained as he pulled onto the main road. "He's the perfect guy to take off in my car and lose the guys with the cameras."

"I see. And you don't worry about him behind the wheel in your car?"

He glanced at her. "No. I trust him."

"You seem to trust a lot of people."

He frowned. "What does that mean?"

"How did the media know you were going to be at the club tonight?"

"Someone at the club probably called them."

"Not one of your friends, though."

"Doubtful. They just want to party. The media showing up kills the party because they know I'll leave."

"But you don't know that for sure. A lot of people want to be photographed with a celebrity. It brings them—at least to their minds—instant fame."

"I trust the people I surround myself with."

"Is this a club you frequent a lot?"

"Yeah. I know all the regulars."

"How well do you know them?"

"Like I said . . . I see them there all the time."

"But it's not like you have them over for barbecues or go to the movies with them or do anything with them other than hang out with them at the club, right?"

He gave her a hard look. "Well, no. So what? They're still my friends."

Lulu had said he was too trusting. Maybe she was right about that. "Do you even know their last names?"

"Do you know the last names of everyone you're friends with?"

"Yes, Cole. I do."

He didn't say anything after that, and Savannah could tell from the tight set of his jaw that he wasn't happy with the direction of their conversation. She made a mental note to bring it up again later.

They met Dave at the pancake house and exchanged cars in the parking lot. Cole pulled out a wad of bills and paid Dave a rather generous tip for his trouble.

"Hey, always fun to drive around in the Lexus, man. Anytime." He winked at Savannah and drove off in his truck.

Cole shot a glance at the pancake house. "Hungry?"

"Not particularly, but if you are I'm happy to accompany you."

He shrugged. "That's okay. It's late and I'm sure you'd like to get home. Plus, I need to get this car off the road in case the media is still circling. I'll grab something to eat after I drop you off."

Once again, he was being polite. Not thinking of himself first. Not at all congruent with the selfish, egotistical man she'd read about in his portfolio.

Something wasn't right here, and she'd have to get to the bottom of it. Either he was playing her, or the reports about him were inaccurate.

Savannah was determined to find out. She couldn't fix his image if she didn't know who the real Cole Riley was.

He drove her back to her house. She started to get out, but Cole did, too.

"You don't have to come in."

"Sure I do. You brought a lot of stuff. I'll help you carry it in."

Again, he confused her. This had to be some kind of ploy on his part. "All right."

She let him inside and turned to him, reaching for her bags. "I'll take those."

"I can handle it. Where do you want them?"

"You can lay them down on the bed." Her Southern hospitality kicked in then. "Would you like a drink?"

"Sure." He went into her bedroom and came back a few minutes later.

"Nice underwear."

She turned. "Excuse me?"

"Hey, it's not like I went rummaging into your drawers or anything, but you had some hot stuff laying out on your bed."

Her face heated. She knew she should have taken her things into the bedroom herself. She handed him a glass of sparkling water. He looked at the glass and frowned. "This is the drink you had in mind?"

"You're driving."

"I'm a big guy. I know my limits."

"You already had shots at the club."

He frowned. "I don't need you monitoring my alcohol intake."

"I wasn't. I was just . . . Okay, I was. And anyway, I thought you didn't drink alcohol during the season."

"It's not the season yet."

"But you'll be reporting to training camp soon, correct?"

"Yeah, Mom."

She rolled her eyes and he laughed.

"You have to get out and have some fun. The serious business starts soon."

"And what—you don't have any fun once the season gets under way?"

He set his glass down on the table next to the sofa and took a seat. "I didn't say that."

She followed, sitting next to him. "And the articles, of course, imply otherwise."

"Of course. According to the media I'm out partying every night, including game nights."

"Which couldn't be true, because of team curfews."

He picked up his drink and took a long swallow. "Don't believe everything you read about me, Peaches. Most of it is hype."

"Don't you have PR people?"

He shrugged. "Here and there. I don't really like the kind of PR they do, so I avoid them."

"So you've fired them, or they've left you because of the kind of bad publicity you garner? Can't be good for their image, either."

"Yeah, it's my fault."

She sighed. "I'm only trying to help you, Cole."

"Not the first time I heard that. A lot of people tell me they want to help. Sometimes PR does more damage than good."

"Elizabeth is a very good agent. She can put you in touch with some great public relations firms who can do so much to help your career. You can trust her."

"Trust is a hard thing to come by."

"And yet you trust your first-name-only friends at the club so easily."

"They haven't screwed me over."

"That you're aware of."

He set his glass down again and turned to face her. "So what am I supposed to do, Savannah? Live in a bubble? Hide out at home and never go out? Put my trust only in you professional people who all claim to know what's best for me and my career? I've done that before—I've put my career in the hands of the experts who said they'd guide me. I've been with three teams so far and it's not going so well. I'm not about to stay home and hide. And I do have friends—people I know on a first-name basis. When I come home, I hang out with them. If I don't know their last names, what's the big deal?"

She laid her hand on his arm. "The big deal is that it seems to me you haven't forged any friendships with teammates, with anyone you feel close enough to invite over to your home. You've never had a long-term relationship with a woman, have you?"

He frowned. "What the hell does that have to do with anything?"

"A lot, I think. Do you even date?"

"Hey, I was out on the dance floor tonight with a bunch of women."

"That wasn't a date. That was an orgy."

He stood and walked to the front window. "My personal life has nothing to do with this."

She rose and followed, stood next to him. "Your entire life has everything to do with what we're doing here. Your background, your feelings, relationships you've built, both personally and professionally. It all ties into your behavior on and off the field. It's all part of your image. Image isn't just surface, Cole. It's who you are not only as a football player, but as a man."

He didn't say anything for what seemed like the longest time. Then he turned to her. "I don't need a goddamned psychologist, Peaches. I don't need you delving into my personal life and my relationships."

"I'm not a psychologist. I'm far from it. But in order to work on your image, I need to know who you are, what shaped you into who you've become to this point. Then we work out from there."

He turned, held his arms out. "You want to know who I am? This is who I am. I never hold anything back. What you see is what you get."

She didn't believe that. He was holding back a lot and they hadn't even begun yet. "If we're going to work together you have to be honest with me."

He laughed. "I haven't lied to you. You're the one who lied to me."

Her eyes widened. "I've never lied to you and I never will."

"You lied to me when we first met. You didn't tell me who you were."

"I was observing. It was Elizabeth's job to introduce us."

"That's bullshit. And what about tonight?"

"What about tonight?"

"Dancing with me?"

She swallowed. "I don't understand the question."

He moved in closer and her heart picked up a rapid beat.

"You and me on the dance floor. You felt it."

"It was just a dance, Cole. Nothing more."

"Was it?" He grabbed her remote and turned on the television, found one of the music stations. He held out his hands. "Prove it."

"What? I'm not dancing with you."

"Afraid?"

"Not at all. This isn't part of my job."

"Not part of mine, either, but you left before we were finished earlier."

She crossed her arms. "It's not a good idea. We need to keep our relationship professional."

"I didn't say I was going to fuck you up against the wall, Savannah. I just want to dance."

Savannah's body went up in flames at Cole's words. Up against the wall? Heat flashed through her and her mind filled with the visuals.

Be a professional. Ask him to leave.

Emotion warred with common sense and she knew what needed to be done here. Cole needed a firm hand, someone who wasn't going to take any of his shit. But he was bullheaded and if she pushed too hard this early, she'd lose him. She had to give a little, too.

She walked into his arms. "One dance. Then you need to leave."

He grinned. "Sure."

She loved jazz music, and the slow, sexy saxophone eased into her bones, making her want to melt against Cole's body. But that would be a very bad thing. Instead, she held herself rigid, refusing to get close.

She wouldn't make eye contact, either.

"Peaches. Look at me."

She tilted her head back to meet his gaze and was lost. His eyes were like the ocean in Mexico. Staring at them mesmerized her, and his off-kilter smile made everything in her lower regions clench in anticipation.

"Relax. It's just a dance."

He was right. And maybe they did need this contact so he'd trust her and open up more.

She released the tension in her muscles and moved in to him, letting herself feel the music, feel Cole, inching her body closer until her thighs pressed to him. When he pulled her in tighter, she couldn't object, not when it felt so good to be held, to feel her breasts against the warmth of his body.

And god, was he ever warm. Rock solid. She looked up at her hand, almost invisible when clasped within his much larger one.

It was just a dance. But when his hand began to roam over her back, his fingertips teasing lightly over her bare skin, it felt like much more. Her skin prickled with sensation, her body trembled as if she'd never been touched before. She definitely wasn't new at this game, but it sure felt like it. She needed to remember that Cole was practiced at this seduction thing, so where he was concerned she was a decided amateur. And maybe it did feel good to be held by someone so big, to feel all those hard muscles under her hands and to have him look at her like he wanted to devour her. He might be the epitome of her every fantasy, but she knew this was going nowhere. He was her client, and she never mixed business with pleasure. They'd already taken it as far—further—than she intended. It was time to end this.

"Cole—"

"You have a beautiful mouth, Savannah."

Her gaze snapped to his. "What?"

"Your lips." He rubbed his thumb over her bottom lip. "I've been thinking about kissing you since the first time we met."

"You have? Oh, that's not good."

He quirked a smile. "So you're a bad kisser?"

"That's not what I meant."

"So, you're a good kisser?"

"Yes. No. Yes. I don't know. Cole . . ."

He slid his hands along her throat. "What you're saying is, you want me to find out for myself."

The "no" hovered. But then his mouth was on hers. All rational thought disappeared and she couldn't remember why he shouldn't kiss her. He kissed her gently, his lips sliding along hers in a delicate tease that made her want to inch up and beg for more.

Her heart pounded as he held her neck between his hands. Could he feel the way her pulse raced as he moved his mouth over hers, deepening the kiss, pulling her tighter against him until her breasts were crushed against his chest? He moved a hand down her back, cupping her butt, letting her feel the ridge of his erection against her sex.

This was everything she imagined. His tongue licking against hers, his cock, hard and rocking against her pussy while the slow wail of jazz music filled her mind with images of the two of them spread out on her bed. She already had a mental list of things she wanted to do with his naked body. She wrapped her tongue around his and sucked. He groaned and lifted her dress to palm her panties.

"You're wet," he said, his tone rough, making her sex quiver as he moved his fingers over her. "I could make you come, Peaches."

He could. Easily. She wanted that. She wanted him, wanted to feel the stretch of his muscles under her hand.

This wasn't supposed to happen. They had work to do. Fucking him wasn't on the agenda.

She pulled away, smoothed down her dress and caught her breath before lifting her gaze to his.

His eyes had gone dark, a storm of hunger in them that matched the fury of her desires.

"We can't . . . I can't do this, Cole. I'm sorry."

She expected anger. Argument. Persuasion.

Instead, all he did was nod.

"You need to leave."

He dragged his fingers through his hair and she sensed his frustration. God knew she felt the same way.

"Yeah. Sure."

She walked him to the door, feeling ridiculous, and angry with herself for letting it go as far as it had. Where had her self-control gone?

Out the window with that first kiss?

Or maybe as soon as he'd pulled her into his arms for the dance.

"I'm sorry," she said again.

He turned to her and his lips curved into a smile. "Don't be."

"I'll call you in the morning."

He walked away without looking back. She shut the door and leaned against it, her body still humming with arousal.

She'd just made a critical error. She'd gotten too close to a client.

FIVE

AFTER HIS WORKOUT THE NEXT DAY, COLE CHECKED his phone and found a message from Savannah, asking him to meet her. He showered and changed, then texted her and told her he'd be there in thirty.

He wondered how this meeting would go after what had happened between them last night. He wondered how it would have gone if Savannah hadn't gotten scared and pushed him out the door.

She was an interesting woman. Cool and remote one minute, and all fiery passion the next. She had these issues about them working together that got in her way.

He aimed to remove those barriers, because he wanted to take her to bed. His dick had been hard all the way home. Jacking off in bed wasn't his favorite pastime and not something he had to do all that often. Or at all. Usually the woman went home with him, or they went to a hotel and ended up in bed.

Not last night, though. Savannah had been eager, and damn, had she been wet. She couldn't deny she'd been ready. But then she'd stopped and he'd read the fear in her eyes. That was professional fear. He understood her not wanting to fuck with her job. He of all people respected that. That's why he was here working with her.

Though he'd rather be doing something else with her.

He knocked at the door and she answered, dressed in tight black pants and a black-and-white-striped top that hugged her breasts and did all kinds of things to his imagination, none of them good nor professional. How was he supposed to keep his distance when she dressed in clothes like that?

"Good morning, Cole. Come in." She looked friendly enough, but he noticed she was wearing her professional mask again.

"Thanks."

Her dining room table was packed with food. A lot of food. He turned to her. "Are there other people here?"

She shook her head. "It's for both of us. I thought you might want to eat after your workout."

"Thanks." He wandered around the table, wondering if she cooked to fill the void left by lack of sex. But no way was he going to mention that. He was already trying to forget last night. Unfortunately, his hand up Savannah's dress was a hard memory to ignore.

He filled his plate with sandwiches and salad.

"Iced tea?" she asked from the doorway to her kitchen.

"That'd be great."

"Have a seat in the living room. Make yourself at home."

When he set his plate down, he noticed she'd had the television on. She must have been watching something, because it was paused. And it was his face on the screen.

"What are you watching?"

"Game films from last season."

He looked at her as she brought the drinks in. "Why?"

"Research." She grabbed her plate, then picked up the remote. "Do you mind if I continue?"

He shrugged. "Go ahead. Always happy to see myself on television."

She pressed the button.

It was the playoff game last season between Green Bay and New Orleans. They'd won that game. He'd played well. The play she was watching was a key third down and seven. Keller, Green Bay's quarterback, was lined up in the shotgun. Cole was set up on the left, the other receiver on the right.

At the snap, Cole took off, sprinting past the cornerback to run his route. He dug his cleats into the turf and headed downfield, only to cut to the center of the field, leaving the defensive back scrambling to catch up. He turned and waited the fraction of a second it had taken for the pass that had come sailing his way.

It had been perfect. The ball landed in his hands and he'd been off to the races, outrunning the safety for thirty-five yards all the way to the end zone. The game had been in New Orleans, and the touchdown had put Green Bay ahead and had silenced the crowd.

Savannah pressed pause on the video. "It was a good play."

Cole nodded. "It was a great play. Too bad Minnesota kicked our asses in the next game, ending our Super Bowl hopes."

She ate and they watched more film, highlights of his season. After they finished eating, she grabbed their plates and put them in the sink, then came back with refilled glasses.

"You had a great season last year."

He stretched his legs out. "Yeah."

"In that game against New Orleans you caught nine passes for over two hundred yards. Last season you had over twelve hundred yards for the year. You were Green Bay's top receiver and were never out with an injury."

"Right. So what's your point?"

She lifted her gaze to his. "A player with your qualifications, with the kind of season you had, and they traded you anyway. Why?"

He planted his feet on the floor and cocked his head toward her. "Number one, I was too expensive. Number two, they'd drafted some guy out of Stanford who'd been a Heisman candidate. Younger, quick feet, great hands, a stellar future player. The team was hyped about this kid."

"You're talking about Cale Lefton."

"Yeah."

She stood, stretched her back, and folded her arms. "What you aren't saying is that the major difference between you and Lefton is that he's a lot less trouble on and off the field."

Cole shrugged. "He got plenty of media attention."

"Of course he did. The media was all over him, but in the right ways. He was an All American, a recipient of the Biletnikoff Award, plus the Campbell Trophy for the top scholar-athlete."

"Uh-huh. He probably walks on water and raises the dead, too."

Savannah laughed. "I doubt that, but he does have a few things you don't, and the number one thing he does have is a positive image. A player like that—someone who not only plays well, but presents well—can do a lot for a team."

"He's young. Give him time."

"Not every player will damage his image like you've done."

"Well aren't you all sweetness and light today?" If anyone needed to get laid and lighten up, it was Savannah. It would improve her mood.

"I wasn't hired to kiss your ass, Cole. I was hired to clean up your image. We can only do that if I tell it to you with honesty. Straight-up, and regardless of you being on what you might consider your best behavior at the club last night, your image isn't clean. We have to fix that."

"There's nothing wrong with my image. My stats show what kind of a player I am."

He could tell she wasn't buying it. She didn't even blink. "That's not enough and you know it. If it was, you'd still be playing for Green Bay."

Logically, he knew she was right. It had been a shock to get cut from Green Bay, and an even bigger blow to be fired by yet another agent. Especially when he felt like he hadn't deserved it. When Liz signed him, he'd wanted to kiss her because he'd been damn scared no one would pick him up, not that he would have admitted that to anyone. He owed it to Liz to give this image rehab thing a chance.

"Okay, so what do you suggest I do?"

"Well, there's obviously nothing wrong with your play on the field."

His lips curved. "Obviously."

"Or your ego, for that matter." She got up and grabbed the remote, rewound it back to his touchdown at the New Orleans game. "But look here. This was a go-ahead touchdown. A game changer."

She replayed him charging into the end zone. After the touchdown, his teammates cheered. Mostly with each other. He got a few obligatory high fives, but it wasn't like they all ran to the end zone and surrounded him like a hero.

Typical.

She fast forwarded. "But look here. When Harrell scored on a running dive from a yard out, they surrounded him. Same thing with Mohan's catch. They were celebrating with him, patting him on the back, banging his helmet. You mostly celebrated your touchdown alone. You ran the ball in and scored, got a few pats, but then the rest of the team went off to the sidelines to celebrate the touchdown—the touchdown you scored. You weren't part of that team."

"I was never part of that team. I never felt welcome."

She leaned back in the chair. "And whose fault was that? Theirs?"

"I didn't say that." He'd never noticed it before she pointed it out, but now that she had, there'd been other instances. He'd kept to himself, worked his magic with the ladies, did the PR gigs he was required to do, but never got involved with any of his team members. It had always been like that. He'd been a one-man wrecking crew, but he never bonded.

It was just the way he operated. He knew what it was like in the NFL. You went from one team to another. No sense in making close friends. And a lot of those guys were assholes, anyway. He got a lot of media attention and they resented it. What was the point in him trying to explain it was part of his job? He owed nothing to them.

"Look. Everyone's out for their own game. That's the way it is."

She arched a brow. "Really. That's how you see it?"

"Yeah. You do your job and leave it on the field. You want best friends, you find them elsewhere."

"Like at the clubs?"

"Something like that."

"I don't think even you believe that, Cole. Those people at the clubs aren't your friends. Not the kinds of friends you get close to."

"How would you know? You don't know who my real friends are."

"Then show me. Introduce me to them, and to your family. Let me see who the real Cole Riley is."

"Is this how you want to do your job? Just follow me around and talk to my friends and family?"

"That's part of it. I told you already that part of me reworking your image requires me to know who you are."

"So you can change me."

"I don't intend to change you."

He stood, raked his fingers through his hair, and paced in front of the television. He stopped and faced her. "I don't get this. I thought maybe you were going to change what kind of clothes I wore or something like that."

"That's not the kind of image we're talking about and I think you know it. This is going to be a deep evaluation into who you are. It's a journey, a discovery not just for me, but for you, too."

"See. You are some kind of shrink."

She laced her hands together in her lap. "I already told you I wasn't hired to psychoanalyze you. I'm here to help."

"You don't need to meet my family and friends."

"Do you have something to hide?"

"No."

"Then what's the problem?"

"There isn't one, except I like to keep my personal life separate from my business life."

"That's an odd statement coming from someone whose picture has been on so many magazine covers."

"With women I party with? Sure. At the clubs? Fine. But with my family? Other than that paparazzi who stalked me when I took my parents out, I keep that life separate."

"But it's part of who you are."

"No. We're not going there."

"That's your choice. But holding a part of yourself away from me isn't going to help me figure you out."

He gave her a sly grin. "Just redo my image as Cole Riley—man of mystery."

Savannah sighed. "More like Cole Riley—major pain in the butt."

"Hey, call me whatever you want. I'm used to it."

"Then we might as well get started with part two, and I'll have to wing it."

"You're the pro. I'm sure you can handle it."

"Fine. We'll get started tomorrow."

"Fine."

He wasn't going to enjoy this. Why couldn't everyone just leave him alone and let him do his job? Why wasn't his performance on the field ever enough?

SIX

SAVANNAH HAD MADE ARRANGEMENTS FOR THEM TO
meet the next night around seven. She told him to dress decently,
because they were going out to dinner.

He had no idea if they were going to meet with some PR people
or not, but he wore a pair of black slacks and a button-down shirt,
figuring he should be ready for anything.

He picked her up at her place. She opened the door, taking his
breath away with her simple summer dress—strapless, to show off
her shoulders. It hit her just above the knee, too, and she wore
heels, accentuating her sexy, beautiful legs. He was stunned at all
the available skin she showed.

It was going to be a long night.

She smiled. "Hi. You look nice."

"Thanks. You do, too."

He focused on her legs as he led her to his car and helped her in.

"So where are we going?" he asked as he started the car.

She gave him the name of a downtown restaurant.

"Fancy."

"Yes," was her only reply.

"Are we meeting someone there?"

"No. Just the two of us."

He frowned. "Is there something I should know?"

"I'm winging it, remember?"

"Okay. Wing away."

When they got to the restaurant, he pulled up to the curb and gave the keys to the valet, then led Savannah inside.

Sure he was about to be blindsided by some marketing or PR gurus, or even worse, the media, he was surprised when they were taken to a quiet table in the corner of the dark restaurant.

Near the windows, the restaurant gave a great view of the St. Louis arch and the riverfront.

"Nice place for tourists," he said.

"I chose it because the food is great, and so is the extensive wine list. You like steak, I assume."

"You assume right."

When the waiter brought the wine list and laid it on the table, Savannah picked it up.

"Would you like to go over the wine list with me? We could make a selection together."

Cole arched a brow. "I'm not much of a wine guy."

She nodded. "I can teach you. Wines are fascinating."

He shrugged. "What if I'm not all that interested?"

"It would probably help if you learned at least a little bit about wine. That way, if you take a woman out who does like wine, you can make suggestions, or even order for her."

"Is this a date?"

Her lips lifted. "No. But if it were, and I were your date, it's possible we could be selecting wine from this list."

"No. If it was a date, we wouldn't be at this restaurant."

"Really? Why not?"

He shifted to face her. "Not my kind of place."

"Really. And what kind of place is your kind of place to take a woman on a date? The club you took me to?"

"What's wrong with the club?"

"Other than your groupies hanging all over you, your bartender-slash-waitress friends acting like bodyguards to make sure no woman gets within a mile of you, no quiet time for talking and getting to know each other via conversation, and the fact that the media knows it's a place you hang out and party so they're more likely to be there to take your picture, there's nothing wrong with it."

"So we're here tonight to do what, exactly?"

"I'm showing you how a normal date with a woman goes."

He laughed. "Seriously? You think I don't know how to treat a woman?"

"At the moment I have my doubts." She leaned in and showed him the wine list. "I'd suggest the sauvignon blanc or the cabernet. They have some lovely brands here. If you'd like, I'd be happy to talk about them with you."

He pulled the wine list from her and set it on the other side of the table. "I can't believe you brought me out here tonight to teach me how to take a girl on a date."

"Woman. Anyone over the age of eighteen is a woman, not a girl."

"Whatever."

"See, the fact that you can't discern the difference indicates your need for coaching."

The muscles in his jaw tightened. "This has nothing to do with my image."

"I disagree. The way you treat women has everything to do with your image."

The waiter came over. "Good evening. I'm Richard and I'll be your waiter tonight. Have you had a chance to peruse the wine list?"

Cole handed the wine list back to Savannah. "I'll have Patron Silver, straight up. Make it a double. The lady would like to choose her own wine."

The waiter nodded, obviously too polite to indicate whether Cole had made some fatal social mistake by ordering his own drink and deferring to Savannah to order wine.

"I'll have the Beaulieu Vineyards Private Reserve Cabernet," Savannah said, "Just a glass, thank you."

The waiter left and Cole took a drink of water, so pissed he couldn't see straight.

"I don't think you got my point."

He leaned toward her and whispered, not wanting to cause a scene. Image, and all. "No, I don't think you got my point. What difference does it make if I order wine or if the woman I'm with orders her own? Do you think it matters to me that I don't know jack shit about wine, or that a woman I take out on a date knows more? It doesn't."

She laid her hand over his and squeezed. "I'm not trying to make you feel inferior. And this isn't about wine. It's merely a cursory overview of what a date might be between a man and a woman. The problem is, you take everything personally, as if it's an insult, when it isn't meant to be."

He had nothing to say to that.

"I merely suggested it might be fun for us to go over the wine list together, Cole. You're the one who made it contentious."

He had nothing to say to that, either.

Except he might have jumped the gun a little.

The waiter brought their drinks. Cole knocked back his tequila and let it burn its way down his throat, settling his irritation. Savannah took a sip of her wine and looked over the dinner menu.

"I might have overreacted."

She lifted her gaze to his over the top of the menu.

"I don't like being told what to do."

She laid the menu on the table. "I don't recall telling you anything."

"You brought me here."

"I did. Aren't you hungry?"

"Yeah, but you know what I mean. It feels like a trap."

"Going out to dinner is a trap? In what way?"

"I don't know. I feel like I'm some monkey you're training. I do know the right silverware to use, by the way."

"Good to know. I'll cross that off the list." She picked up the menu again.

He opened his mouth to fire back a reply, but the waiter returned to take their order. Cole hadn't even looked at the menu yet, so while Savannah ordered, he scanned, and ended up ordering a nice, thick steak.

Obviously, he was going to need the protein to engage in this battle of wills tonight.

When their salads arrived, he took his napkin out and made a production of showing Savannah how he placed it in his lap.

She rolled her eyes.

"Did I do it right?"

"That's not necessary, you know. I haven't scheduled you in for a manners and etiquette lesson."

He picked up his fork.

"Yet," she added.

She started eating, and he caught the tips of her lips curling into a smile.

Smart-ass. He should eat the damn salad with his fingers, but with his luck someone would take a shot of it with their camera phones and it would end up in the tabloids.

Then he *would* get compared to a monkey, and Savannah would be proven right.

He'd be damned if he let that happen. So instead, he ate and stewed about how he'd been suckered into coming on this non-date.

By the time dinner arrived and he'd plowed through his steak, he was more settled.

And more than a little curious.

"What makes you think I don't know how to treat a woman on a date?"

Savannah sipped the coffee the waiter had brought her, then set the cup in the saucer. "I didn't say you couldn't. But as I've been trying to explain to you, image is everything, including how you treat the women you go out with. This was merely my way of assessing your treatment of women."

"Yeah? And how am I doing so far?"

Her brow arched. "Do you really want me to answer that?"

"No. Because this isn't a real date. You and I went at it right away because we're in business together. If this had been a date, I'd have treated you differently."

She clasped her hands together on the table. "Really."

"Yeah."

"And what if the next media personality who interviews you tough is a woman? Will you treat her the same way you treated me tonight?"

"Did I treat you badly tonight?"

"No, but that's not my point. My point is you're reactionary. Instead of calmly discussing an issue, you get angry and perceive an insult where there might not be one."

"And you accuse instead of asking for an explanation."

She turned her head in question. "Do I? How so?"

"I felt dumb for not knowing anything about wines, but instead of asking me, you plowed ahead, assuming I was pissed off instead of embarrassed."

Now it was her turn to go quiet for a minute. "You may be right. I'm sorry. I would never intentionally make you feel stupid. Not everyone is knowledgeable about wines. I'm certainly no wine connoisseur. I only know a few brands that I've tasted and like very much. I've been put to shame on vineyard tours by friends of mine who are experts in wine."

He nodded. "You also assume I treat all women badly just because I hang out in clubs. You never gave me a chance to show you how I could treat a woman I was taking out on a date. Instead, you blindsided me."

"All right. Show me."

"Now?"

"Yes. We've only had dinner. The night is still young. Show me."

"And you'll correct me if I do anything wrong."

"Not until the end of the evening."

He rolled his eyes. "So I can do anything I want with you."

She laughed. "Within reason."

"Okay." He signaled for the waiter, who brought the check. Savannah reached for it.

Cole gave her a look. "You're kidding me, right?"

"This night was my idea," she said. "I'll pay."

He pulled the check across the table and took out his credit card. "I don't think so."

Savannah grinned. "Does the idea of a woman paying for dinner offend your masculinity?"

"Hell, yes. Deal with it."

After he paid, he led her out to his car. The drive was short, since they were already downtown. When he parked across from the Arch, Savannah's lips curved. He held the door for her and walked her toward the curved icon that symbolized the gateway to the west, the beautiful silver arch that had stood on the banks of the Mississippi River for as long as he remembered.

"Ever been?"

"Actually, no. I've always meant to go, but I'm always too busy."

He laid his hand at the small of her back and guided her inside, where he paid for them to take the tram up to the top of the Arch.

"We have some time to kill before our scheduled trip up," he said. "Care for a little history?"

Her eyes gleamed with excitement. "Of course."

They wound their way through the exhibits from the 1800s. Cole had been here before when he was a kid, had remembered enjoying seeing all the stagecoaches and fur traders and guns and everything associated with the exhibit.

It was even more fun looking through it as an adult, now that he had a more thorough knowledge of history. Plus, seeing it with Savannah was enjoyable. She made comments as they wound their way through each section, ending with a recap of the construction of the Arch.

"So fascinating," Savannah said as they got in line to take the elevator ride up.

"Growing up here, I always take it for granted, but it's a pretty unique piece of architecture. Wait till you see the top."

They rode up and Cole helped Savannah up the ramp toward the windows.

She leaned forward to look out.

"It's beautiful. I can't believe it took me so long to get here."

She moved between the east and west windows, wandering in between the tourists who'd accompanied them. Cole leaned against the carpeted sill so he could look out over the lighted city, never more glad to be back home. Seeing the river on one side and the city on the other relaxed him.

This is where he belonged. This felt right to him. It was going to be a good season.

They left the Arch and Cole drove them a few short blocks to one of his favorite places.

The club was dark and had a moody atmosphere. He hadn't been here in a while, had almost forgotten about it because he usually went to the other club these days.

This challenge with Savannah had reminded him of some of the old places he used to frequent, like this one.

Savannah gave him a dubious look as they grabbed a booth in the back of the club. It was quiet right now. The band must be on a break.

"Someplace else your groupies hang out?"

"I used to come here a lot. Not so much anymore. No idea who hangs out here."

The waitress came by and they ordered drinks.

Savannah gave the place a once-over. Very dark wood paneling graced the walls. There was no ear-splitting loud music. Not a strobe or neon light in sight. The waitresses wore dark pants and tuxedo-like shirts and vests. There were business people in here. Some folks were dressed up. It was . . . classy.

Very much *not* a Cole Riley kind of place.

Several guys stepped up to the band area, pulled up trumpets and trombones and bass and guitars and started playing a slow, very mellow song. A woman got up and started singing, her voice melancholy and filled with lost love and regret.

Surprised, she looked at Cole. "It's blues music."

He raised his glass to her. "Yeah."

She listened for a while as the song sank deep into her bones. She closed her eyes and let the lyrics and the notes fill her as she sipped her most excellent wine. The singer's voice was deep and throaty and filled with pain.

She turned to Cole. "I love this."

"I thought you might."

Then she smiled. There were obviously facets to Cole she hadn't explored yet, parts to him he didn't let people see. All the media saw was the party Cole, the angry Cole. That side of him was definitely present, but she'd enjoyed seeing the city from the top of the Arch tonight. It had been so thoughtful of him to take her there. There was nothing more fun than playing tourist, especially when a native indulged you like that.

And this club? Heavenly. She relaxed into the booth and every bone in her body melted into the music.

"What kind of music do you like?" Cole asked.

She sat up and faced him. "All kinds, really. Everything from classical to hip-hop."

"Eclectic, aren't you?"

"A bit. How about you?"

"I'm a fan of country, blues, and jazz."

"And yet you go to the clubs. Where the autotuned, electropop, dance music plays."

He laughed. "Hey, I hang out at the clubs. I didn't say I liked the club music."

"Then why do you go there?"

"I like the people."

"Because they're such good friends of yours? The ones whose last names you don't know?"

"You're going there again?"

She decided to take a different approach. "Okay. Now that you're home, tell me about your friends. Any friends from high school you still hang out with?"

"Not really. My two best friends from high school both live out of state now."

"That's too bad. So you don't see them anymore?"

"One lives in Denver, and the other in Chicago. Whenever I have games there, we meet for dinner. Otherwise, no. They come home to see family over the holidays, and I'm usually home in the off-season, so our visits don't coincide."

"I'm sorry. I suppose now that you're back you'll make new friends."

He rimmed the tip of his shot glass with his fingertip and gave her a lazy smile. "I already have."

"At the club."

He shrugged. "Sure."

"Those are groupies, not friends. You can make the distinction, can't you?"

"I think you're hung up too much on the friends thing. Guys don't need close friends like women seem to. With guys, wherever we are, that's who our friends are. We don't call guys on the phone to chat for hours. We don't go shopping together. Guys don't need the bonding rituals that women seem to need."

"Maybe you're right." She'd let that one drop . . . for now. But she'd get back to it, because he was wrong. He'd isolated himself for years, and there was a reason for it. Tonight wasn't the night to discuss it in-depth.

Not when there was great music and amazing ambience. Instead, she listened to the band play and the singer belt out more mournful songs that filled her soul. It was captivating. This place was lovely and, though crowded, it was understated. No one came up to Cole and bothered him. He blended in and they were able to enjoy the band without being bombarded with women or the media.

"It's still early," he said, holding out her chair for her. "Let's go take a walk."

"Sure."

He held the door for her, but instead of taking her to the car, he led her across the street. There was a festival going on near the riverfront about a half a block away.

"Can you walk in those things?" he asked, directing his gaze toward her heels.

She grinned. "Of course."

"I think I should hold your hand."

She lifted her gaze to his. "Why?"

"First, because I'm afraid you're going to trip and fall. And second, if this was a real date, that's what I'd do."

"All right."

There were tents set up with beer and food, a live band up on a stage as well as crafts and all forms of entertainment. It was lively and the area was packed with people enjoying the festival.

Savannah was definitely overdressed, but she didn't care. She loved watching the people mingle. The band was playing some very loud rock music, and the crowd was electrified.

Cole held tight to her hand as they strolled among the vendors hawking pottery, jewelry, artwork, and the like. Savannah enjoyed fairs like this, loved to stop at each tent to see what they were selling.

"Is this what you'd really do if you were out on a date?" she asked as they stopped to buy a drink from one of the food carts.

"Sure it is."

She took a drink of the lemonade. It was tart and sweet. Absolutely perfect on a hot night. "Somehow I can't see you doing a riverfront fair."

"Why not?"

"I don't know. It doesn't seem your type of fun thing to do."

"You don't know me all that well, Peaches."

He was right about that. She only knew him on paper. "That's what this exercise is all about. Getting to know you better so I can clear up any misconceptions I might have about you."

"Yeah, well, it seems like you have a lot of them."

She tilted her head back to look at him. "Do I?"

"Obviously. You thought all I liked to do was hang out in nightclubs and have orgies with women."

She gasped. "Now how could you possibly make that kind of generalization?"

"I don't know. How could you?"

She rolled her eyes. "You know, Cole, for a man you're awfully sensitive."

"And you're a typical woman who judges on first impression."

"It's a good thing I'm not easily insulted," she said with a laugh. "And if this is how you talk to the women you date, it's no wonder you frequent the clubs."

"What does that mean?"

She caught the frown and the way his body straightened as he tensed.

"It means in a club atmosphere it's mostly groups. It wouldn't be a one-on-one type of situation, so you don't have to get close to anyone. The so-called date we had tonight was quieter, more time for one-on-one conversation, which allows a woman to ask probing questions, to become more intimately familiar with you."

"And you're saying I don't want that?"

"I don't know. Do you?"

"Hey, I like intimately familiar."

"I'm not talking about sex."

"Neither was I."

Her lips curved. "Liar. You were, too."

"Okay, maybe I was."

They walked across the street to his car. She climbed in and he started the engine.

"So what would be your next move—if this were an actual date?" she asked.

He was silent as he pulled onto the highway and headed west. "I'd take the woman home."

He did just that, and walked Savannah to her door. She took her keys out of her purse and was about to tell Cole good night.

"And if this were a real date, this is where I'd go in for the kiss."

Before she could object, he had his arms around her, tugging her close, his mouth coming down on hers.

It wasn't a forceful, demanding kiss. Instead, he brushed his lips across hers.

Shocked, all she could do was hold on to his arms. She opened her mouth and he slid his tongue inside. Warm pleasure spread throughout her body, wrapping her in a foggy sensation of want and need.

For a minute she forgot all about the purpose of this night. Instead, all she thought about was the way Cole held her, the way he lazily stroked her back when he kissed her. Up close, he smelled like everything she loved about a man—crisp, clean, and sensual. She lost herself in the way his lips moved over hers, the magical way his hands cupped the back of her head and tangled in her hair when he deepened the kiss. And when he pressed her against the door, his body aligning with hers, lord have mercy but she thrilled to the feel of him, all hard angles and planes.

All hard. All over, especially between his legs, where he rocked against her sex, making her wet and quivery.

She'd invite him inside, where he'd pull the zipper down on her dress and fill his hands with her breasts. She could already imagine his mouth on her nipples, his hand inside her panties, coaxing her to the orgasm she so desperately needed.

She whimpered.

"Invite me in, Peaches," he whispered against her lips.

And then reality set in, and she remembered she wasn't on an actual date with Cole.

He wasn't hers to do with as she pleased. And she certainly didn't belong to him.

She splayed her hands on his chest and gave him slight pressure.

He took a step back.

She swallowed, her body, her senses, still filled with him. She fought for breath, willed her rapidly beating heart to slow down while she made eye contact with Cole and silently begged for understanding.

He straightened, then his lips curved in a hint of a smug smile.

"And that's what I'd do with a woman I was out on a date with, Peaches. Except it wouldn't end there."

He turned and got into his car, started up the engine, and pulled away.

Savannah opened the door, the cold of the air-conditioning inside doing nothing to quell the blast of heat burning inside her body.

No, it definitely wouldn't have ended here.

Not if they'd been on a real date.

Not if he really belonged to her.

SEVEN

COLE HAD A WORKOUT AT THE TEAM TRAINING FACILITY the next day. It was his first time being with the entire team, to see how the offense would mesh together.

It was mainly drills today and working with the conditioning coaches. There'd be no formations, unfortunately. He was eager to get in a line and take a pass from Cassidy, show the Traders what he was capable of.

This was going to be the year he'd become a star. He was home now and this was the right team. It might not be game time yet, but something was gelling for him. There was a renewed sense of fire in his gut that he hadn't felt since he was a rookie. And if he had to grind his cleats over all the other wide receivers to show the team how good he was, that's what he'd do.

He'd noticed Liz and Savannah on the sidelines watching the drills, decided to ignore them both while he worked out with the coaches. No distractions today, not when he was focused on work. He tuned them out until four hours later when he was drenched in sweat and every muscle in his body screamed in pain from the non-stop drills and sprints they'd put him through.

"You're done," the trainer said to the wide receivers. "Hit the showers."

Thank god. He pulled off his helmet and walked to the sideline for a drink.

"You're huffing and puffing like an old man," Liz said, leaning her hip against the drink table. "Too tough for you out there?"

He downed the drink in two gulps, then tossed the cup in the trash and grinned at her. "Nope. Just the way I like it."

He shifted his gaze to Savannah. "What are you doing here?"

"Observing."

"Did I pass or fail?"

"You didn't punch any of the coaches or any of the other players, so I'd call it a good day."

He laughed. "Come on. I'm not that bad, Peaches."

"Aren't you? I've read your file. You're not exactly known for playing well with others."

He rolled his eyes. "I'm going to take a shower."

"Then we'll take you to lunch," Liz said.

He shrugged. "Fine with me."

He showered off the grime and pieces of turf, changed clothes, and met Savannah and Liz in the parking lot. He wasn't sure, but this felt a little like some kind of intervention. "You're not both here to gang up on me, are you?"

Liz linked her arm in his. "Afraid of two small women?"

"Normal women? No. You two? Yes."

Liz gave him a diabolical laugh. "Good. You should be wary of us. We've been plotting."

He shifted his gaze to Savannah, who cast an innocent look his way.

Bullshit. He wasn't buying it.

"Christ." He raked his hand through his damp hair. "All right. Let's get this over with."

They drove to a restaurant. It was past lunch hour, but too early for dinner. Still, he was starving so he was glad the place was open. He was in the mood for a giant burger, which he ordered as soon as the waiter showed up to take their drink order.

Liz grabbed the bread basket, then pushed it aside. "No. Wedding. Must fit into my dress."

Savannah gave her a smile. "Just one piece?"

"Don't enable me. I'm resisting carbs until after the wedding. After that I'm going to devour an entire loaf of French bread. Possibly an entire bakery of bread. Poor Gavin. He might have to take me to a bakery on our wedding night."

Savannah laughed. "You're a stronger woman than I am. I wouldn't be able to do it."

Cole frowned. "Why can't you have the bread?"

"You're such a guy. You don't understand. My dress fits me. I mean really fits me. I have to watch everything I eat right now."

He shook his head. "Women."

"It's only a few days," Liz said, then turned to Savannah. "I'm dreaming of bread and pasta, though."

"I would be, too," Savannah said with a sigh. Then reached for the bread. "Sorry."

"Bitch. I hate you. I'm going to watch you eat every bite."

Women were odd creatures. He wasn't even going to try to figure that out. Instead, he ate his salad, glad to be eating something and ignorant of the female species.

"So let's talk media interviews," Savannah said after they'd all filled their stomachs.

Content after the giant hamburger he'd devoured, Cole pushed his empty plate to the side and took a drink of iced tea. "What media interviews?"

"One of the local news stations wants to do a piece on your coming to the Traders for their ten o'clock sports cast."

He looked at Savannah, then shook his head. "Me and the media don't mesh."

"They're going to have to," Liz said. "You can't avoid PR forever just because a few guys with cameras have pissed you off in the past."

"This is true," Savannah added. "The whole purpose of me working with you is to get you media ready. You're going to have to do interviews."

He leaned back in the chair. "The media makes up shit about me. They're going to go into this with preconceived notions about me. You know they're going to bring up everything that's happened in the past."

Savannah nodded. "That could be. I'll coach you on how to handle those questions, downplay the negative and accentuate all the positive aspects of you being with the Traders this year."

"This doesn't sound like a good idea." He'd never volunteered for media interviews. Not since they started going south on him.

"It's necessary," Liz said. "The sooner you get started working with the media and turning your image around, the better it will be for you."

"Maybe we could feed them the questions to ask."

Savannah shook her head. "You can't limit the media. That will only make them suspicious and more difficult to deal with. It's best to be an open book. The more honest you are, the less negative they'll be."

Before he could object, Liz piped up with, "This is why we brought Savannah in. She's an expert in this area."

He knew he was going to get ganged up on. Good thing he'd already eaten lunch because just thinking about sitting down with sports media had his stomach clenching. "Fine. When?"

Savannah checked her phone. "In about two hours. They want it for the broadcast tonight."

"You set me up so I wouldn't have time to think about it."

"Of course we set you up," Liz said with a sly grin. "What kind of an agent would I be if I didn't maneuver you into doing my bidding?"

He turned to Savannah. "How long have you known about this?"

She frowned. "What are you talking about?"

"That date we had last night. Was that to mellow me out and make it more likely I'd be cooperative?"

She frowned. "I didn't know anything about the interview last night. Liz called me this morning about it."

Liz glanced from him to Savannah. "What date?"

Savannah waved her hand. "It was nothing. An exercise."

"Uh-huh. Whatever. I'll leave you two to work on the specifics of the interview. I have wedding stuff."

Liz kissed Savannah's cheek and stood, glaring at Cole with her fiercest agent look. "Behave and don't fuck this up."

"Yeah, yeah."

"I'm serious. And I need *you* to take this seriously."

"Jesus. I said I would and I will. You two are like my grandmother. Nags. Go play bride-to-be and leave me alone. I'll be good."

She laughed. "See you later."

After Liz left, he turned to Savannah. "Okay, get me the hell ready for this inquisition."

She stood. "Let's go to the studio. They've offered us private space for preparation prior to the interview."

"I don't think so. We'll go to my place. I don't want them bugging the room or popping in to see how we're doing and asking a bunch of nosy questions. They'll get my time for the interview and nothing before that."

"Paranoid much?"

"Yeah, totally. I don't trust the media. They've screwed me over too many times."

She followed him back to his condo. He cleared a spot at the table and they grabbed some water and sat.

"All right," Savannah said, pulling a sheet of paper from her briefcase. "Since this is local news and not national, they're likely just going to ask you about you being with the Traders this season. Remember, their job is to talk up their local team, not just you. I've met Hal Marbrook and have worked with him on behalf of the team before. He's been with this network sports outlet for fifteen years. He's a nice man, and also very knowledgeable about the Traders. He's aware of the team's needs and what they've risked bringing you on board. So while he'll cut you some slack because of his dedication to the Traders, he might press you about your past altercations. Be prepared for that."

"I'm always prepared for anything when it comes to the media. And I don't doubt for a second that no matter how nice a guy Hal Marbrook is, it's his job to get a juicy story."

"Just don't go into it thinking negatively. He could make you look good."

He wasn't buying it. "It's not the media's job to make players look good. It's their job to gain viewership. Controversy gains viewers. If you got him an interview with me as an exclusive, I can guarantee you he's coming after me."

She nodded. "It's a possibility, but I don't think so. So don't plan on a fight when you might not get one. Be pleasant, be courteous, and above all, smile. Take a lot of deep breaths and pause before you answer each question. Think about your answer. Remember, you need your hometown in your corner. You're not going to get them if you piss them off before you ever take the field for your first preseason game."

He couldn't tell if this was her normal way of dealing with her clients, or if she was covering all her bases because she was afraid he was going to explode into some chair-throwing maniac on the air.

"You know, just because I got into a few altercations with some of the media doesn't mean I'm going to implode every time someone with the press interviews me. I really do know how to handle myself in an interview."

"Really? Because you haven't shown much of that lately."

Okay, she had him there. "Trust me. I'll prove it to you."

"You're going to have to, because I was hired to rework your image, and a large part of that involves your relationship with the media, which you have to admit hasn't always been a friendly one."

"I'll admit to that."

"Upper management expects that to change."

"And that sounds an awful lot like an 'or else.' "

"I don't deal in 'or elses.' That's for upper management."

She leveled a sweet-as-pie smile at him while delivering that not-so-subtle threat. He'd have to be brain-dead to miss it.

He wasn't brain-dead. "I'll handle it."

"I'm sure you will. Would you like to go over some practice questions so we can work on your potential answers?"

He laughed. "Not a chance in hell. I'd rather go off the cuff."

"Uh-huh. And that's what's gotten you into trouble in the past. I'd much rather have you well prepared for any possibility."

"And you know as well as I do that you can't prepare for what they might throw at me."

"No, but we can practice."

He stood and grabbed his phone. "Look at the time. I should change clothes so we're not late."

"Cole." She stood, the warning tone in her voice making her unhappiness very clear to him.

"I'll be right back, Peaches." He stopped, turned to her. "Unless you'd like to come into the bedroom and dress me, too."

She crossed her arms. "I'll pass."

* * *

SAVANNAH HELD HER BREATH AS HAL SHOOK HANDS with Cole. She had to wait outside the recording studio, which seemed like miles away.

Not that she could do anything for Cole even if she was sitting right next to him. She couldn't put the right answers in his mouth. Whatever he said, he'd have to own.

Hal started slow, talking about Cole's hometown connection to St. Louis. Obviously tense at first, Cole seemed to relax under Hal's easygoing style of questions about how Cole would fit into the Trader lineup. Cole handled those answers just fine. He had enthusiasm, really talked up the Traders, kept his points to discussing the team and how excited he was to be a part of such a great organization.

It was perfect.

"So tell me, Cole. Given your past and the fact you've often been in the limelight for all the wrong reasons, why do you think the Traders took a gamble on you?" Hal asked.

Uh-oh.

She saw the change in Cole's expression, the way he leaned back in his chair.

Please think before you answer, Cole.

He opened his mouth, then looked across the room to the booth where she sat. He took a deep breath and said, "Well, Hal, you can't believe everything you hear about me."

"So all those previous media reports are lies?"

He gave Hal a grin. "Of course they are."

Hal gave Cole a disbelieving look. "Nothing printed about you previously is the truth."

"Hey, I'm no Boy Scout. Like I said, you can't believe everything that's been said about me. But some of those things happened when I was younger. I learned a few lessons."

"So you're turning over a new leaf with the Traders."

"Clean slate. New start. And in answer to your question, the Traders took a gamble on me because I'm one of the best wide receivers out there."

Hal laughed. "Pretty bold statement considering there are three awesome receivers on the team."

"I'm confident in my skills. Obviously the Traders are, too. Otherwise they wouldn't have picked me up. But rather than just talking about what I can do, I hope you and the Trader fans will tune in to *see* what I can do."

Savannah relaxed her shoulders. Excellent answer. And Hal wasn't a contentious interviewer, so he didn't get into the negatives about Cole's past. Cole and Hal shook hands after the interview and Cole met her outside the booth.

He gave her a smile. "Did I pass?"

"You did okay."

"I did better than okay and you know it."

They walked toward the front door and outside. "Hal was easy on you. He's not going to besmirch anyone with the Traders because he doesn't want to risk his press pass to the locker room. The real test will come when you have to face national media. But as a first test, you passed."

"Good enough."

"We need to work through some of the questions that will come up when you do have those interviews." She pulled her phone out of her pocket and scrolled through her calendar. "I have some free time tomorrow afternoon."

Cole shook his head. "Can't. I have Gavin's wedding coming up and I'm one of the groomsmen. I have all this . . . wedding stuff to do over the next few days."

"Oh, that's right. Fine. We'll start on Monday."

"That'll work."

"I guess I'll head out, then."

She walked to her car and he opened the door. "Savannah."

She turned. "Yes."

"You wanna talk about last night?"

"What about last night?"

"That kiss between you and me. And what happened the other night at your place."

"Nothing happened, Cole. Nothing that's going to be repeated, anyway, so there's nothing to talk about."

"If that's the way you want to play it."

"It is. It's best if we keep our relationship strictly business." The chemistry between them scared her. She had to be on her guard around him to make sure what happened never happened again.

And he knew she was attracted to him. She caught the hint of a smile, but then it was gone.

"Sure. I'll see you Monday."

He turned and she slid into her car. Now it was her turn to smile. He'd see her well before Monday.

EIGHT

COLE STOOD IN THE SMALL, SUFFOCATING ROOM IN the back of the church, feeling claustrophobic and wishing this were over already so he could be at the bar. But he'd do anything for his cousin Gavin, including hanging back here to wait for the ceremony that was already ten minutes late.

"Leave it to Liz to need to make an entrance," Gavin said as he looked out the window.

"Maybe she bailed on you."

Gavin shot his brother, Mick, a glare. "She'll show up. Or I'll hunt her down and kill her."

That made Mick laugh. "You do realize you're in church."

"And God knows Elizabeth. He'd forgive me."

Cole shook his head. Weddings were so not his deal. It was hot and humid today and wearing this tux didn't help. Nor did being packed in like sardines in this tiny little room with a bunch of men, one of whom was pacing.

Mick's phone rang and he picked up and listened. "Okay, babe.

Smile pretty when you come down the aisle." He pocketed the phone. "Tara said we'll start in about ten minutes."

Gavin groaned.

"Hey, at least she showed up," Cole said.

"Yup. It'll be over before you know it. And then your lifetime of servitude begins."

Dedrick, one of Gavin's teammates and best friends, shot Gavin a huge grin.

Gavin laughed. "I hope so, Deed, because we have a game on Friday night."

"I can't believe you didn't get married during the off-season," Cole said.

Gavin gave Cole one of those looks. "You obviously don't know my soon-to-be wife and your new agent all that well yet. She wanted the wedding now, in July, and by god she was going to have one, even if it's in the middle of baseball season and on a Wednesday night. She arranged it around the All Star break so there'd be a few days off."

"She had to plan it around our season," Tommy, one of the other teammates said as he buttoned and unbuttoned his jacket. "My wife, Haley, said Liz was kind of determined."

"So I guess you'll be delaying your honeymoon?"

Gavin shrugged. "Yeah. But we're heading to Fiji in November."

"After we win the World Series," Dedrick said.

"Hell yeah," Tommy said, high-fiving Dedrick.

"If you don't have her pregnant by then," Dedrick added.

Gavin laughed. "I'll do my best."

"You guys are crazy." Mick came over to Gavin and straightened his tie. "And so's your fiancée."

"Tell me something I don't know," Gavin said. "But I love her. What can I do? July wedding it is. She doesn't care that much about the honeymoon, anyway. To her it's all about the wedding."

Mick nodded. "Tara, too. It's all she's been able to talk about since our own wedding. That and baby stuff now that she's pregnant. She was freaking out about having to have her dress altered."

Cole shook his head. "Women and love and marriage and weddings and babies? I remember when all we could think about was sports. And getting laid."

"You find the right woman, you still get laid," Dedrick said, waggling his brows.

"Damn straight," Mick said, patting Cole on the back. "Just you wait, cousin. Your day of reckoning is coming."

Cole let out a derisive snort. "Not me. Not interested."

Mick shot Gavin a knowing look. "Seems it wasn't that long ago we both thought the same way."

"Yeah. He's gonna fall hard when it happens."

"All married men say the same thing. Mark my words. I'm staying single."

Mick arched a brow. "Care to lay some money on it?"

Cole rolled his eyes. "Sure."

Gavin put his arm over Cole's shoulders. "I'm in for a hundred."

"Me, too," Mick said.

"You're on. Easiest money I'll ever make."

"Sucker," Dedrick said as he walked by. "You'll meet your match. Every guy does."

"Not this guy. I like my life just the way it is."

SAVANNAH THOUGHT THE WEDDING HAD BEEN AMAZing. Elizabeth was stunning on an ordinary day, but today she looked like she belonged on the cover of a bridal magazine. In a soft white with a dropped waist, her strapless organza dress was simple, but elegant. Her red hair had been pulled up, with a few strands softly framing her neck and face. She took Savannah's breath away, so she could only imagine the impact she'd had on Gavin, who'd looked awestruck when Gavin's father had walked Liz down the aisle.

Cole hadn't looked too shabby as one of the groomsmen, either. Whether sweating it out at the gym or dressed up to the max in a tux, he was simply mesmerizing. She couldn't take her eyes off him, which was no doubt why he had the reputation he had—like all the Riley men. There was no doubt it was a devastating gene pool.

The ceremony had been lovely as Elizabeth and Gavin had shared tender words of love and commitment. And even though the wedding was on a weeknight, the hotel where the reception was being held was packed full of family and friends and Gavin's teammates. It probably helped that their next series was a home game.

The hotel ballroom was decorated in a mix of pale yellow and purple, the dark purple matching the bridesmaids' dresses. The flowers throughout the ballroom, highlighted by breathtaking orchids, were simply stunning. The wedding party was introduced to a fanfare of shouts and applause, then Savannah nearly swooned to the romantic first dance. It was clear Elizabeth and Gavin were very much in love.

She'd love to have a man look at her like that someday—like she was the only person in the room and no one and nothing else existed.

Did love like that exist? It must, because it was evident on the faces of this newly married couple, and others spread across the room. She could feel it, though she had never experienced it either for herself or in relationships close to her.

As her gaze drifted over the wedding party that surrounded the bride and groom, she caught sight of Cole, who happened to be looking at her at the same time.

She smiled at him, but he frowned, then looked away.

Interesting.

The wedding party danced, pictures were taken, and Savannah found her seat at the table with some of Gavin's teammates and their wives.

Cole sat at the head table next to one of the bridesmaids—

Elizabeth's new sister-in-law Jenna. She was Cole's cousin, if Savannah remembered the family tree correctly. Jenna was perfectly adorable. She had short dark hair with purple streaks at the tips that matched her dress. And some very hot and gorgeous guy came up to her and kissed her, causing Jenna to smile.

"Are you having fun?" Elizabeth and Gavin were making their rounds from table to table.

"It was a beautiful wedding. I've never seen two people who are obviously so much in love."

Elizabeth grinned. "I know. Kind of nauseating, isn't it?"

"Not at all. It's very romantic."

"I can't help it. It's everything I ever wanted, the stupid fairy tale and all." She grasped Gavin's hand and introduced him to Savannah. Gavin shook her hand.

"You have an incredible new wife."

"So she keeps telling me," he said with a grin, then planted a kiss on her lips.

Elizabeth elbowed him in the ribs. "And here I thought he'd be charming for the rest of the night."

"You know me better than that." Gavin wandered off to talk to his teammates and Liz took a seat in one of the vacant chairs next to Savannah.

"I love designer shoes and all, but my feet are killing me. All those pictures."

Savannah laughed. "I'm sure the photographs will be aweworthy. I love the purple dresses on the bridesmaids."

"Totally Tara's idea." Liz looked over her shoulder at Tara, who was talking to someone across the room. "Isn't she adorable? And that baby bump. I'm not even a baby person and it makes my biological clock do a fast tick-tock."

"Do you and Gavin want to start a family?"

Elizabeth nodded. "We will be eventually. The poor kid. Me for a mother."

Savannah grasped Liz's hand. "You'll make an amazing mother."

"I hope so. Now that Tara's pregnant, and Jenna's planning her wedding to Tyler—it's like the whole Riley crew is fast-forwarding into family mode. I can't believe I'm thinking about making babies already. If it was up to Gavin I would have been pregnant already, but we decided to wait until after the wedding so his parents wouldn't kill us."

Savannah laughed. "Sometimes doing it the old-fashioned way is fun."

Liz shrugged. "I guess so. But I'm throwing my birth control pills away after this month. I couldn't care less if I'm pregnant on my honeymoon."

Liz was positively glowing. "You sound so happy. And so relaxed."

"I know. If you would have told me a year ago I'd be married and talking about making babies, I would have laughed in your face. I guess the laugh is on me now."

"Love changes you, I guess. At least that's what I've heard."

"Oh, you just wait, Savannah. When you meet the right guy, it's like an explosion. It knocks you back on your heels."

"What are you girls gossiping about?"

Savannah looked up to find Tara leaning over. She was so beautiful, and pregnancy only added to the glow on her face.

"Men. Marriage. Babies," Liz added, rubbing the slight bulge on Tara's lower stomach.

"Oh, god. I don't look pregnant. I look like I ate too much pasta."

Savannah let out a laugh. "You totally look pregnant. You're glowing all over with it."

Tara cupped her cheeks. "Do I? I feel all glowy. It's wonderful. After Nathan—" She shifted her gaze to Savannah. "Nathan's my son." She pointed him out in a group of teens across the room.

"He's so handsome," Savannah said.

Tara grinned. "Thank you. He's seventeen and mortified that his mother is—how did he put it?—oh, yes. 'Knocked up when you're so old, Mom.' " She laughed.

"Anyway, after having Nathan so long ago, it's like starting all over again." Tara looked at both of them, then shrugged. "Hell, it *is* starting all over again. What was I thinking?"

"That you love Mick and want to have his babies?" Elizabeth asked.

She sighed. "Yes. That's what I was thinking. And I'm so happy to be doing it all again."

Savannah pulled out a chair. "Sit. Tell me all about babies and doing this twice."

"Thank you. I like this spot in the corner. I can hide from my husband and my son."

"I doubt for long. I imagine Mick is very protective of you."

Tara grimaced. "It's horrible. He watches what I eat, monitors where I go, what I lift. He treats me like I'm fragile and I'm going to break. I'm glad football season's starting and I can get him out of my hair. Though Nathan is just as bad keeping his eagle eye on me. You'd think this was the first time in history that a woman had been pregnant. I'm hardly an egg. I'm very healthy, the doctor says everything's fine and I can go about my business like normal as long as I don't plan on doing any bungee jumping, which wasn't on my upcoming agenda anyway."

Liz laughed. "Damn. And I was so going to get you that for your birthday."

"Har-har. Soon I'll be as big as a house. I got huge right away with Nathan, and his father—though tall—wasn't nearly the size of Mick. I'm doomed."

"I can't believe you're all hiding out here." Jenna came over and pulled an empty chair over. "No one told me we were having a girl meeting."

"It's impromptu," Liz said. "I'm resting my feet."

"I told you those were going to hurt," Jenna said, pointing to Liz's shoes. "But no. You insisted they were gorgeous."

Liz lifted her dress. "They're not just gorgeous—they're fucking gorgeous and I'll deal with sore feet. But right now I'm taking a few sit-down minutes with the girls."

"They are beautiful shoes," Savannah said, admiring the silvery stilettos adorned with Swarovski crystals. "Well worth a few blisters."

Liz lifted her chin and glared at Jenna. "See?"

Jenna rolled her eyes. "I'd rather be barefoot."

"You would. You'll probably get married at some park, or in a meadow, or something disgustingly bohemian," Liz said with grimace.

"Likely. I'll be sure to add 'barefoot' to my wedding list, knowing how much you'll love that."

"Bitch."

Savannah laughed. This must be what it was like to have sisters and a close-knit family. She ached for the camaraderie, the sharing of secrets, and the familial bond she'd never had. It must be a pure thrill for Tara, Liz, and Jenna to have this.

"Come on, wife. Time to dance." Gavin came over and dragged Liz out of the chair.

She rolled her eyes. "Look how he thinks he owns me now." She might have voiced a complaint, but the warmth and love in her eyes was obvious. She grinned and slid into his arms, gliding out onto the dance floor as a slow song played and the photographer snapped pictures.

"God, they're so perfect for each other," Jenna said. "I'm all teary-eyed."

"Your day is coming."

A tall, gorgeous dark-haired man kissed the back of Jenna's neck. She turned around and grinned. "Not soon enough."

Jenna introduced Savannah to her fiancé, Tyler, who Jenna said played for the St. Louis Ice hockey team.

"Sports must be in the Riley family blood," Savannah said. "You even marry into it."

Jenna laughed. "Believe me. I tried my best to avoid it."

"True, but I wore her down with my charm," Tyler said. He pulled Jenna from her chair. "Let's dance."

Mick found his way over and grabbed Tara. "Feel like showing the rest of them how it's done?"

"What? You're going to allow me to dance? Are you sure it isn't against your mountainous list of things I'm not supposed to do?"

"Hey, I'm only taking care of your precious cargo."

"The precious cargo is fine. And I'd love to dance with you, as long as you don't try to carry me around the dance floor." She walked away with her arm in Mick's, winking at Savannah.

Savannah sighed as the remnants of love and family surrounded her.

Speaking of family . . . She searched the darkened ballroom. She spotted Cole, standing next to a couple who must be his parents.

He'd been avoiding her and she knew why. She stood and headed toward him. His back was to her as he stood with his mother and father and a stunning brunette who looked to be a few years younger than him.

"Hello, Cole."

He turned and looked decidedly unhappy.

His parents smiled at her, then looked expectantly at Cole.

"This is Savannah Brooks. She works for the team, and with me. Savannah, these are my parents, Jack and Cara Riley, and my sister, Alicia."

Savannah shook their hands. "It's very nice to meet all of you."

"Nice to meet you, too, Savannah," Cara said. "What exactly do you do for the Traders?"

"Public relations."

Cole rolled his eyes at her.

"Oh. That's nice. So you'll be working on some things with Cole."

"Yes, I will. Since he's new to the team, it's my job to work closely with him, get him acclimated to the team, associate his image with the Traders."

"Good deal," Jack said. "He's a great player, and we're happy as hell to have him playing for the home team now."

"I'm sure you are. The team is very happy to have him."

His mother put her arm around Cole's waist. "We've missed him since he started playing football. He travels so much and is rarely home except in the off-season. It'll be nice to have him around for family dinners. You should come, too, Savannah."

"No."

Everyone looked at Cole.

"Cole, that was impolite."

"Sorry. But you know how I feel about work and home life mixing."

She smacked her son on the arm. "And you know how I feel about you being rude and obnoxious." She turned to Savannah. "Since the season hasn't started yet, do come. Sunday dinner is at five o'clock."

Cole would hate that. What a perfect opportunity to get to know him better through his family. "Thank you for the invitation. I'd love to."

She could feel Cole's gaze on her, but decided to ignore him. Instead, she turned to his sister. "Alicia, what do you do?"

"I'm in sports medicine. I'm working with the St. Louis Rivers baseball team. It's a relatively new position for me, so I'm very excited."

"Oh, what an excellent field."

"We're so proud," Cara said, obviously beaming with pride.

"It's a great career," Alicia said with a grin. "Fortunately, my family has always been filled with jocks for me to experiment on."

Savannah laughed. "I'm sure that's true. And the Rivers. What an amazing team. Congratulations."

"Thank you. I'm thrilled to work with them. They have an excellent team of doctors and therapists."

"And athletes," Savannah added. "They're lucky to have you. I'd love to know more about what you're going to be doing for them. Sports medicine is such an interesting field."

"Let's dance." Cole grasped her arm.

She tore her gaze away from Alicia. "What?"

"Dance. Music. Dance floor."

"Oh. Sure." She looked at his parents and sister. "Excuse me. It was lovely meeting all of you."

She knew what he was doing. She could have said no to the dance, but that would have been impolite, and he was doing a fine job of that, so she didn't want to add to it.

He swept her against him—tight. "What are you doing here?"

"I was invited."

"You didn't mention that the other day."

She shrugged. "You just assumed I wasn't going to be here."

"And so you finagled an invitation from Elizabeth."

She sighed. "I've known Elizabeth for five years. She and I have become friends. She invited me to her wedding. Would you like me to dance you over to her so she can confirm that?"

"No."

His body was tense as they swayed to the music.

"What was that all about with my parents and sister?"

She lifted her gaze to his. "I introduced myself to your family."

"And I said no."

"It would have been inappropriate for me to ignore you. We work together."

"No one needed to know that."

"You hardly need to shove me in a closet, Cole."

He lifted his head and looked around. She squeezed his hand to grab his attention. "What you and I do together is between us. I didn't say anything to your family that you need to worry about."

He gave her a terse nod.

"Though I don't think you need to be ashamed of it."

"I'm not ashamed of anything I do."

"Are you sure? Why do you feel the need to hide me away like I'm some deep, dark secret?"

"I told you. I like to keep my personal life separate from my professional life."

"It seems to work out just fine for your cousin. Look at all the friends Gavin has here at his wedding. So many from his team."

"That's his deal, not mine."

"Maybe it should be your deal. If you make friends with your teammates, it makes for better game play—"

"There's nothing wrong with the way I play."

"May I finish?"

He clamped his lips together.

"It makes for better game play and fosters a sense of team camaraderie. Surely you know this from playing organized sports since you were a kid, through high school and then again in college. A team needs to be a cohesive unit in order to operate at prime efficiency. If one cog in the wheel is broken, the entire team suffers."

"I line up where I'm supposed to, and I catch the ball like I'm supposed to. My stats speak for themselves."

He looked away. She squeezed his hand again to get his attention.

"So does your behavior and the fact that no team has bent over backward to keep you in the entire time you've been with the NFL. That speaks volumes."

"I didn't come here to work tonight, Savannah."

Frustrated at where this conversation was going, she let go of his hand. "You know what, you're right. Neither did I. Relax and enjoy your cousin's wedding."

SHIT.

Cole watched Savannah walk away. He'd hurt her feelings.

Then again, maybe he hadn't. She was cold and precise and doing her job, no matter what she told him about being invited to the wedding.

She might look beautiful in a black dress that showed off her curves and her amazing legs, but she'd come here tonight for one reason and one reason only—to keep an eye on him, to monitor his behavior and report to the team.

She was his worst goddamn nightmare, and just as bad as the media stalking him.

A tap on his shoulder made him turn away from Savannah's retreating form.

It was Elizabeth, dancing with Gavin.

"Hey, beautiful," he said, replacing his sour expression with a grin. "And you look nice, too, Liz."

Gavin snorted. "You can have my bride for a few since you're standing in the middle of the dance floor with no partner. I need to talk to the photographer."

"Glad to." He took Elizabeth in his arms and swept her around the floor.

Liz laughed. "Lose your dance partner?"

"She needed to . . . uh . . . take a break."

"Uh-huh."

He twirled her around, hoping they weren't going to discuss Savannah.

Liz's arched a brow. "Aren't you smooth."

"All football players are, honey."

"Yeah, yeah. That's what they all tell me. So how's it going with Savannah? I saw the two of you dancing."

"It's going just great."

"From the tight set of your jaw I'm thinking you're lying to me."

He met her curious gaze. "It's your wedding day. Let's not get into this."

"Oh, let's do. Tell me what's going on."

He blew out a frustrated breath. "Look, I'll put up with her invading my work life, but she had no business being here tonight. I don't like her butting into my personal life."

She laughed. "Your ego never fails to amaze me. She's here tonight because I invited her. Yes, she's someone I recommend to players, but she's also a good friend to me and has been for years."

"Huh."

Liz rolled her eyes. "You are such a dumbass. You thought, what? That she was stalking you or something?"

"Or something."

"I don't think you're that important to her. You're just a job, Cole. Quit acting like such a douchebag. And believe me when I tell you this, because you're family now. Otherwise I wouldn't bother because you're already a pain in my ass."

He looked down at her, caught the sparkle and grin, and laughed. "Yeah. Okay. I'll fix this."

"You do that. I'm going to go find my sexy husband. Oh, god. I have a husband now. Maybe I need a shot of tequila first." She lifted up, kissed his cheek, and wandered off.

Yeah, so he was an asshole. And overly sensitive like Savannah had told him. He grabbed a beer and found Savannah at her table nursing a glass of wine. He pulled up a chair.

"Okay, so I was wrong. Again."

She smiled at him, obviously not hurt or upset. "I'm amazed you didn't choke getting those words out."

"Hey, I know how to apologize when I'm wrong."

"Then we're taking a step in the right direction, aren't we?"

"*We* as in you and me, or me as in my . . . image?"

She lifted the glass to her lips and took a sip. "I thought we already established that I wasn't here to work tonight."

He leaned back in the chair and took a long swallow of beer. "So you're here solo tonight?"

"Yes."

"Dating anyone?"

"Not at the moment."

"I imagine someone as beautiful as you has a pretty active social life."

She frowned. "Cole, you're not by any chance hitting on me, are you?"

He smiled at her. "Nope. Just trying to get to know you. If we're going to work together, this should be a two-way street. I figure I should find out a little more about you, too."

"I don't think that includes discovering anything about my dating life."

"Why not? You get to know all about mine."

"You don't have one."

It irked him that she seemed so confident in that statement. "I could have a girlfriend."

"But you don't."

He cocked a brow. "How do you know?"

"That's part of my job."

He leaned forward. "You know all about me, but I don't know nearly enough about you. I'll be more comfortable working with you if I get to know you."

She swirled her drink around the glass. "Nice try."

"So you have secrets."

"No, I don't."

"Everyone does, Savannah."

"I have nothing to hide. I just don't think my personal life is any of your business."

He enjoyed this sassy side of her, but he wasn't sure if she really wanted him to mind his own business, or if this was her way of coy flirting. Only one way to find out. "Now see, when you say that it makes you mysterious, like you have juicy skeletons in your closet."

Especially when she gave him that cold Southern stare.

"Maybe an ex-husband, or some scandal?"

She covered it up with a salty smile. "Remember, Cole, this is all about you. Not me." She stood and grabbed her bag.

"You're leaving?"

"Yes."

"Party's not over."

"It is for me."

"So you're a coward."

She stilled. "I am not."

"Then why are you running as soon as I try to dig into your personal life?"

She laid her bag down on the table. "That has nothing to do with my life. I thought you were more content to avoid me tonight. Didn't you want me out of the way?"

"I want you out of my personal life."

"That's not going to be possible. So make up your mind what you want."

What he wanted was her stripped naked and in his bed. He supposed that was as personal as it got. But he could also separate her from the rest of his life. If he could manage that and do what he wanted to do with her, then he'd be satisfied.

When a slow song played, he held out his hand. "Let's take another shot at that dance."

She looked up at him. "You weren't so good at it the first time."

"Now I'm insulted. I need to redeem myself." He took her

hand and led her onto the dance floor, pulled her against him, and wrapped an arm firmly around her back.

Her gaze met his, and like always when he was close to her, he breathed her in. The smell of peaches surrounded him. She felt good in his arms, like she fit. Her skin was soft, and it was a little bit perfect in the way their bodies nestled against each other. She didn't grind against him or run her hands all over him like the girls at the club did. Instead, she let him lead, content to just "be" in his arms.

He had to admit he liked that, too. There was no frenzy involved in this, even though he had a lot of dirty thoughts running through his head at the moment.

"I'm being honest with you now, Savannah. I'd really like to get to know you. We spend a lot of time talking about me. Tell me about you."

For a flicker of a second, he saw wariness in her eyes before she masked it. "Not much to tell. I was raised in Georgia, went to school there. Right after college graduation I got my first job in PR, which evolved into my current career as an image consultant. I've been doing that ever since."

"That's a brief bio."

"I'm very good at being concise. I can work with you on that. You might find it useful in interviews since you tend to run at the mouth."

She was good at deflecting. "I like talking about myself. Obviously more than you do, which leads me to believe you have something to hide."

Again the wariness crossed her face before she carefully shuttered it behind a smile. "I'm just not an egomaniac like some people."

"That was subtle." He turned her around as the tempo increased.

"I'm never subtle."

"Then tell me what's on your mind."

Her gaze was direct. "You wanted me to stay because you think you can get me into bed."

He arched a brow. "And?"

"Not a chance."

That made him smile. "You want to know what I think?"

"Would it matter if I didn't?"

"Probably not."

He caught the slight curve of her lips. "Then go right ahead."

"I think not only do you have secrets, but you're sexually repressed. That's why you have this job helping other people. Focus on someone else so you don't have to deal with your own issues—whatever the hell they are."

She let out a soft laugh. "I can guarantee you I'm not sexually repressed. I know exactly what to do with a man in the bedroom, and am given multiple opportunities to do so. But thank you for offering to save me, Cole. Unfortunately, I'm in no need of saving."

She started to pull away, but he held her tight. "I'm not throwing you a line, Savannah. I'm attracted to you. And I know you're attracted to me. What I want to know is why you fight so hard to deny what's between us."

"Because we work together. A line has to be drawn."

But she hadn't denied the attraction. That was progress.

She pulled away again, and this time he loosened his hold on her.

"You're leaving me on the dance floor again?" he teased.

She paused, then slipped her hand in his. "Walk off with me. Let's go to the bar and get a drink."

He went with her to the bar. She ordered a glass of champagne, while he ordered a whiskey. She perched on one of the bar stools while he leaned against the bar.

"You've met my family. Tell me about yours."

She sipped her champagne, staring out over the dance floor. "Not much to tell. I had a very unremarkable childhood."

There was a lot she wasn't saying in that statement. "No brothers or sisters?"

"No. Just me."

"How about aunts and uncles or grandparents."

"None of those, either."

"So . . . what? You're an orphan?"

"No." She finally looked at him. "It was just my mother and me."

"Oh. Did your dad die?"

"I have no idea. I never knew him."

"Ouch. I'm sorry, Peaches."

She shrugged. "Don't be. You can't miss something you never had. I managed just fine without him."

"Still, I imagine it was hard to grow up without one of your parents."

"I have no idea. Like I said, I never had him so it wasn't like I missed him or anything."

"So your mom pitched in and did double duty?"

She looked away, and it was clear her mind wasn't on the present anymore. "Something like that."

She downed the contents of her glass of champagne in two swallows, then slid off the bar stool. "Now I really do need to go. Good night, Cole."

He wasn't going to let her get away. He'd dug open this wound and it was up to him to close it. He caught up to her.

"Wait."

She stopped, looked up. "What now?"

He winced at the raw pain in her eyes. "Let's take a walk out back. You just poured down a pretty hefty glass of champagne. How about you let that settle before you drive?"

She paused, then nodded. "Fair enough. I do need to clear my head a little."

He grabbed a bottle of water on the way out the back door.

The gardens were nice, with a path fringed by overhanging

trees and bushes lining the sides. There was a waterfall at the end of the path, lit up by twinkling lights above. Romantic, he supposed, but what he liked about it was the privacy. And even better, no one was out here, so he tucked her arm in his and they took a leisurely stroll. A breeze had kicked up, obliterating the hellish heat that had blanketed the city during the day. They could at least breathe without the humidity suffocating them.

She wasn't talking, so he let her simmer in silence for a few minutes while they walked the path.

"I don't need you to handle me."

He paused, turned to her. "Isn't that your job?"

"Excuse me?"

"I'm taking a beautiful woman who's upset for a walk. You're the one who handles people."

She rubbed her temple. "You're right. I'm sorry."

"No. I'm the one who's sorry. I shouldn't have pried into your personal life. Not my business."

She looked away to stare at a rosebush. "It's my fault. I never talk about it."

"Maybe you should."

When she turned to him, he saw sadness in her eyes and wished he could turn back the clock, erase the time when he'd pried about her past.

"It's best if I don't."

He didn't agree. Things held inside festered. "Look, I'm like the worst person in the world to give advice since you obviously know I have character issues, but that shit boils inside you. Eventually it'll find its way out."

She laid her hand on his arm. "There's nothing wrong with your character, Cole. Nothing that I've seen of your behavior indicates you're anything but a fine, honorable man. Remember, it's all about image."

He liked what she'd said about him. It struck something deep inside him that was rarely touched. He also liked her touching him, didn't want to do anything to change it.

But he wasn't going to take advantage of her when she was vulnerable. That would make him the asshole the media portrayed him to be. "Well, my image needs work. That's why I have you."

He covered her hand with his and continued walking down the path.

"You confuse me," she said.

"Do I?"

"Yes."

"How's that?"

They stopped at the end of the path where the water fountain and lights met. Benches surrounded the fountain, so he sat her down, opened the bottle of water, and handed it to her. She took a couple sips, then recapped the bottle and handed it to him.

"You're angry and tense half the time, and the other times just so damn sweet. I don't know what to make of you."

"I'm just a regular guy, Savannah. Not perfect, but not the big bad ogre the media makes me out to be." He shrugged. "I have flaws. Maybe mine go under the microscope more than the average guy."

She shook her head, then raised her hand and swept it along the side of his face. He actually found himself holding his breath, and he never did that. Not for any woman. But he did for Savannah, because her hand was like silk across the roughness of his face and he wanted to lean into that buttery softness so she'd continue to touch him.

"No, you are most definitely not just a regular guy, Cole."

He shouldn't do this. In fact, he'd just made a mental promise he wouldn't. But he couldn't help himself. He laid an arm around Savannah's shoulders and tugged her against him. She went willingly and her head tilted back.

This time, she knew what was coming. Her lips parted, and he took the kiss.

He'd meant to just brush his lips across hers, something brief, and then he'd let her go. He wanted to give her comfort, a little reassurance. But that's not what this was about, because a hunger took over, especially when she touched him.

Heat burned through him, and when she leaned into him, the inferno burst. He groaned and hauled her onto his lap, deepening the kiss, letting his hands roam over her back and down her sides.

She felt good. He wanted to feel more of her, wanted to taste more than her sweet, sassy mouth. His tongue dove inside and tangled with hers, and she whimpered.

He swept his hand across her rib cage. As he listened to the sounds of approval she made, he palmed her breast. She arched against him and his cock, already hard and straining against his pants, jerked.

He slipped his fingers inside the opening to her dress, inside her bra and found her nipple. He brushed his thumb over the taut bud and Savannah whimpered, sucking against his tongue.

Jesus. She made his balls throb. He could take her right here in the garden, undo his pants, pull out his cock, and pull her astride him. She could ride him until they both came. He needed her so badly he was shaking. Her lips licked across his, her tongue taking his in a frenzy of need and desire.

She wanted this as much as he did. He felt her desperation.

But the breeze whipped her hair across his face, reminding him where they were.

Outside. In the garden at his cousin's wedding. Where anyone could come out. And as hot and oh-hell-yeah ready as he was to slide inside her, he wouldn't do that to her out here in public.

He pulled his hand away and righted her dress, leaving his hand on her rib cage to feel the hard thump of her heartbeat. It felt good to know she was in this as fiercely as he was, that it wasn't one-sided.

Savannah drew her lips from his. Her eyes were glazed with passion, her lips swollen. She pressed her fingertips to her lips, her tongue flicking over them. He saw the shock on her face as the cold slap of reality hit her, too.

Goddammit, but he wanted to lay her out, undress her, and put his mouth on every part of her until she came apart for him. The desire was written all over her face. If only they'd been in the right place, he could have taken his time with her, undressed her piece by piece and discovered all her secrets.

But he damn well wasn't going to do it here. He needed hours with her. All night.

"I know, we got carried away. Let's go to my place."

He felt her shudder. "I can't. I'm sorry. I shouldn't have done this. I keep losing control with you. I don't know what's wrong with me."

He swept his hand over her back. "There's nothing wrong with you. We both want this."

She slid off his lap and stood, adjusted her dress with shaky hands. "I don't. I mean I do. God, Cole. I'm not a tease. You have to know that. But my job means everything to me. It's the only thing I have and I won't sacrifice it."

He saw the regret in her eyes before she grabbed her bag from the bench and turned away from him, walking down the path back toward the reception hall.

Cole stood and watched her walk away. His cock was still hard and throbbing. He'd need a few more minutes before he went inside.

He knew better than to pressure a woman who said no. But there was more than just her job standing in their way.

He didn't know what it was, but he intended to find out.

NINE

SAVANNAH HAD ALMOST CHANGED HER MIND ABOUT going to Cole's parents' for dinner.

But she always kept her promises, and since she'd been invited, she was going to go. It might be a little uncomfortable considering what had happened between her and Cole the night of Gavin and Liz's wedding, but she was a professional. She could handle it.

She'd thought long and hard about that night. Okay, she'd thought of nothing but that night since it happened, since it burned in her nonstop. Her body still throbbed from Cole's kisses, from his touch on her body.

Damn man. And damn her inability to stop kissing him.

It wasn't going to happen again. She had a career trajectory and it didn't include screwing up her job by having sex with one of her clients.

Good god she could ruin her career if she was caught.

No more. She was pushing hot Cole out of her head and only client Cole was going to remain there.

She brought a plant over to Cole's parents' house for Sunday dinner. A bottle of wine was so provincial.

Cole's mother seemed pleased. She beamed with delight and thanked Savannah profusely.

Cara was beautiful, and Savannah guessed her to be in her mid-fifties. She had long, thick, very dark hair that she pulled into a ponytail, the most expressive brown eyes, and she was always smiling.

"Come with me into the kitchen." Cara led her through the hallway.

The house was modern and beautiful, with marble flooring in the entry, wood throughout the expansive house, and dark tile in the kitchen. There was a definite Italian influence in the décor. The kitchen was filled with stainless steel appliances, a dark granite countertop, and a center island with a sink and a seating area.

"I love your home, Cara."

"Thank you. So do I. We used to live in a tiny three-bedroom in South City that Jack and I had bought when we first got married. Over the years it had gotten run-down and in need of repair, but with Jack's income as a welder and mine as an office assistant, there was only so much duct tape we could put on the old house to keep it together. We put all our money into the kids and making sure they got college educations. Of course it helped that Cole got the football scholarship."

"I'm sure it did."

"When Cole got his first contract, he bought us this house. It was my dream house. I'm Italian, so I decorated it with my love of my heritage."

"I see the Italian influences. It's lovely."

Cara gave her a smile. "Thank you. I love this place so much, and there's plenty of room for the kids—though they don't live here anymore—and any grandchildren they might bless us with some-day. Sadly, neither of them seem in any hurry to settle down."

"Busy with their careers, I imagine."

"True. Though Cole will be thirty this year. Alicia is just getting started on her career. I'm just anxious to hold some babies and fearful both of them will focus on their careers instead of love, marriage, and those grandchildren I want to have."

Savannah laughed. "I'm sure it'll happen eventually."

Cara went to a pot on the stove, stirred, then replaced the lid. "Maybe. Maybe not. Honestly, it's up to the two of them. I try not to interfere. Much," she said with a wry smile. "So tell me about you, Savannah. I love your Southern accent. Where are you from?"

Savannah took a seat on one of the cushioned bar stools at the island. "Georgia."

"Where in Georgia?"

"Macon."

"Do you have a big family? Any brothers or sisters?"

"No, it's just me."

"And your family still lives there?"

"Yes, they do." As far as she knew. She hated making up stories about her family, but the truth wasn't something she ever shared.

At least not typically. She'd shared too much with Cole and that had been a disaster. It was always better to make up lies than to tell the truth. After all, image was everything, and often the truth was painful.

"It must be hard to be away from home."

"Not too hard. I travel a lot so I'm used to being away from home."

"Oh. So you don't live near your family anymore?"

"No. I haven't for years."

"That must be difficult. Do you miss them?"

She paused. "Yes. Of course."

Cara got out a cutting board and started slicing tomatoes. "I know it was hard for Cole to move away, though it's something he had to do to play football."

"I'm sure he missed all of you."

"He likes to play at being tough and independent, but at his heart he loves his family."

An interesting observation, which was why she'd wanted to meet his parents.

"And here I am monopolizing your time. Let's go into the family room."

The family room was huge and spacious, with a super-large flat-screen television and copious amounts of seating. The Rileys must entertain a lot.

Savannah was certain Cole didn't believe she'd show up, or maybe he hoped she wouldn't, but when Cara led her into the family room, Cole frowned.

He stood and greeted her, but it was obvious he wasn't happy to see her.

Cole's father shook her hand, and Alicia gave her a hug.

"I'm so glad you came," Alicia said. "Now I have someone to talk to. They're watching baseball." Alicia sighed.

"You're not a sports fan?"

"Oh, of course. I love sports. I just watch it for different reasons. I pay attention to their physical mechanics—the way they move their bodies, checking for strains or injuries or how they could hurt themselves." She motioned for Savannah to take a seat next to her on the sofa. "So many of these guys continue to play while hurt."

"That's because we're tough," Cole said from his chair.

Alicia rolled her eyes. "And then they wonder why their careers are so short."

Savannah laughed. "I've discovered in my work with sports players that they're not very fond of listening—especially when they feel they're being lectured to—by a woman."

"So not true." Cole pinned her with his gaze. "When whoever's talking knows what the hell they're talking about, we listen. Sex doesn't matter."

She had a feeling she'd just been insulted.

"Well, you listen to Mom, and she's a woman, but only because she's scary." Alicia looked at Savannah and winked.

"Who's going to say no to her? And besides, moms don't count."

"I heard that." Cara came in bearing a tray of iced tea. She poured a glass for Savannah, and refilled everyone else's glasses.

Savannah was content to sit back and watch the family dynamic unfold, but apparently that's not how it worked in the Riley household.

"Tell us in more detail about what you do for the team, Savannah," Cara said after she took a seat on the sofa, sandwiching her between Cara and Alicia.

She noticed Cole watching her out of the corner of his eye, though he had his focus on the television. She knew he was listening in, no doubt afraid she was going to spill his secrets.

"I do public relations, both for the team and the individual players."

Cole rolled his eyes. At the television. Ha. She knew better.

"That sounds fun," Cara said. "So you juggle both?"

"My main job is to look out for the team's image, so yes."

"And how does that relate to you working with Cole?" Alicia asked.

Oh, she was smart. "I'll be working with him, teaching him about the Trader brand. What the team stands for, who their charities are. Basically, I'll be making him a St. Louis Trader."

Alicia grinned. "In other words, you'll be indoctrinating him into the cult."

Savannah laughed. "More or less."

"I'm going to go see about dinner," Cara said.

Savannah stood. "Let me help you."

"That's not necessary. You sit here and visit. Alicia can help me."

"Really, I love the kitchen. It's one of my favorite places."

"Oh, you've saved me," Alicia said with a grin. "I hate cooking."

Cara gave her daughter a look. "That means you're on dishes."

Alicia grimaced. "So I'm not saved after all. Cole can help me with dishes."

"Joy," Cole murmured.

Savannah followed Cara into the kitchen. "What can I do?"

Cara handed her a loaf of bread that looked and smelled heavenly, following up with a bread knife. "You can slice the bread."

She washed and dried her hands and got to work on the bread. "It all smells so good."

"I made lasagna. I hope you like Italian food."

"Love it."

"I imagine you miss your mama's Southern cooking."

She resisted the snort that stuck in her throat. As if her mother would have bothered fixing a meal. "I do a lot of that myself, so I get plenty of Southern home cooking."

"Oh, really? I'd be thrilled for you to fix some dishes for me sometime. I love Southern cooking."

"I'd be happy to."

She helped Cara take the dishes into the dining room. The table was already set, so all they had to do was lay out the salad, lasagna, and bread.

"Let's eat," Cara said.

The television went off and everyone piled into the dining room.

"Savannah, you sit next to Cole right there," Cara directed.

She took her place and Cole sat, but still didn't seem happy about it. Not that she minded. This was a fact-finding mission, not a date, no matter what had happened at the wedding. She was here to see how he interacted with his family. Nothing else.

"When does practice start up?" Jack asked him.

"Already doing conditioning and drills with the team. We start practice next week."

"You ready?"

"Yeah." Cole took a slice of bread from the basket Savannah passed him. She smiled at him and he gave her a glare.

He was not happy. One would think he'd be over it by now. She was here and they were sitting next to each other, so he should make the best of it.

Savannah listened in while they talked of family and friends, about things going on with Jack at work. Idle chitchat, and, of course—football.

"I hope this season goes well for you, Cole," Alicia said. "Maybe the Traders will keep you."

He focused on his plate. "I don't see any reason why they wouldn't."

"Others haven't."

Cole shrugged. "Not the right fit."

"What do you think will be different this time?"

He pinned his sister with a cold look. "Why don't you mind your own damn business?"

"Cole." His mother shot him a warning glance, and he looked down to scoop up more lasagna.

"Hey, I was only asking."

"Quit asking," he said to his sister. "You have your own shit to deal with."

"I'm dealing with my shit quite nicely, thanks."

"Then why are you bothering with mine?"

"Because you're my brother, you moron. And all I did was ask a damn question. What crawled up your ass?"

"Cole. Alicia. This is not appropriate conversation for a meal. And we have a guest, so it would be really nice if the two of you didn't act like a couple of squabbling eight-year-olds."

Cara, though seemingly sweet, obviously raised her children with a firm hand because they both clammed up. But now the dead silence at the dinner table was unnerving. Savannah ate and tried to make herself as small as possible. She had years of experience doing that.

"Sorry, Savannah," Alicia said, obviously unruffled. "I hope you're not offended. This is normal mealtime conversation around here."

She smiled at Alicia. "I'm not offended at all. I'm used to dealing with athletes."

"Hey, don't talk to me like I'm not even here," Cole said.

"Actually, I wasn't referring to you."

"Amazingly," Alicia said, "not every conversation is about you. I know you and your tremendous ego find that hard to believe."

"And you and your superior intellect think you have to be the star of every show. Why don't you talk about something medical and leave football out of the equation?"

"Enough," Jack finally said, giving a hard stare to both Cole and Alicia.

Cara shook her head. "You two. Always at each other like wild dogs. Can't you be nice?"

Alicia looked at her mother. "I was being nice. He's being an ass."

Savannah didn't disagree, but there was no further commentary on the topic. It was interesting that Jack only had to say one word to silence the bickering.

She wished it had been so easy at her house when she was growing up, but there had been no one to run interference on her behalf, no one to silence the endless arguments.

Until one day it had just stopped. Her mother had stopped it, but not in the way Savannah had wanted.

But that was long ago, and over, and she'd buried it. No sense dredging it all up again just because she was having a meal with a nice family.

After dinner, she rose to help clear the table, but Cara stopped her.

"No, that's Cole's and Alicia's job. You can come sit in the living room with Jack and me."

"I don't mind helping."

Cara took her hand. "And deny them the pleasure of dishes?"

Alicia groaned, then winked at her. Savannah tried to get Cole's attention, but he was obviously still sulking.

Fine. They could talk later. Maybe he needed some bonding time with his sister in the kitchen.

Hopefully, they wouldn't go after each other with knives.

She went into the living room with Cara and Jack. Cara regaled her with stories about how she and Jack met. It was sweet and romantic.

Fifteen minutes later, she heard Alicia shrieking, then laughing.

"Do you think they're all right in there?"

"Oh, no doubt," Cara said.

"So . . . they fought and then made up over washing dishes?"

Cara grinned. "Washing dishes is the great equalizer. It solves many a dispute."

"I see." She really didn't, since, when he left the dining room, Cole looked like he was ready to murder his sister.

Being an only child, she clearly didn't comprehend family dynamics.

"I think I'll see what's going on in there."

"You go right ahead," Cara said.

Savannah moved down the hall toward the kitchen, where she heard both Alicia's and Cole's unabashed laughter. As she rounded the corner she saw Alicia dumping a handful of bubbles on Cole's head. He retaliated by rolling up the dish towel.

"Don't you dare," Alicia said, giving Cole a warning look and backing away, but her expression was filled with mirth. She ran toward the container of spatulas.

Cole snapped the towel her way and she grabbed at it with the spatula.

The two of them battled back and forth. It looked like a very unconventional sword fight. Cole, obviously much bigger than his sister, lunged and grabbed her, then tickled her. She burst into laughter.

"Oh, god, stop. You know I hate when you tickle me."

"You started this by throwing dishwater at me."

"It wasn't dishwater, you moron. It was bubbles."

He held her firmly in his grip. "Whatever. Do you give up?"

"Screw you. I'll never surrender."

He lunged for the towel and she whacked him on the back with the spatula. He turned to come after her again, but spotted Savannah leaning against the wall.

He dropped the towel.

Alicia, still trying to catch her breath, leaned against the counter. "Please tell me you've come to save me. He's trying to kill me."

Savannah's lips lifted. "I don't know. From where I'm standing it looks like you held your own."

Alicia pushed off the counter and headed her way. "He cheated. He knows my weaknesses. But I'm still running like hell." She winked and walked by.

Savannah walked into the kitchen. "Abusing your little sister?"

He folded the towel and hung it up on the holder. "She's hardly little anymore, and she started it. Plus, she's mean with that spatula."

"You sound like a ten-year-old making excuses."

"So now I'm in trouble for roughhousing with my sister? Does that go in your report?"

She folded her arms. "What report?"

"I don't know. Whatever report you're making about your visit today."

"Cole, my visit today was because your mother invited me. This was not about work."

He leaned against the counter. "So you're here just to get to know me better."

"Yes."

"Why?"

"Because it's part of my job."

"Then it's work."

He had her there. "I suppose you're right. But I'm not judging you on your family and how you relate to them. Seeing you with your parents and your sister helps me formulate your image in a much better way than just reading a paper bio. It's more three-dimensional. I can't help your future without knowing about your past."

"If you have questions about my past, just ask."

"All right. Tell me how you got started in football."

"That's all in my bio."

"It's more engaging coming from you."

"Pee Wee league. I was five."

She took a seat at the center island. "You played every year?"

"Yeah. I loved it. It was physical and loud and I was always a fast runner. My parents said I had all this excess energy. Which in parent speak means I was an unruly pain in the ass. Football gave me an outlet for it."

She could picture him as a rambunctious kid. "I imagine it would. What did you do when it wasn't football season?"

He quirked a smile. "Mostly got in trouble."

She laughed. "I see. Did you play any other sports?"

"Yeah. When my parents figured out that sports equaled the outlet I needed, they signed me up for soccer and baseball, too. I didn't like those as much as football, but it was something to do to pass the time until football started up again."

"We have photo albums with all of his sports photos. Would you like to see them?"

Savannah turned around to see Cara coming in to refill the iced tea pitcher. "I'd love to."

Cole frowned. "Mom. No. Don't drag out the old albums."

Cara waved her hand at him, grabbed another pitcher of tea, and started toward the doorway. "Oh, come on. What fun is it to be your mother if I can't embarrass you?"

Curious, Savannah slid off the stool and followed Cara into the family room. Alicia and Jack were playing a card game. Alicia looked up when Cara crouched down and opened up the lower cabinet of the bookshelf.

"Oh, god, Mom, not the photo albums."

"Yes. I'm going to show Savannah the ones of Cole when he was younger and in sports."

Alicia cast Cole a sympathetic look as he trailed in. "Sorry, dude."

Cole grimaced at Savannah. "I hate when she does this."

"Have a seat on the sofa," Cara said, then took a spot next to her and laid one of the thick photo albums on her lap. "This is Cole playing Pee Wee football. His first year. He was five."

Savannah watched the pride cross Cara's face as she flipped the pages, stopping every now and then to smile and lay her hand on a photo of Cole when he was small.

Oh, heavens. Savannah was struck with such a fierce sense of longing. This was a mother's love, a mother's pride in her child. So this was what it was like.

She hadn't known, had never felt it. Her heart ached with wanting something she'd never had—would never have. She was shocked when tears burned her eyes. She hurriedly blinked them back and shook off the melancholy. This wasn't about her. This was about Cole.

Focus on Cole and stop feeling sorry for yourself.

She returned her gaze to the photo album, concentrating on the pictures as Cara turned the pages.

Cole was adorable as a kid, with dark shaggy hair, kneeling for the cheesy photo with his helmet in his hand and a wide grin.

"You were so cute," Savannah said.

Cole, who'd taken a seat across from her, said, "So, you're saying I'm not cute now?"

No, he was definitely not cute. More like devastatingly handsome. "I didn't say that."

Cara flipped through the pages and Savannah got to see Cole progress from year to year. It was amazing to see his growth spurts, from adorable child to losing his teeth to adolescence to his high school photos. In college, he'd added more muscle—and even more good looks.

She lifted her gaze to his. "Didn't you ever have an ugly phase?"

"No," Alicia answered. "It's disgusting. He's always been perfect and beautiful. I, on the other hand, had braces and acne and was chubby."

Cole laughed. "That's true. You did. You were lucky to have me as your older brother. It's the only thing that saved your social life in high school."

"Yeah, thanks. Didn't help me much with the guys, though. They still weren't interested in dating me."

"Not until you grew boobs and lost the baby fat."

"And by then I wasn't interested in them because they were all egotistical, single-minded pricks. I was a virgin until I got to college."

"Way too much information, Leesh," Cole said.

"As opposed to you, stud muffin, who likely got laid before you got your driver's license."

Cole grinned. "It was Melissa Petry. And I was fifteen, as a matter of fact."

Cara sighed and gave Savannah a look that spoke volumes. "The things you learn about your kids after the fact. Always so enlightening."

"And so many things you don't want to know," Jack said, giving pointed looks to both Cole and Alicia.

"Oh, come on, Dad," Alicia said. "We're both adults now. It's not like there need to be any secrets."

"Yes, there do," Jack said. "Especially with my only daughter. As far as I'm concerned, you're always going to be my baby. Innocent and untouched."

Alicia rolled her eyes. "Such a double standard. You'll probably pat Cole on the back."

"No comment," Jack said, reaching for the crossword puzzle.

Savannah adored this family. They squabbled, said too much sometimes, but the love was evident. Cara was clearly so proud of both of her children. It was obvious they had been raised in a stable, loving, but firm environment. And Jack, though quiet, clearly loved his kids. Both parents had worked hard to give their children the tools they needed to succeed.

And despite Cole's recent turmoil with his image, he didn't appear spoiled or entitled. She didn't quite know where his issues had come from, but apparently not from his upbringing, which seemed warm and generous.

She was envious of his family life. It was as different as night and day from hers.

After visiting for a while longer, she stood. "Thank you for inviting me for dinner, Cara. I had a lovely time."

"Do you need to leave so soon?"

"I'm afraid so. I have some work to catch up on."

She said her good-byes to Cara, Jack, and Alicia.

"I'll walk you out," Cole said, surprising her since he'd been so distant with her throughout the evening.

"All right."

When she got to the driver's side door of her car, Cole slid his hand in hers. Shocked, she turned to face him, but he'd only grabbed her keys out of her hand.

"You were nice to my family. Thanks."

"Did you think I'd come here to interrogate them?"

He raked his fingers through his hair. "Honestly? I didn't know what your intentions were in coming here."

She laid her hand on his arm. "Just to have dinner. To get to know you better."

"Why?"

"To help me help you."

"You put that much effort into your clients?"

If she were honest with herself she'd say no. Not as much as she was putting into Cole. She didn't know why she was pushing so hard with him. Maybe because he was so resistant? Maybe because he didn't believe in her.

There couldn't be another reason, could there?

"Yes. You're going to have to start trusting me, Cole. Have some faith in me. I really am here to help, not hurt, your career."

He walked down to the end of her car. She followed. He leaned against the trunk and folded his arms. "I'm not easy to deal with."

"Is that right? I hadn't noticed."

He gave her a hint of a smile that caused her pulse to kick. Really, this would be a lot easier if she didn't find him so incredibly attractive. She'd worked with good-looking athletes before who'd never gotten her motor running. So what was it about Cole that got to her?

"I like you, Savannah. I think you're beautiful and smart and you seem to be able to put up with me. Not a lot of people can stick it out."

Uh-oh. "I like you, too, Cole. But remember, I'm being paid to stick it out."

"There've been other people paid to stick it out who haven't."

She offered a smile. "I don't give up easily. Maybe you will."

"Is that a challenge?"

"It might be. We haven't even started the real work yet. Maybe you should reserve judgment."

"Why? Thinking of putting me through some grueling image makeover paces?"

"Something like that."

"I think I can handle it."

"I don't think you like being told what to do, and that's exactly what my job entails."

"So you're already setting me up for failure before I even start?"

"I didn't say that. Maybe this is the problem you have with the media, Cole. You're contentious and see things that aren't there."

He pushed off the trunk and bridged the gap between them. "I never see things that aren't there. I'm pretty smart for a dumb football player. I think you like to challenge me."

"I don't think you're dumb. And I'm not challenging you. I'm preparing you."

He picked up a lock of her hair and rubbed it between his fingers, his gaze holding steady on her face. "I'm ready for you, Peaches. Bring it on."

Was he deliberately being seductive, or did it just come naturally to him without his even realizing what he was doing? This had to be a practiced move. It was a good one, too, because her breasts swelled, her nipples tightened, and she was ready to fall into his arms and take a nibble out of his lower lip.

Lord have mercy but the man was tempting. Tall, with a rock-hard sexy body, and there was something about his neck she found so enticing. He smelled good, his eyes mesmerized her, and he was clearly the devil in blue jeans and a tight black T-shirt. She needed to stay far, far away from him.

She took a step back. "May I have my keys?"

He dangled them in front of her. She snatched them and unlocked the door, then slid in.

He shut the door, then leaned his arms against it, so close she could count his eyelashes and inhale his scent.

Get a grip, Savannah. She turned to face him.

"I'll call you in the morning."

"Sure. Good night, Savannah."

His face was inches from hers. If he dipped his head in just a little bit, he'd kiss her. If she tilted her face up a little . . .

No. What was she thinking? After the night at the wedding, she'd vowed that wouldn't happen again. She'd been so close to giving in, and that would have been a disaster. If they hadn't been outside in a public place when he'd kissed her that night, she'd have been naked and he'd have been inside her in minutes.

And she wouldn't have objected.

"Good night." She started up the car and put it in gear. He paused for a second, then pulled away. She backed out of the driveway and finally released the breath she'd held for what had seemed like an eternity.

What was wrong with her anyway? She needed to gain control of her runaway libido. This was going to be a very tough assignment. She'd never been attracted to one of her clients before.

And she was determined to fight the attraction to Cole. She was stronger than this, rigid in her dedication to her job.

Work had always come first, and it always would.

COLE SMILED AS HE WATCHED SAVANNAH DRIVE OFF.

There were a lot of things he didn't know about, but there were things he knew a lot about. One of those things was women.

Savannah had wanted him to kiss her. It had been written all over her blushing face. The intent had been in her eyes and in the way she positioned her head. He could read signals clearly. It was part of his job as a wide receiver. Body language was everything. If she'd leaned forward a fraction of an inch he would have had his mouth on hers in an instant.

But she hesitated. He could have initiated, of course, and he doubted she would have balked, but this was her game to play, at least for now. He had no problem simultaneously working and playing with her, but obviously she did.

He'd wear her down.

Grinning, he pivoted and headed back into his parents' house.

TEN

COLE'S PHONE RANG AT SIX GODDAMNED O'CLOCK. HE picked it up and growled at it, then looked at the display.

It was Savannah. He punched the button.

"What?"

"Your schedule says you have team practice this morning."

"Yeah. So?"

"I'll be on the field to watch."

"So you called just to tell me that?"

"Yes."

"Fine. See you there." He hung up and flung the phone on the bed, diving back under his pillow. Practice wasn't for three more hours, which meant he could sleep two more hours.

Or not.

Shit. He tried, but he couldn't go back to sleep, so he got up, took a shower, and fixed himself eggs and bacon for breakfast, then headed to the practice facility to do a workout before drills.

The offense was there, including his competition—Jamarcus,

Lon, and the new kid, Kenny Lawton, a hotshot rookie out of Texas who'd been covered nonstop by the media. According to the press, the kid was a future star wide receiver. He'd run a 4:32 in the forty-yard dash at camp before the draft, and everyone wanted him. The Traders were lucky to pick him up.

And now Cole, at twenty-nine years old, was going to have to compete with a twenty-one-year-old who was younger and faster.

Even worse, the kid was polite as hell with no obvious skeletons in his closet.

Cole had a lot to prove. So maybe it was a good idea to have Savannah on board.

He nodded to the other guys as he moved from the workout room outside to the practice field and started doing warm-ups. Bill, the athletic trainer, came out to work with the players. Since Jamarcus and Lon were returning veterans to the team, Bill got them set up on some reps, then came over to work with Cole.

"Let's see what you've got today," Bill said, putting Cole through warm-ups, then conditioning drills to test his endurance and skill set.

After an hour, Cole was dripping with sweat, his breath sawing in and out from running one end of the field to the other.

And Cole thought Mario was the devil? Bill was a tough trainer.

He didn't know when Savannah had shown up. Dressed casually today in capri pants, tennis shoes, and a short-sleeved top with her hair in a ponytail, she was on the sidelines in conversation with Coach Tallarino. Coach had his clipboard and whistle and, despite needing to run his team, he was having an intense conversation with Savannah. Occasionally, he'd look over at Cole and nod while she talked.

"That your girlfriend talking to Coach?" Jamarcus pulled up next to him.

"She's not my girlfriend."

"Who is she?" Lon asked, stopping short after a long run.

"She's my . . . assistant."

"Yeah? They let your assistant come on the field during practice? And, dude, that's one hell of a good-looking assistant. How come she gets to talk to Coach?"

"They know each other."

"How do they know each other?"

He was digging the hole deeper and deeper with every lie. "I don't know. By marriage or somebody's cousin or something. I didn't get the details. I just know she knows his family or something."

"Huh." Jamarcus studied her. "She's talking to him for a long time. They must be close."

"Who's the pretty girl?" Kenny asked, not even winded from his drills.

Bastard.

"Riley's assistant," Lon said.

"No kidding. Someday maybe I'll be important enough to have an assistant. Hope she's as good-looking as yours, Riley."

Kenny ran off to do more drills. Before he got himself into even more trouble, Cole headed toward the sidelines.

"I was just talking to Savannah. She said the two of you have already gotten started," Coach said.

"We have."

"Good. I have high expectations of you this year, Riley. Don't fuck this up."

"I don't intend to, Coach."

Coach wandered off, leaving him with Savannah.

"Looks like you were playing nice with your teammates this morning."

"They asked about you."

"Did they? And what did you tell them?"

"That you were my assistant."

She arched a brow. "Really. Would you like me to fetch you a drink to really sell it?"

"I don't think that'll be necessary."

She went over to the table where cups were set up. "I insist."

She handed him a drink. "I'd hate anyone to find out my real job here. I know how that worries you, so I'll stay stealthy for you."

He rolled his eyes at her, but took the cup from her hand and downed it in two swallows. "Thanks."

"My pleasure."

She lifted her warm gaze to his.

"So what were you talking with Coach about?" he asked.

"The team in general. His plans for the season."

"Yeah, I'm sure he shared all that with you."

"You might be surprised what he shares with me."

He wanted to ask her what they'd talked about in reference to him, but he wouldn't. "I need to get back to work."

"Go ahead. Play nice with the other kids."

He headed back onto the field. He worked with the other receivers on the designated plays he'd learned, watching the other guys at wide receiver to size up his competition.

Kenny was good, but he was green. He was fast, but he had a lot to learn. He wasn't going to be competition for a year or two yet. Jamarcus and Lon, however, were seasoned, fit well with the team. Blockers respected them, they were in sync with Grant Cassidy, the quarterback, and their timing was good.

They were going to be his fiercest competitors. He'd have to watch out for those two, make sure he could beat them so he'd end up the number one receiver on the team.

When it was time for the tight ends to do their drills, he headed over to the sidelines to get another drink while Jamarcus and Lon huddled up with Kenny.

"You keep yourself separate from your teammates."

He downed one drink, reached for another, then turned to Savannah. "Huh?"

"Look on the field. The other wide receivers are together and talking. You're over here."

"I was thirsty."

"You need to hang out with them."

"No. Why should I?"

She sighed. "Because you're part of a team. That's what you do. When practice is over you rehash with the other players in your position."

He shrugged. "That's not how I do it."

She took his arm and led him away from the other guys. "Maybe not in the past, but it's how you need to do it now. Part of your image needs to be that of a team player. We alter your image—the one everyone's had negative issues with—by showing you've changed since coming to the Traders, that you're more willing to play ball, so to speak."

"I'm not going to change who I am, Peaches."

"That's exactly what you're going to do. That's why Elizabeth and the Traders brought me in. To change who you are, at least on the outside. Who you are in here"—she laid her hand on his chest—"that doesn't change."

Tension coiled up inside him. "I don't see any reason why I have to be friendly with those guys. They're my competition. We're all after the same thing—the ball. Playing nice with them doesn't gain me anything."

She took a deep breath and let it out. "You need to become friendly with everyone on this team. From the quarterback to the offensive line to every player on the defense and special teams, you're all after the same thing—that big trophy on the last game of the season and a Super Bowl ring on your finger. The only way to get those is to work as a cohesive unit. The way you've gone about it in the past is all wrong. You on one side and everyone else on the other is only going to guarantee two things. One, you don't get the ball in your hands as much as you want, and two, the potential for your team to lose is greater because of inner turmoil. Is that what you want?"

"No."

"Then at least give it a try. Be nice. Talk them up."

He glared down at her. "About what?"

"Oh. My. God. You have no idea how to go about doing this, do you?"

"I'm not a moron."

"I didn't say you were. But you've never gotten close to anyone on any team you've ever played for. Start with the new kid—Kenny Lawton."

"What about him?"

"He needs guidance. He's the one out in the cold and craves leadership. Who better to offer it than you, a veteran in the game and in his position? Do you really want him bonding with the other two receivers and leaving you the one out in the cold?"

"You make me sound like an old man."

"And you need to quit taking everything so personally. You're not going to play football forever. No player does. Part of your responsibility to the game is to bring up the younger players—to pass the torch and make sure they're ready to play as good or better than you did."

"Kind of defeats the purpose of me being the best on this team."

"You know as well as I do it'll be years before he's as good as you are. That doesn't mean you can't show him the ropes. Don't you remember what it was like your first year?"

She had a point. It sucked being brand-new. His first year in professional football had been awful. He didn't know anybody and he'd felt left out of everything. He'd barely been able to find his ass with both hands. If not for the guys who'd taken pity on him and showed him the way, he'd have been lost. He still remembered those guys today.

"Fine."

"And while you're at it, try to be nice to Jamarcus and Lon.

You're all after the same thing and there's a lot of intel you can share with each other. Like it or not, they're the veterans on this team. They can help you."

Who made her an expert on football all of a sudden?

He went back out on the field and joined the other receivers.

"Giving her some instruction?" Lon asked, a teasing glint in his eyes.

"She's competent. Knows a lot about football. She's an asset to have around."

"She does have a nice ass, that's for sure," Lon said, nudging Jamarcus.

Cole's blood boiled. He was two seconds away from shoving his fist in Lon's face. But he glanced over at Savannah, who frowned and shook her head, so he stopped in his tracks and took a deep breath. But he still wasn't going to let Lon insult Savannah. He got in Lon's face. "Look. I like you. I think you're one of the better wide receivers in the game. I'm new to this team and I'm trying to make a go of it, so for that reason alone I'm giving you a pass. But understand this: You make another personal remark about Savannah and I'll lay you flat. You got me?"

Lon raised his hands. "No harm, man. I got you. Sorry. I didn't know your relationship with her was like that."

"It's not like that at all. She's a nice woman and she's out here doing her job. You don't need to ogle her and you don't need to talk shit about her. Just keep your mind on your business."

"Okay. I'm sorry again. Really."

He could tell Lon was sincere this time. Now he had all this anger and no way to vent. Normally, he'd have had a fight by now, or he'd go walk off and do something to get rid of the tension. But heeding Savannah's advice, he nodded. "Fine. Let's go see if Bill can run some drills with us. Kenny and I could use some help getting the layout."

"Okay. Sure." Lon grabbed his helmet and he and Jamarcus walked off.

"Kenny," Cole said.

"Yeah?"

"You're a little slow on your timing. You need to push off harder and watch your left. Safety's getting to you every time on the double six play."

He could see the lightbulb go off in the kid's eyes. Kenny gave him a tentative smile. "I didn't see that. Thanks. I'll work on it."

Okay, so maybe that hadn't been as bad as he thought it might be.

Jury was still out on how friendly he'd allow himself to be with these guys.

But Savannah might have had a point. There was no sense in making enemies when it was to his advantage to make friends.

At least on the surface.

ROUND ONE DOWN. SAVANNAH BREATHED A SIGH OF relief.

She knew working with Cole was going to be tough. He wasn't a marshmallow, and he wouldn't take all her suggestions as easily as he'd taken this one. But the offensive line was running plays, Cole was getting the ball, and even the other receivers were blocking for him.

So far, that meant he hadn't pissed off anyone. Not bad for day one. Maybe if she stuck close to him she could avoid a disaster. The coach still had reservations about Cole, despite her reassurances that she had it all under control. She'd told him Cole had changed, and it wouldn't be long before he had an image as shiny as a bright new diamond.

Coach seemed dubious about that, and he told her actions spoke louder than promises.

Savannah never failed. If she had to move in with Cole and watch him like a first-time mother hovering over her newborn, that's what she'd do. Her reputation was on the line.

Which meant instead of leaving during his practice, she decided to stay for the day. She pulled up a chair near the coaches and watched Cole practice.

Not a hardship, really. Tight pants, great ass, and a lot of sweat. There was no doubt he worked hard, and even though he was the oldest wide receiver on the team, if she could convince him to keep his head in the game, he could be the best. His reflexes were quick, he was in excellent health. He'd suffered no injuries during his career. Just watching his calves work made her mouth water. It was obvious his legs were still in prime shape.

So were his hands. He seemed to have an instinct about the ball, as if they were of the same mind. Wherever it was thrown, there he was. He had a light touch and he never dropped it. When he took off into a sprint, even the young defensive players had a difficult time keeping up with him as he dashed toward the end zone.

She'd underestimated him. Admittedly, she'd thought he was average—a player at the midpoint of his career with the attitude and chip on his shoulder to match. Watching him today she realized he was anything but.

With his talent, health, and stamina, Cole had a lot of seasons left. He could be an MVP if he concentrated more on the game and positive influences and less on getting in trouble.

That's why she had her job. She was going to make sure this was a great season for him and just the beginning of great things.

She met him outside the locker room after he took his shower. "You still here?"

"I am." She followed him down the hall. "You had a great practice today. You looked amazing."

That got a twitch of a smile from him. "Honey, I *am* amazing."

"Your modesty touches me."

He laughed. "I did have a good day today. Thanks for your help."

She craned her neck to look up at him. "My help with what?"

"I spent some time with the other receivers, and I offered advice to Kenny. It wasn't as bad as I thought it would be."

"I'm glad."

They headed outside.

"You'd make a good coach," he said.

She let out a soft laugh. "That's not really my area, but thank you for thinking so."

He walked her to her car, opened the door for her. She turned to face him. "Do you have plans for dinner tonight?"

He'd put on his sunglasses so she couldn't see his eyes, but she imagined he was surprised by her question. "Uh, no. Why? Are we still on the clock?"

"I'm on the clock twenty-four hours a day. I thought we'd have dinner."

"All right. What did you have in mind?"

"Actually, something simple. If you don't mind, I'll bring some food over to your place and cook for you."

"You cook?"

"I do."

He leaned an arm against the top of her car. "Are you a good cook?"

"I'm an excellent one."

"It just so happens I like food. Fixed by excellent cooks. Come on over."

"Does seven work for you?"

He seemed to be staring at her, and she wished she could see his eyes. "That works fine. See you then."

She slid into the car and he shut the door, then walked away.

She couldn't help the thrill of anticipation, but tamped it down immediately.

This was work, not a date, which she mentally reminded herself all the way back to her place. Her body, though, had other ideas. It tingled in all the wrong places.

Work.

Not. A. Date.

ELEVEN

COLE PICKED UP THE HOUSE, WASHED THE DISHES IN the sink, and even ran the vacuum cleaner in anticipation of Savannah's arrival. On impulse, he changed the sheets on his bed, then laughed, wondering what the hell he was doing.

Savannah wasn't going to end up in his bed tonight. She was cooking him dinner. That was all.

But she had been throwing out some pretty clear signals lately. And despite what happened that night at the wedding, she'd wanted him to kiss her at his parents' house.

Or maybe that was just his imagination. His imagination liked to think that every woman wanted to get into his pants.

He'd sure as hell like to get into Savannah's. But it would be a smart idea to keep things between them professional. She'd made some keen observations about him on the field today. He could use her expertise, and screwing things up between them with sex might fuck up their relationship. He could end up losing her, and right now that would be bad.

He needed her. He might not know much about this whole image consulting thing, but he knew a good thing when he had it, and so far Savannah's advice hadn't hurt.

Getting his carrer on the right track was his number one priority and he needed to be smart and remember that.

Then again, when had he ever done the smart thing?

He threw on a pair of jeans and a T-shirt, then organized the living room so it wouldn't look like a jock lived there.

When the doorbell rang, he did a once-over of the place and decided it was going to have to be good enough.

He opened the door and held his breath. Her hair was down, like a waterfall of gold around her shoulders. She wore a yellow sundress and sandals—cute and casual, but she still managed to look elegant and beautiful.

He took the grocery bag from her hands. "I would have bought this stuff."

"It's no problem. Next time, you buy."

"Deal." He led her into the kitchen.

"I assume you have pots and pans."

"Yes. My mom insisted I not live on take-out food. I know how to make basic stuff."

Savannah laughed. "I can imagine her saying that to you."

He showed her the layout of his kitchen and she started grabbing things while he unpacked groceries.

"I like steak."

"Good, because you're cooking them. I also made an assumption that you have a grill."

"You assumed right."

She got out a plate and did some basting and seasoning to the steak, but not a lot, which made him happy. Meat should taste like meat, not like other junk. She slid the steaks off to the side, then pulled out lobster.

He arched a brow. "Aren't you fancy."

"I like seafood."

She set water boiling in two pans. One for the lobster and one for the rice dish she was making.

"You get your grill ready. I've got everything covered in here."

He shrugged. "Okay."

He went outside to start the grill, watching her through the sliding glass door.

It was interesting having a woman in his kitchen, something that had never happened here before. She looked—cute. Domestic. Comfortable. He sure as hell never had a woman come over and cook for him. He hadn't been lying when he'd told her he didn't invite people over to his place. It was too personal. If he spent the night with a woman, it was at her place, or at a hotel. There were no sleepovers here, no fixing breakfast in the morning together, no spending the day together. That had always seemed too close to a relationship and he steered clear of those. Building his career was enough of a full-time job. Dragging a woman into the mess that was his life would be more than he could handle. He wasn't ready.

Though he sure seemed to be doing a lot of relationship-type things with Savannah. Going out for dinner. Having her over to his parents' house. Dancing with her at his cousin's wedding. Then again, maybe all those things were coincidence—just the nature of her job and the fact they always seemed to end up together lately.

And relationships were things he sure as hell didn't want to be thinking about right now. Or ever. Time to focus on food, work, and keeping his priorities straight.

Once the fire was hot enough, he went inside.

Savannah was conducting a symphony. Music played on her iPod. She was dancing as she moved from one task to another. Pots littered the stove. She was preparing lettuce, slicing strawberries, and boiling something that smelled really good. He stayed still, leaning against the doorway to watch as she hummed along to the music, comfortable in his kitchen.

There was that word again—*comfortable*. He waited for his own discomfort to set in. It didn't.

She turned around and spotted him. "How long have you been there?"

"Awhile."

She grinned, not at all concerned that he'd been spying on her routine. "I can't help myself. Being in the kitchen relaxes me." She handed him the steaks. "Go cook. I like mine medium."

"Yes, ma'am." He got out of her way and did his thing, and let her do hers. By the time he brought the finished steaks in, she had the lobster tail on plates, along with rice and a bed of lettuce for the steaks.

He gave her the plate and she scooped the steaks onto the lettuce, then poured sauce over them, sprinkled a little cheese and a few strawberries over the top of the meat. He frowned.

She laid her hand over his. "I know—you like your steak naked. But trust me." She handed him a plate and they moved to the table.

She'd already poured wine for both of them, so they sat and he dug into the steak, his first inclination to brush away the stuff on the top of the meat. But he didn't want to insult her, so he scooped the strawberries and cheese into his mouth along with the steak.

"Oh, god," he said after he swallowed. Who knew those flavors would go so well together? "What the hell is this sauce?"

She took a sip of wine, then smiled. "I told you to trust me. I wouldn't ruin a great steak. It's just a balsamic reduction, some blue cheese, and the sweetness of the strawberries bring out the flavor."

"It's really good." So was the lobster. Perfectly tender, and she'd even provided melted butter. "Can you come over every night and cook for me?"

"I thought you said you cooked."

"Eggs. Bacon. Tuna. Burgers. Basic stuff. I'm no gourmet cook like you."

Her cheeks darkened pink. "I'm hardly a gourmet cook. I do

like to dabble here and there with different recipes when I have some free time."

"You're very good at it. This is great food."

"Thank you."

"Where did you learn to cook like this?"

"Television cooking shows, the Internet, and a lot of practice."

He ate everything on his plate, and what was left on Savannah's that she didn't finish. After that he did the dishes, since she'd done most of the work on the cooking, though he wasn't able to kick her out of his kitchen. She stood by and helped him load the dishwasher, and when she wasn't doing that she was cleaning off the stove, counter, and table and putting things away, despite his suggestion that she take her glass of wine and sit down.

"Don't you ever relax?" he asked as he dried his hands on the dish towel.

"This is relaxing for me. It's what I do after a long day. I cook. I clean up."

He shook his head. "This is work."

She laughed. "Not to me it isn't. I travel so much that most of the time I eat restaurant food or room service. To be able to eat a home-cooked meal is heaven for me. To cook it myself is a double bonus."

Women were odd creatures.

No, Savannah was an odd creature. Most of the women he went out with were perfectly content to have him take them out for a pricey dinner. Not once had any woman offered to cook him a meal.

She was unique.

He led them into the living room. Savannah took a seat at the end of the sofa. He almost sat in the chair across from her, to maintain that professional distance and all, but decided on the sofa, too. "What you said about being at home? I know what you mean. Once the season starts we're either on the road and when we have a home game we're at practice. Not that I'm a big cook to start with, but I'm tired by the time I get home, so I'll grab something on the way. I eat a lot of take-out food. Don't tell my mom."

Her lips lifted. "Your secret is safe with me." She kicked off her shoes and tucked her legs under her on the sofa.

"You're a woman of many talents, Savannah."

"Not really. I just like to cook. And men are easily impressed by a woman who knows how to cook. It caters to one of their base needs."

"Food and sex."

"Exactly."

"So you're saying I'm easy?"

"No. I'm saying you're a man."

He laughed. She had a dry wit and could send a subtle zinger with her sarcasm using that sweet Southern voice of hers. He had to admit, he liked that.

But he liked strong women, not ones who would cry if you looked at them the wrong way. She wasn't the type of woman to manipulate a man with tears to get what she wanted. He couldn't see her ever doing something like that, since she was so straight-up honest. She was sweet on the outside, but she was tough. He'd given her a hard time in a lot of ways and she hadn't yet folded.

She set her wine on the table and shifted to face him. "I want to talk to you about some suggestions I have."

"Work-related suggestions?"

She cocked her head a little to the side. "Of course."

"Not tonight." He stood and grabbed her wineglass, went into the kitchen and refilled it. When he came back, he could see she was confused.

"Look, Peaches. I appreciate your cooking me dinner, and I enjoy your company, but I'm not all about working twenty-four hours a day." He handed the glass to her. "Sit back and relax."

She took the glass from him. "My job is to work with you to repair your image."

"And we are working on that, aren't we?"

"We've barely scratched the surface. I have a plan."

"I'll just bet you do. But we're not going to get into that tonight."

"Really. And what are we going to get into tonight?"

He liked the sound of her voice, the soft, sexy way she asked that question, almost in invitation. He didn't think he was reading anything that wasn't there. He was smart enough to know the difference between a woman who was interested and a woman who wasn't. And while he'd promised himself he was going to keep it professional, she was the one opening the door now.

"I thought maybe we'd just hang out together tonight. Get to know each other a little better."

The look she gave him almost made him laugh. She looked tense, maybe even a little horrified.

"Okay, I can tell that's not what you want to do. Did you have something else in mind?"

She put her glass down again and stood. "Yes. Work."

He stood, too, came over to her. "No work tonight, Savannah."

"Then I should definitely go."

"You're afraid of me."

She let out a snort. "I am definitely not afraid of you."

"So it's just men in general?"

She rolled her eyes. "Don't play me. We had a nice night. Let's just leave it at that."

She went into the kitchen and he followed. She grabbed her purse.

"No, really. Is it all men, or is it just me?"

"It's just you."

"I make you—what? Uncomfortable? Or do I make you realize it's been a while since you've been with a man?"

Her eyes blazed hot. He liked to see the cool Southern belle spitting a little fire. "You're presuming a lot, Cole."

"Maybe I am."

"Don't." He was blocking the doorway, so she laid her hand on his chest to move him out of the way. He grasped her wrist and she halted.

He felt her pulse racing and he knew it wasn't because she was mad. He could see it in her eyes, the way her pupils dilated, the way her lips parted. And when she took in a breath, it wasn't so she could spit out words of anger.

She was turned on. So what held her back?

"Look," he said. "I know we work together, but I'm good at separating the two."

"I don't mix business and pleasure."

He moved in closer. "Have you ever tried it?"

"Cole. We've already tried this and agreed this was a bad idea."

"No. You thought it was a bad idea." He lifted her hand around his neck, swept his arm around her back and tugged her close. "But you already know I never do the right thing."

He bent, hesitated, waited for her to object. He didn't feel any resistance, so he took her mouth in a kiss. He'd been dying to taste her all night. She tasted like sweet wine and mint, her lips as soft as her skin. She melted against him, her hand sliding into his hair.

This time they weren't outside, weren't in public, and there was nothing to stop them from taking this further.

Nothing except Savannah, and all he felt from her this time was surrender.

SOMEHOW, SAVANNAH HAD KNOWN THIS WAS GOING TO happen. Maybe she'd even subconsciously orchestrated it by planning this dinner at Cole's place tonight.

Despite trying her best to not put herself in this position, here she was, letting Cole kiss her.

Oh, who was she kidding? There was no "letting" going on here. She wasn't passive in all this. She was a full-on participant, pressing herself up against him. She'd dropped her purse to the floor and sifted her hands through his hair, holding on like she was afraid he'd disappear if she let go. She was all in on this and nothing was going to stop her from having him. He'd been a fixation since that first night she laid eyes on his sexy body, since the first time he hit her with those gorgeous, sinful eyes of his.

She'd wanted him, and now she was going to have him, damn the consequences.

He waited, tensing as she shifted. Did he think she was going to run? He likely did since she'd pulled back so many times before. But not this time. She moved in closer, sliding her other hand around his neck, tangling her fingers into his hair. And when she released a sound of pleasure from the back of her throat, he relaxed.

He flexed his fingers against her hip and her knees weakened. She loved the sensation of his hands on her and wanted a lot more of it. He let his other hand roam up her back, teasing the bare skin there, before sliding his fingers into her hair.

She tilted her head back, met his gaze. He brushed her hair away from her face and traced her bottom lip with his thumb.

"I'm sorry," she said.

He frowned. "For what?"

"For waiting so long. For pushing you away all those times. I'm not going anywhere this time, Cole."

He let out a groan with his exhale, then leveled a devastating crook of his lips on her that made her knees weak.

"You have a pretty mouth, Savannah." He kissed her again. She loved the way he kissed. It wasn't savage or demanding, but more of a lazy, exploratory taste, rubbing his lips against hers, teasing her with his tongue. And while he did it, she was getting dizzy, everything inside her heating up to boiling point. Her butt rested on his kitchen table, and Cole had maneuvered himself between her legs, all that denim-clad muscle inching ever closer to her sweet spot.

She quivered with anticipation, moaned with it when he pushed her back on the table, grabbed her butt, and pulled her closer to the edge, drawing her pussy right against the hard ridge of his erection.

Lord have mercy, but if she rubbed herself against his delicious cock, she could come. Just the thought of her rocking against him while he watched—both of them fully clothed—made her clit throb and her nipples tingle. It was one of her hottest fantasies.

She tilted her head back and wrapped her legs around him, delving into the thought of doing just that. And when he laid the palm of his hand at her rib cage, where her heart beat a hard rhythm, she opened her eyes and met his gaze.

"Tell me what you're thinking," he said, his voice as dark as his eyes.

"That if I rubbed myself against you I could come."

He inhaled sharply and tilted his head down. His lids went to half mast, and he looked like the devil himself.

Which only turned her on even more.

"Yeah, that could be fun," he said, his fingers clenching and unclenching on her hips. "But I'm gonna be the one to get you off tonight. More than once."

Heavens. She'd just bet he could, too. There was an air of confidence about Cole, one of the things she liked most about him. She believed he could do what he said he could, and she looked forward to the hands-on experience.

When he pulled her to sit up and slid his fingers in her hair, she realized she never really enjoyed that whole hands-on thing. Oh, foreplay was nice of course, but she was always in a rush to get to the good part. She loved sex, loved everything about it, but she most enjoyed having a man inside her. It was the one time she felt the connection she'd spent her life searching for.

Now, with Cole's hands buried in her hair, his body pressed full-on against hers and his mouth doing delicious things to hers, she felt one zinger of a connection, and they weren't even close to the good part yet. She still had her clothes on, for one thing. But the way he massaged her scalp when he kissed her, she realized she'd never tingled before, except in all her girlie parts, of course. But her head tingled, and so did her lips. She was one giant nerve ending of feeling, from the top of her head all the way down to her uncharacteristically curling toes.

And when he scooped his hands under her ass and picked her up, she wrapped her legs around him and held on, nearly swooning, as his lips were still joined with hers and he was carrying her out of the kitchen toward—no doubt—his bedroom.

Her sex pulsed with anticipation, but then he stopped in the hallway, pressed her against the wall and kissed her so deeply she was dizzy.

She'd never been so fully involved in a kiss before, or so aware of every part of her body. Cole aligned his body with hers, and her breasts rubbed against his chest, her nipples tightening in an agonizingly pleasurable way. When he moved his mouth from her lips to her throat, she banged her head against the wall, the pain only heightening her pleasure.

"I think I might take you right here in the hall," he said, his voice rough and low. "I don't think I can wait." He licked along her collarbone, his tongue dipping into the swell just above her breasts. "What would you think about that?"

Think? She had no thoughts. Her mind had gone liquid, like the rest of her. She couldn't believe he was still holding her, that every part of her body quivered, and that she was so close to an orgasm that one touch, one lick, would set her off. She swallowed past the dryness in her throat and fought for an answer.

"I think you can do whatever you want to with me."

He laughed, the sound wicked and devilish. "I'm planning on it."

He set her on her feet and she wasn't at all surprised to feel her legs trembling. He held on to her with one hand, while the other pulled down the straps of her dress to reveal her bra.

"Pretty," he said, his gaze caressing the black and yellow lace-and-satin demi-bra she'd chosen tonight. He drew one cup down and her breast popped free, her nipple already hard and aching.

"Even prettier." He captured the bud between his lips and, lord have mercy, she thought she might die right there in his hallway.

She wanted to close her eyes and focus on the sensation, but she couldn't help herself—she had to watch what he was doing with his amazing mouth. She looked down, watched her nipple disappear between his lips, felt the suction as he captured it between his tongue and the roof of his mouth. The sensation shot right to her clit, the aching tingle unbearable. And when he released, she gasped.

He looked up at her and grinned. "You taste good, Peaches."

She didn't even get a chance to catch her breath, because he pulled the other cup down and flicked his tongue over her nipple, caught her breast in his hand and played with it, toyed with the bud until her legs were so wobbly she'd have slid down the wall if he hadn't been pressed against her, holding her there.

She might be in charge of making over his image, but he had full mastery over her body right now. She didn't have a problem with relinquishing control over to him, not when he sipped at her nipples and ran his hands down her sides to lift her dress.

He let loose of the bud he'd been suckling to drop to his knees and run his hands over her sides, drawing her panties down to her ankles.

"Step out of these for me."

She shuddered and obeyed, feeling sinfully sexy standing in his hallway with the top of her dress dropped to her waist, her breasts bared, and her panties now gone. Anticipation made her swell with heat and arousal, especially when he pulled her dress down over her hips and it dropped to the floor.

"I want to see you."

When he pressed a kiss to her hip bone, her already weakened legs wobbled a little more.

"Damn, you're beautiful, Peaches." He leaned in and slipped his tongue along the folds of her pussy, before tilting his head back to meet her gaze. "And you taste as good as you look. Tell me to make you come."

That one lick made her quiver. She wanted so much more. Without hesitation, she said, "Make me come, Cole."

He raised up, grabbed her ass, and put his mouth on her. His tongue was warm and wet across her clit, flooding her with heat and sensation and a trembling, aching need for more. His fingers dug into the cheeks of her ass, and she was overcome with the sheer pleasure of his touch and his mouth on her.

Mercy, but the man had a talented mouth. And the things he could do with his tongue should be outlawed. Or at least forbidden from use on any other woman but her for the rest of his natural life, because she was going to take him home with her, lock him in her bedroom, and never let him go.

He had a way of using his tongue that defied logic. He rolled it over her, slid it inside her, and dragged it slowly over her sex, swamping her with sensation until she arched against him and came with a wild, unexpected cry. Through her unabashed climax he held tight to her, never once relinquishing his hold on her.

Panting, she pressed her palms against the wall for support, but she didn't need to worry because Cole stood, slid an arm around her, then planted his mouth on hers. She wound an arm around his neck and kissed him back, trying not to appear as desperate as she felt. Normally, she played it cool and unruffled, but he had definitely ruffled every part of her. She was hot and perspiring and shaking all over. Her normal calm had been replaced by a frenzied need to get him naked so she could run her hands and mouth all over his fine body. And then she wanted—no, needed—him inside her.

It couldn't happen soon enough for her liking.

He lifted her and carried her the rest of the way down the hall. She held back on rejoicing, but she was closer to getting exactly what she wanted. They fell onto the bed and she rolled him over onto his back. She undid the clasp of her bra and pulled it off, tossing it to the floor.

"I like where this is going," he said, reaching for her breasts.

She pushed his hands away. "No."

He frowned, but then she slid her hands under his shirt, and his lids shuttered halfway down. There was something very dark when he looked at her like that . . . something elemental and wicked that made her want to climb on his very erect cock and do very nasty things with him.

She licked her lips and spread her fingers, exploring his firm, muscled abs as she raised his shirt up. She leaned down and pressed a kiss to his bare stomach, snaking her tongue out to follow the trail of soft hair that led to his belt buckle.

He hissed and grabbed a handful of her hair. Mercy, but she liked the feel of his power. She undid his belt buckle and drew the zipper down, feeling the hard ridge of his erection pressing against the seam. Anxious to release him, but also knowing how much he wanted this, she lifted, meeting his gaze as she rubbed against his cock with the heel of her hand.

He gave her a warning glance. "Savannah."

She rubbed again, feeling the length and thickness of him. She shuddered out a sigh and cupped him through his boxer briefs. "This is very nice."

He glared at her, lifting against her hand. She bent and pressed a kiss to the open vee of his jeans, inhaling the musky scent of him. So very male, so potent and arousing.

She rose and reached for his pants. He helped her by shrugging them down his hips. The unveiling was like watching a work of art. Tan skin, then white, a few scars here and there, but the mars only highlighted his beauty.

His nose was a little crooked, and he had a scar across his chin. Another scar ran the length of his forearm and there was a jagged one on his thigh, too. Perfection was overrated. She much preferred a man who wasn't so perfect that she'd feel inadequate. After all, she was hardly a fashion model. She was full bodied, and he was all muscle, yet lean, and oh so thick in one place. He made her mouth water.

He raised up so she could remove his shirt and continue her worship of his sculpted shoulders. She loved a man's arms. There was something absolutely delicious about the deltoid muscles and biceps. She'd felt his strength when he'd held her up in the hallway. She was certainly no light-as-a-feather woman, yet he hadn't strained holding her.

She ran the tips of her fingers over his arms, then across his chest, snaking them down his stomach to where his cock jutted up, proud and hard and tempting. She wound her fingers around him, lifting her gaze to his face.

He was watching her hand, his gaze focused on her stroking his shaft. She squeezed harder at the base, lightening her touch when she got to the soft crest, where she circled her thumb over the silky top.

Nestling onto her stomach, she shouldered her way between his legs and traced her thumb over the thick vein that ran along the underside of his cock.

"Your cock is beautiful," she said.

"It's not beautiful. It's tough and manly."

She laughed. "Okay. It's tough and manly. And beautiful." She licked the tip, then rose up to put her lips over the wide crest. When her mouth slid over him, she heard his harsh breath.

He slid his hand in her hair, grabbing a handful of it to hold on to as she wound her tongue around his shaft, licking her way from base to tip, then going down on him again, taking him deep until he let out a strangled groan as she felt his cockhead bump the back of her throat.

Sucking him was magical, turning her on almost as much as it had when he'd had his mouth on her pussy. There was something about giving pleasure to him that she found incredibly arousing. She wanted him to come, to feel that burst of pleasure like he'd given her. And when he tightened his hold on her hair and began to pump with short, quick bursts between her lips, she knew he was close.

"Savannah. Goddamn. I'm gonna come in your mouth if you don't let go." His voice was gravelly and hoarse, telling her all she needed to know. She gripped the base of his cock and stroked him, tightening her lips around his shaft.

He let out a groan as he came, shoving his cock deep into her throat. He held her, pumping his cock deep. Savannah swallowed as he jerked against her until he was completely empty. She loved that she could give him that kind of pleasure.

He went lax and stroked her head as he panted in recovery. She climbed up his body, learning every muscle and plane as she mapped her way to his mouth, where she planted a hot kiss on his lips. He wrapped his arms around her and rolled her over, kissing her so deeply she lost all sense of time and place. Their legs were tangled, his feet playing with hers. She would never suspect him of being so playful, so willing to make a kiss so long and thorough or of taking his time in the lovemaking process. While she'd wanted him inside her, she certainly didn't object to some extended foreplay.

And oh, what foreplay it had been. But for some reason she'd pegged Cole as a guy who'd want to strip her down, slide inside, and get right to the action.

She'd been so wrong about him—about everything. At least, so far. Because his hand was lazily fondling her breast, his mouth was devastating hers with a deep, passionate kiss, and his foot was teasing her calf. He acted like he could go all night at this, and there was his cock, slowly growing harder against her thigh, while she was primed and ready to go off like a rocket if he so much as got within an inch of her pussy.

And when he slid his hand from her breast to her rib cage to her belly, she wasn't about to object. In fact, she rolled onto her back and spread her legs, hoping he'd get the message.

He lifted his lips and gazed down at her. "Something you want?"

"Yes. Well, I have a list, actually."

His lips lifted in a devastatingly wicked half smile that made her clit quiver. "Care to share that list with me?"

"Your hand on my pussy would be a good start."

He glided his hand down, cupping her sex, using his fingers to rub over her sensitive flesh. She arched against him, reaching for his wrist to hold him where she needed him the most.

"Feel good?" he asked.

She turned to look at him as he brought her right to the edge. "Yes."

"Ready to come?"

She was. It was so fast, but it had been a long, dry spell without a man, and she needed this. She wasn't about to hold back, not knowing when she'd have sex again. "Yes."

He tucked two fingers inside her and pumped, rolling his thumb over her clit, then using his magnificent hand to cup her, tease her, and take her right to the edge.

She exploded, this second climax even more intense than the

first had been. She tightened around his moving fingers as her orgasm peaked.

When Cole removed his fingers, he slid them into his mouth and licked them. "I like the way you taste, Peaches."

She shuddered, still throbbing from the aftereffects. Her nipples were tight, aching peaks, her entire body taut with expectation. And when Cole reached for a condom on his nightstand, she licked her lips, so ready to feel his cock inside her that she almost whimpered with the need for him.

She took the condom from his hands and rolled it on, her gaze locked on his. Intimacy like this wasn't something she had all that often, so she wanted every part of the experience. She wanted to touch him, to taste him, as much as she could tonight.

He rolled her over onto her back and used his knees to spread her legs, pressing his body on top of hers. His cock wedged at the entrance to her pussy, his hips against hers.

He looked down at her and their gazes met. He reached for her hair, brushing it away from her face, the action so brutally intimate it made her heart clench.

"You are beautiful, Savannah," he said, then slid inside her, his eyes shuttering closed just as he drove home.

Oh, god. The intimacy was more than she could bear. Feeling him inside her, the way he'd spoken to her, shattered her.

Savannah reached up to slide her fingers in the silky softness of his hair, watching the features of his face tighten as her pussy gripped his cock.

She wasn't often driven poetic over the act of sex, but there was something magical about Cole being inside her. She'd never felt such an amazing thrill about a man fucking her. Sex was perfunctory. Fun and certainly a wonderful release, but being connected to Cole like this, having his gaze touch hers in such an intimate way as he pulled back and thrust so deeply inside her, filled her with passion—and more than a sense of wonder.

This was what she'd always read about, what sex was supposed to be like—a joining that was both physical and emotional, so powerful in its intensity that she was caught up in its storm.

Cole dipped down and brushed his lips across hers, then cupped her butt and lifted her to grind against her. As the storm intensified within her, she tightened, sparks of lightning shooting through her nerve endings. Taut with impending release, she dug her nails in Cole's skin. His answering growl only heightened her senses and rushed her along the path to orgasm.

When he sank his teeth into the soft skin of her shoulder, she cried out, her climax sending her flying into the sweet darkness. She wrapped her legs around Cole's hips and arched, dragging him along with her, his answering groan a blissful balm in the maelstrom.

He kissed and licked her neck and shoulder, bringing her back down from one of the wildest rides of her life. He left her for only a few seconds, then came back and pulled her against him.

There were things that needed to be said, things she knew he was likely thinking about, too. Reality-type things. Logical-type things.

She wasn't going to talk about them now. That conversation could wait for later. For now, she was going to enjoy being held and caressed by a man who'd just rocked her world.

SAVANNAH WAS QUIET AS COLE HELD HER AND SWEPT his hand over the softness of her back.

He knew what that meant. She was thinking.

Likely regretting.

He had no regrets. Tonight had been nothing short of amazing. She was a wildcat in the bedroom. She had no reservations about sex, great communication skills, and she was as beautiful as he'd imagined.

But knowing Savannah, by morning—if not within the hour—she was going to call this all a mistake.

Cole planned to argue that point, because sex this good was never a mistake.

He was pretty good at arguing his point, especially when he knew he was right.

For now, he intended to keep this luscious woman in his arms—and his bed.

TWELVE

"NO."

"Cole . . ."

"I said no. There's no point in discussing it."

Cole had thought they'd end up arguing about sex. But surprisingly, Savannah hadn't said a word about it. She'd actually stayed all night, though she'd hurried out of his condo the next morning, uttering no more than a few words about him needing to get to practice and her having things to do. Though she'd been vague about what those "things" were.

Ironic, considering that was usually *his* behavior after sex. He normally couldn't wait to get away. Instead, the roles had been reversed, because waking up to Savannah's warm butt nestled against his cock had made him hard. He'd pulled her against him, figuring they could have a nice morning replay of the night before.

Yeah, that hadn't happened. She'd rocketed out of bed, grabbed her clothes, climbing into them while simultaneously mumbling about how great it had been the night before, and she'd call him later. Then she'd shot out the door like a lit firecracker.

It had been damned uncomfortable being on the other side of that fuck-'em-and-leave-'em treatment. Now he knew what it felt like.

It didn't feel all that good.

He climbed out of bed, making a mental apology to all the women he'd done that to.

But he wasn't finished with Savannah, and if she thought that all they were going to have was one night and she was going to forget it happened, she was wrong.

After practice, she'd been waiting for him. That's when he'd expected the argument.

Instead, she dragged him upstairs to the conference room and shut the door.

"What's up?"

"Have a seat."

This was where she was going to tell him that last night had been fun, but it was only a one-time thing and couldn't happen again. He knew this talk. Hell, he'd given it a hundred times before.

He was already preparing his rebuttal.

"How are you with a hammer?"

He looked up. "What?"

"I have you—well, us, actually—scheduled for a local home-building charity project."

"Uh . . . why?"

"Because it's for a worthwhile cause. Actually, several of the team members are doing it, along with coaches and staff. Saturday."

"And we're doing this because . . ."

She rolled her eyes. "Image, Cole."

"In other words, media will be there."

"Yes."

"And you think this will somehow help repair my image?"

"It certainly won't hurt your image to have you seen doing something for your community."

"I do plenty for my community."

She leaned back in her chair. "Really. Like what?"

"I give to a lot of charities."

"Give . . . how?"

"I write checks."

She let out an audible sigh. "That's not visible. You need to be seen being charitable. Besides, don't you want to get more involved and centered in your community?"

He shrugged. "I guess."

She stood. "I wonder about you sometimes, Cole."

She headed for the door. He stood. "What the hell does that mean?"

She turned to face him, her hand on the door handle. "It means I wonder why you're so reluctant to get involved."

"Because I don't want it to be bullshit."

"Excuse me?"

"Look. I understand charity. My parents taught my sister and me that it's important to give back. I do plenty of that. I just don't think we need to stick our faces in cameras to show how charitable we are. It seems dishonest."

She frowned. "So you think what the team does is dishonest? That we're just doing this for publicity, and not actually helping?"

"I give generously to multiple charities, but I don't make a big deal out of it. I don't think it's anyone's business."

"I think you confuse a publicity stunt with actual helping out. Not everything can be accomplished by writing a check, Cole. I'll show you the difference on Saturday."

"Fine."

"Fine."

He watched her walk out the door and realized that the conversation hadn't gone at all like he'd expected. She always made him feel like he was doing it wrong.

His mother gave him that feeling, too.

Comparing Savannah to his mother was a place he refused to go.

And now he was going to have to build a house on Saturday. And no doubt deal with the media on his ass at the same time.

He dragged his fingers through his hair.

Great.

SAVANNAH HAD A LUNCH DATE SCHEDULED WITH LIZ, who bounced in beaming, her cheeks rosy pink, a wide grin on her face as she threw her purse into the chair next to her.

"You seem awfully happy."

She ordered an iced tea. "I am happy. I have a successful career and a hot man to sleep with—whenever he's in town. Life is good."

Savannah pushed her irritation with Cole to the side and smiled. "I'm so happy for you. You deserve this."

"I never thought I could feel this way. Or that I deserved it. But you know what? You're right. I do."

Sometimes Savannah wondered if she'd ever feel that sense of contentment that seemed to surround Liz.

"So, how are things going with our problem child?" Liz asked.

"Oh, they're going fine." She opened up a packet of sugar and added it to her tea, then decided today was the kind of day she'd need two sugars.

Liz arched a brow. "Two sugars doesn't signal fine to me. What's going on?"

She met Liz's probing gaze. "Nothing. Cole's being cooperative."

"Cooperative is good, but what aren't you telling me?"

A lot. But she wasn't the type to share intimate secrets. Instead, she plastered on her brightest smile. "He gave a great interview to the local television station last week. Did you see it?"

"I did. And you're still hiding something. We might do business together, Savannah, but we're also friends." Liz reached across the table and laid her hand on top of Savannah's. "Tell me what's going on."

Savannah's shoulders slumped. "I slept with him."

"With Cole?" Liz's eyes widened. "That's an interesting development."

"That's an understatement. I tried so hard to deny the attraction. I'm a professional. I should know better."

The waitress brought their chicken salads, but Liz leaned forward. "Honey, I'm the last pot to call the kettle black in this instance, since I did the very same thing with a client who is now my husband. Tell me all about it."

She picked at the pieces of grilled chicken, feeling miserable about everything. "I don't know what happened. I had a handle on it—on Cole—but he's just so darned attractive. I don't think I tried very hard to resist him."

"Well, those Riley men can be persistent as hell." Liz waved her fork at Savannah. "Once you fall for one, you don't stand a chance in hell."

"I'm not falling for him. We've only had sex once and it isn't going to happen again."

Liz gave her a wry smile. "Isn't it?"

"No. I'm determined to finish this assignment, make him the best wide receiver the Traders have ever had, and get out of his life."

"Uh-huh. Famous last words. You and me need a night out with Jenna and Tara. The four of us need to have a talk about sports jocks and the irresistible testosterone factor."

Savannah lifted her chin. "I'm a strong woman. I can resist."

"Sure you can, honey."

This conversation with Liz was not helping. "My career is my number one priority. I won't let any man get in the way of that."

"So was mine. Until Gavin came along."

"Your situation isn't the same as mine. You were already in love with him."

"I was. But he didn't know that when he came after me."

"It still affected how you interacted with him once the two of you became involved."

Liz took a swallow of tea, then set the glass down. "You're right. It did. I was scared to death, afraid he'd find out how I felt, afraid the whole situation with Mick would blow up in my face. I'd already lost one client. The last thing I wanted was to lose another. I tiptoed around like a ballerina on pointe, waiting for the inevitable stumble of my career."

Savannah took it all in, listening to Liz talk about her fears. "But it all worked out for you. You got the guy and kept your career."

Liz nodded. "It turns out I was worried for nothing. I was afraid to fall in love, afraid I'd lose who I was, afraid he wouldn't love me back. We were both so stupid." She took a bite of salad and swallowed. "And I know with your background you must have triple the amount of fear I did."

She shrugged. "I try not to let it influence my decision-making and the way I live my life, but I know it does."

Liz squeezed her hand. "You know I'm a big old busybody and I want to interfere where my friends are concerned, but I'll try to stay out of your way. Just know if you need me to talk to, I'm always here for you."

"Thank you."

"But just one piece of advice, if I may?"

Savannah smiled, knowing Liz wouldn't be able to control herself if she didn't interfere just a little. "Sure."

"Open yourself up to the opportunity. Let him in and see what happens. If nothing else, you go back to doing what you were doing before, with no change to your life. I'd hate to see you spend your life alone because you're afraid."

And she'd hate to hurt as much as she had when she was a child. She'd been left and rejected once. She wasn't sure she ever wanted to go through that again.

Sometimes never taking a chance at all was a better option than taking one and facing that rejection.

She was a strong woman in a lot of areas. In her career, she was fearless, going toe to toe with some of the biggest names in business and sports.

But in matters of heart and emotion, she was a big ol' sissy, afraid to step away from the shadows of the past.

Maybe Liz was right, though. Maybe it was time to let that all go.

How else was she going to have a bright future?

"In time, I'll be sure to do that. When I'm ready."

"But not with Cole?" Liz studied her with that probing gaze she used on her clients.

"Not with Cole. It's a conflict of interest. I just can't risk everything I've built."

"Up to you, sweetie, but I say don't pass up a golden opportunity. They don't come around all that often, and you don't know when you might have another chance."

Savannah smiled at her. "There are a lot of men out there."

"Yes. But has any other guy made you feel like Cole does?"

She stared at her tea. "Never. Not yet, anyway."

Liz laughed. "Trust me, Savannah. There aren't that many men in this entire world who can put that kind of look on a woman's face."

She lifted her gaze. "What kind of look?"

"That sexed-up, pink-cheeked, dreamy-eyed, oh-boy-was-it-good kind of look."

Savannah palmed her cheeks. "I do not have that kind of look."

"Of course you don't. I'm making it up."

"Sometimes I hate you, Elizabeth Riley."

Liz grinned and lifted her glass, saluting Savannah. "Why, thank you, Miss Brooks. That's the nicest thing anyone's said to me all day."

THIRTEEN

SAVANNAH KNEW THAT WORKING WITH COLE ON SOME of the image makeover ideas she had wasn't going to make him happy. He was resistant to thinking he was anything less than perfect.

Then again, he was a man, and men didn't like to be told they needed to make changes in their lives. Ego and testosterone and all.

She understood that and she was trying to finesse this, but there were a few things that couldn't be finessed, and he was just going to have to suck it up and take it.

It had dawned a miserably hot day, and even at seven a.m. Savannah knew it was going to be the kind of brutal day that made you wish you could stay inside, hibernating in the air-conditioning.

The site had no trees—at least not yet—so they'd have zero shade today. She fought back a grumble and sucked down her iced latte, determined to focus on Thomas and Selena Rogers, their three children, and the new house they were going to get.

Selena was beyond excited and Thomas was grinning ear to ear.

Savannah had worked with both of them on a couple other house builds as well as the start of their own. They were quiet and soft-spoken, generous with their time, and willing to do anything to help others. They were also still shocked and grateful to be so close to having their first home. They currently lived in a one-bedroom, which wasn't at all comfortable for raising three children.

But they were together. Selena worked a full-time job and was in night school. Thomas worked two jobs and yet Savannah had never once heard them complain. And their kids were an utter delight. So smart and happy, always with smiles on their faces no matter their circumstances. Seeing those kids filled Savannah with joy.

Because they had love, hope, and most important, parents who loved them.

That counted for so much.

The crew was arriving, it was getting noisy, and as Savannah turned, she caught sight of Cole pulling his SUV onto the street. He greeted the foreman, who checked him off the list and got him set up with what he'd need for the day.

Lord. He wore jeans, a sleeveless shirt, and a ball cap he'd turned backward. He also had on scuffed, dirty work boots. When he strapped on the tool belt and headed her way, Savannah's knees weakened.

She'd already resolved that their one night together was going to remain exactly that—one night. Her body apparently thought otherwise, because parts of her were tightening, throbbing, and jumping for joy.

She was stronger than her libido. She was. She could contain herself and not go over there, leap on him, and take a long, slow lick of his neck.

She took a deep breath and met him on the sidewalk.

"Good morning," she said.

"Mornin'. Ready to pound some nails?"

She was ready to pound something, but it had nothing to do with nails, unless she was going to nail him. Which wouldn't be appropriate in front of all these people.

Well. So much for her resolve, which was quickly melting in the morning heat. Thinking about business would help.

"Before we get started," she said, "I want to talk to you about the media."

"What about them?"

"They're going to be here to cover the house building today, but also because members of the team are here."

"Okay. So?"

"Make this about the house and not you, okay?"

"I will if they will."

He started to walk away, but she touched his arm to stop him. "You know they won't. They're going to want to dig at you. Don't let them."

"So, what am I supposed to do, Peaches? Stand there and take the shit they dish out about me and my career?"

"For the most part, yes. Talk about the house project and the Traders' involvement in it. Tell them how happy you are to be participating. Concentrate on the positive aspects of you being with St. Louis and downplay all the negatives of your past."

"And what if that's not what they want to talk about?"

"Then keep directing them toward the project. It'll make them look bad if they keep badgering you about your past. As long as you smile and you're positive, they'll have nothing to say."

He shook his head. "I'll try, but I don't think it's going to play out like you think it will."

"As long as you don't argue with them or start a fight, it'll be fine. Trust me. The less you engage with the media in a negative way, the better."

"All I can tell you is I'll do my best."

She smiled at him. "That's good enough. Let's go build a house."

Cole walked away and got started on the framing. Watching his body work was like visiting an art museum. He was all fluid motion, the play of muscles in his arms and back as he moved lumber and pounded nails a beautiful sight to behold. He worked alongside his teammates, something Savannah arranged for because this was also a team-building exercise as well as a charitable undertaking.

It worked, too. And looked amazing with the team working together to raise the frame of the house alongside the other volunteers. The media took pictures, which Savannah knew would make the local papers.

Good for the team. She grinned, put down her own hammer, and brought sandwiches and drinks to everyone as they stopped for lunch. She stayed out of Cole's way because he was hanging out with Grant, Kenny, Jamarcus, and Lon as well as several members of the Traders' offensive line. She wanted him to have that bonding time, so she ate her lunch with a few of the players' wives who'd come along to help.

She was deeply engaged in conversation with Missy Sandell, one of the linebackers' wives, when she saw a couple reporters bearing down on Cole.

"Excuse me, Missy," she said, pushing back her chair to move closer to where the players were being interviewed as they ate lunch.

"We never saw you doing any charity work while you were with Green Bay," one of the reporters asked.

"Maybe that's because you're a St. Louis reporter," Cole answered.

Savannah winced.

"It would have made the national wire," the reporter shot back. "You're in the news a lot."

"Only the negative stuff."

One of the reporters laughed. "Well, face it, Riley. You do give us plenty to report on."

Cole took a long swallow of water, then caught Savannah's sharp frown. "But I'm here now, and happy to be working on this house today. The Traders are an amazing organization who put a lot of time, effort, and money into charitable efforts. I'm honored to be a part of this one."

She exhaled. Good answer.

"Does this mean you're turning over a new leaf?" one of the national news outlets asked.

Cole stood, wadded up his trash, and tossed it into the nearby bin. "Watch me and find out. In the meantime, we're all headed back to work. Why don't all of you drop those microphones, cameras, and recorders and put a little muscle into helping out this family?"

He walked away with the rest of the players. Savannah grinned. The interview started out shaky, but it ended perfectly.

There might be hope for Cole after all.

COLE LOVED WORKING WITH HIS HANDS.

Even in this brutal heat and humidity, sweat pouring down his back and getting in his eyes, he was focused on seeing this house take shape.

Besides hanging out with his teammates off the field today, which made him realize they were all pretty nice guys, he got to spend time with Thomas and Selena Rogers, the soon-to-be owners of this house they were building. They were great people. Enthusiastic, dedicated, and willing to give back to their own community.

They were also huge football fans, so they were ecstatic the Traders had showed up today to help work on their house. When the guys signed a football for them, gave them all jerseys and tickets to one of the games, Selena was touched and Thomas was as excited as their two boys.

It made him realize Savannah was right. He hadn't spent a lot of—okay, any—time in the communities he'd been a part of all the years he'd been playing. Other than writing checks to a few charities here and there, he hadn't taken the time to get to know any of the people who were his fans.

That sucked. And needed to change.

He was beginning to see a lot of things needed to change.

"Feel good?"

He turned toward Savannah, who'd come up to stand next to him. She'd worn jeans and a Traders T-shirt today and had pulled her hair up in a ponytail. With her tennis shoes on and very little makeup, she looked fresh and sexy and gorgeous. And she had dirt on her nose. He used his thumb to swipe it away.

"I feel great, though I'm hot and sweaty and I probably stink."

"I hadn't noticed. Everyone probably stinks."

She still smelled like peaches. He had no idea how she managed that.

"I need a shower and a beer. Want to come over for burgers?" he asked.

"Sure. But I need to take a shower, too. I'll do that and meet you at your place in an hour."

"Sounds good."

He stopped at the store, then went home and jumped in the shower, scrubbing off the sweat of the day. He felt a lot better after he changed clothes and downed a couple bottles of water.

Savannah arrived about thirty minutes later. She'd changed into a tank top and very sexy shorts, her hair down and loose around her shoulders. That peach smell made him hard. He wanted to bury his face in her neck and lick the scent from her skin. All her skin.

He took a step back. "How about a beer?"

"Sure."

He pulled two beers from the fridge and popped the tops off, handed her one and took a couple long swallows from the other. The icy cold brew tasted like heaven after the hellish day. "Now that's good."

"I thought you didn't drink once the season started."

He set the beer on the counter. "It's beer. It doesn't count, and I'm only going to have one or two." He frowned. "Are you going to monitor my drinking now?"

She laughed. "Not in the least. I was just curious."

"Good. I'll go grill the burgers."

"What would you like me to do?"

"Uh . . . nothing."

She frowned and pursed her lips. "I can't do nothing. How about a salad?"

"Sure. I think there're salad fixings. See what you can scrounge up out of the fridge."

He took the burgers out and tossed them on the grill, taking a long swallow of his beer after he'd flipped the meat. He could see Savannah working in his kitchen, mixing up the salad and slicing tomatoes.

He was getting used to having her around, seeing her in his kitchen. Kinda weird considering he usually didn't like people at his house.

And okay, he wanted to get in her pants again, so there was that objective. One night wasn't enough with Savannah. But he liked what she had to say, and she didn't take any of his bullshit. He pushed, she pushed back. He didn't always agree with her or her methods, but that didn't really matter. She wasn't one of those pleaser people who kissed his ass. Mostly she kicked his ass. He liked that about her, too.

He finished the burgers and brought them inside. Savannah had the table set and was leaning against the counter, staring off into his living room.

He set the burgers on the counter. "What are you doing?"

"You have such a nice, open place here. You should have a party."

"Huh?"

She turned to him. "You should invite your offense over. Have a party."

He frowned. "I don't do parties."

"You should. You're the new guy. It would be a chance for you to bond with the players."

He took the burgers into the dining room. "I don't think so."

They fixed their burgers and he piled salad on his plate. She'd poured iced tea for them, too, so he pushed his near-empty beer bottle to the side and took a swallow of tea.

Savannah ate without saying much, until she was halfway through her burger.

"Why don't you like to have people over here?"

He knew she wouldn't drop the subject. "This is my private getaway. No media, no team players, no girlfriends."

"So it's your man cave."

"I didn't say that. I just don't do parties over here."

"It would be great for your image. Show your guys you really want to be part of the team."

"No." He finished off his meal and pushed his plate to the side, following up by emptying his glass of tea.

"I'll do all the heavy lifting. We can even hire a caterer. No cooking, they do all the cleanup, too. All you have to do is be here to hang out with the guys."

She was like a dog with a meaty bone. She refused to leave it alone. "Why is this necessary?"

"Team building is necessary for your image rehab. Not once have you been actually part of a team you've played for."

"Sure I have."

"Did you ever do things with your team members? Go out with them? Do activities with them off the football field? Charitable or personal?"

She had him there. "No."

"It's time we change that. If you don't want to do the party here, we can do it at my place. I don't mind."

"That kind of defeats the purpose of it being all about me, doesn't it?"

He saw the corners of her mouth lift. "Kind of."

He looked around at his place, imagined it filled with a bunch of linebackers and receivers. The thought both excited him and filled him with dread. "I don't know, Peaches. I'm not much for entertaining people."

"Look. You don't have to strip naked and dance on top of your coffee table. Just some food and drinks, music, and you already have the fun video games. A little conversation and you invite wives and girlfriends. Trust me, this will go a long way to cementing your position within the team."

He leaned back in his chair. "You think so."

"I know it."

He already knew he was going to cave, so he might as well get it over with. Savannah wasn't going to let this go. "All right. When?"

"How about Wednesday night after practice? That'll give me several days to put everything together."

"You don't have to do all the work."

"I told you I would. I'm a Southern girl. This is what we do."

He shrugged. "Fine."

"Great. You won't regret this."

"Uh-huh." He grabbed their plates and went into the kitchen, Savannah right behind him. She was talking details about the party, from who to invite to what kind of food they'd have. He mostly tuned out the details and focused on how excited she was.

Her enthusiasm was cute. After loading the dishwasher, he turned to her.

"You like entertaining."

She stopped mid-sentence. "What? No. This is to help you."

He grabbed her hands and pulled her toward him, wrapping his arms around her. "You see yourself married with three kids and throwing big parties, inviting all the other kids' parents over and having those big bouncy houses in your backyard."

She tried to pull away, but he held her tight in his arms. "I do not. And how did you get married with kids out of me planning a party for you?"

"You're practically glowing all over doing your party-planning thing. Your eyes are bright, your skin is flushed, and you can't stop talking."

She laid her arms on top of his. "Hey, there's a lot to do to plan a party in a few days. I'm just running some ideas by you."

"And now you're embarrassed."

"No, I'm not." She shoved at him. "Let me go."

"You are embarrassed. It's sweet, Peaches."

"You're being an ass."

"I know. I can't help myself. You should probably kiss me to shut me up."

Her eyes widened. "Oh, no. We already discussed this."

"No, *we* didn't discuss this. You ran like hell out of here after that night and we never talked about it." He swept his hand over her back. Just holding her against him made his cock surge to life. He liked being close to her, feeling her heart beating against him.

"I think it was obvious that what happened between us was a mistake."

She said the words, but her nipples were hard points against her shirt, her eyes dark and filled with desire. He didn't understand why she wouldn't give her body what it wanted—what she wanted.

"It wasn't obvious to me. I like you. I want to spend more time with you."

She laughed. "We spend almost every day together, Cole."

He slid his hand into her hair. "In a business way. I'm talking about getting personal."

He pulled her closer, waited for her to tense. Instead, she yielded, and he moved in for the kiss.

Her lips were soft and warm and she opened them willingly for him, sighing as he slid his tongue in to move against hers. He pressed his hand against the small of her back with one hand while exploring the silkiness of her hair with the other. Her breasts crushed against his chest and he felt the wild pounding of her heart—same as his.

She excited him. The soft, exploratory kiss turned wild and she wound her hands around his neck and into his hair, yanking on it, telling him she wanted more. Control was lost as he lifted her shirt over her head.

Pink bra tonight, her breasts spilling over the tops.

"You make it hard for me to breathe."

She smiled. "Judging from this," she said, palming his erection, "I make a lot of things hard."

He loved the ballsy way she approached sex. She might be reluctant at first, but once she was in, she was all in.

"Yeah, you definitely make me hard." He reached between them and flicked open the button of her shorts, drew the zipper down and shoved her shorts to the floor. Just as he imagined, matching pink panties. He could stare at her hot underwear for hours, but right now he wanted her out of them.

He traced the outline of her breasts, teasing the edges of the top of her bra, watching the way her breasts rose and fell with her deep breaths. He lifted his gaze to hers and undid the front clasp of her bra, pulled it apart and cupped the globes, using his thumbs to tease her nipples. Her lips parted and he leaned in to kiss her, her bare breasts brushing his chest.

He pulled her bra off and pressed his hand against her butt to draw her closer to his throbbing erection. She was so soft, curvy, his hand gliding over each slope like an exploration into how their bodies were different. He liked how her waist dipped in and her hips were so full. And he loved her ass, loved grabbing it and holding on to it with both hands as he rubbed his dick against her.

He especially loved the sounds she made when he moved against her. He wanted to hear her cry out when she came.

He lifted her up on the counter and stepped between her legs so he could put his mouth on her nipples. Being this close to her skin put him in direct contact with whatever peach body soap or lotion she used—whatever it was that gave her that scent. It intoxicated him like a drug, made him suck hard on her nipples until she grabbed his head to pull him closer, moaning when he nibbled on the bud with his teeth.

He popped the nipple out of his mouth and worked on the other, grasping her breast in his hand to slide his tongue across.

"Cole."

He liked when her voice went low like that, the way she tilted her head back, revealing the soft column of her throat. He kissed the hollow of her neck, sucked it, then grasped her ear with his teeth and tugged. She groaned and lifted her head to stare at him.

"You drive me crazy."

He laid his palm against her sex. "Honey, I haven't even started yet."

She reached for his head, cupped his cheeks between her hands and laid one explosive kiss on him that made him rethink this slow seduction. Because right now he could think of nothing but unzipping his pants and shoving his cock deep inside her, then pumping hard and fast until they both got what they needed. But he knew he wanted to tease her, to take her right to the edge, then watch her fly.

"Lean back, babe," he said.

When she did, he bent over and rolled his thumb over her sweet sex. Her panties were moist, her scent filling the air, making his dick throb. He pressed his nose to her panties and blew a soft puff of warm air against them.

"Oh, Cole," she whispered. "Please."

"I do like it when you beg in that sweet Southern voice of yours, Peaches," he teased. He pulled her panties off, slid his hands under her butt, then put his mouth on her soft, wet pussy.

She shuddered against his lips, cried out when he shoved his tongue inside to lap up her juices. She was quivering all over, and when he slid a finger inside, she tightened around him.

His pretty little Southern peach was ready to explode. But he wasn't yet ready to let go of this, so he swept his tongue around her clit, teasing her with gentle strokes of his finger.

"Please." This time, a little less sugary-sweet.

He flicked his tongue over her plump lips, pulled one into his mouth and sucked it, got a little closer to her clit, but avoided it.

"Cole."

Yeah, she wasn't sweet at all now. She was desperate, lifting her butt against his face, trying to direct her clit to his mouth. He shoved two fingers inside her and clamped his lips over her clit, using his mouth and tongue to pleasure her, to turn her irritation to pure pleasure.

She dropped down on her elbows, let out a whimper, and shuddered.

"Oh, yes. Yes, that's it. I'm going to come."

He laid his tongue over her clit and she let go, shoving her pussy against his face. He gripped her hips and held her while she cried out with her orgasm, licking her gently as she shuddered and trembled. When her muscles finally relaxed, he pressed a kiss to her hipbone and belly, then undid the zipper of his pants and pulled her off the counter. He drew her into his arms for a long kiss before turning her around and bending her over the counter.

"Stay like that. I'll be right back."

He went into the other room and grabbed a condom, put it on and was inside her in one thrust, holding on to her hips as he stilled for a minute, basking in the feel of her still spasming pussy clenching around him.

Savannah gasped at the feel of Cole's cock entering her. Her pussy quivered, then tightened, grasping his shaft and holding on as he began to move inside her.

These sensations undid her, her skin flushing with heat when he was inside her. It was more than just a "Hey, this feels great" kind of thing. It was an all-encompassing explosion of warmth to her entire body, and the sense of something monumental going on in her mind.

Which was likely all in her imagination, because as Cole pulled partway out and slid ever so slowly inside her again, she figured this was just really great sex and nothing more. She was just being overly emotional about how great said sex was, and likely because she hadn't had really good sex in a very long time, and there was no doubt Cole was an expert lover. He was in tune with her body in a way she'd never experienced before, that was all.

But then he wrapped his arm around her middle to shield her body from the counter. He leaned over her back.

"Do you know how damn good it feels to be buried inside you like this?" he asked. "Do you know how tight you are, how wet your pussy is?"

He withdrew, and thrust deep inside her. "You make me want to come hard right now, Peaches. But I want to fuck you all night long, stay connected to you like this for hours. Your body is so sweet, you smell so good, and I love being inside you."

Oh, god. She loved the way he talked to her, the deep whisper of his voice sending chills down her spine. He made her tremble inside and out and she bucked back against him, letting him know just how much she enjoyed having his cock inside her.

He swept her hair away from her neck and licked the side of her throat, flicking his tongue across her earlobe.

"Do you have any idea how good you smell?" he asked. "Just being around you makes my dick hard, makes me want to get you naked so I can suck your pretty nipples and lick your pussy."

He gave her goose bumps when he thrust his cock in deeper, inciting her wild imaginings with the way he talked to her. "You make me come hard when you lick me."

"I know. I like watching you let go. You're so wild and free when you come. It turns me on."

He pulled out, turned her around and slid his cock into her, his gaze glued to hers. She held on to the counter while he eased in, then out.

"I want to watch your face when you come." He ground against her, rolling his hips to give her maximum pleasure. Her pussy quivered and clamped around him like a vise.

"Keep doing that and I will."

He kept doing that. And she did. The intimacy of meeting his gaze as she climaxed, of seeing his eyes narrow and his jaw tighten as he went with her, was nothing short of a molten volcano of liquid pleasure.

Out of breath, she fell into his arms, feeling the jackknife rhythm of his heart beating against her chest.

She was sweating. So was he.

That had been more than enjoyable. It had been intense. Maybe a little earth shattering.

And totally wrong.

When he withdrew, he grinned down at her, obviously satisfied and happy. He bent to kiss her, but she pulled away. "I need to go clean up."

"We could take a shower together."

"I really need to go." She grabbed her clothes, but he stopped her.

"Savannah. What's wrong?"

"Not a thing. This was a lot of fun. But I really should go."

She scooted down the hall and shut the bathroom door, appalled at what she saw in the mirror.

Her bra still hung halfway down her arms. Her hair was a mess, her makeup was smeared and there was a blush all over her skin. Cole had left marks on her and—oh, god—was that a hickey on her neck?

How old was she, anyway? She wasn't a teenager in the throes of first passion. She was an adult. A sensible, capable, professional who should not have had sex with her client in his kitchen.

That was twice now she'd utterly lost her mind.

She washed up and got dressed, took a couple deep breaths, and went back out. Cole was having a glass of water in the kitchen.

"Here, I poured you one. Figured you might be thirsty."

"Thank you." She took a couple long swallows to lubricate her parched throat. "Now I really should go."

"Want to tell me why you run every time we have sex?"

She paused, feeling awful that she kept doing this to him. She owed him an explanation. She turned, faced him.

"Because we shouldn't have sex."

"Why not?"

"You know why not. Because we work together. I'm supposed to act professionally around you, not jump on your cock every time we're alone together."

His lips curved. "I like you jumping on my cock."

"How are you going to take the work we do together seriously if we're sleeping together?"

"So far, there hasn't been a whole lotta sleeping."

"Not funny, Cole." She grabbed her purse and started for the door, mentally kicking herself for ever allowing her libido to have free rein.

He moved beside her. "I'm sorry. I can tell this bothers you, but I don't know why. I can keep professional and personal separate."

She opened the door and walked outside, but turned to give him a regretful look. "That's the problem. I'm not sure I can."

He leaned against the doorway. "You know, Peaches, I'm not buying your practiced speech about professional and personal. You're running because of something else. And if we're going to keep seeing each other, eventually you're going to have to start trusting me with your secrets."

Savannah gave Cole a pained look that told him she really wanted to do that.

Cole wished she would, but instead, she turned and walked to her car. She got in and started the engine, her gaze meeting his for a brief second.

Come on. Come back inside and talk to me.

But she put her car in gear and pulled away.

He dragged his fingers through his hair and shut the door.

For a second there, they had been so close. Hell, for the entire night they had been close. Good dinner, great conversation, amazing sex.

And then she'd slammed the door in his face as soon as the sex was over.

If he were the kind of guy who'd get all emotional over shit like that, his feelings might be hurt. He might even take it personally.

But he wasn't that kind of guy, and he knew this wasn't about him.

This was about Savannah. And it had nothing to do with him being her client.

He'd been making progress. He might not really enjoy taking instructions from her, but he'd seen the light. He was beginning to see the wisdom in her suggestions. He might not be the sharpest tool in the shed, but he wasn't a total dumbass, either. A lot of what she'd been trying to tell him made sense. So he'd been listening, putting those words into action, and it was working.

Which had nothing to do with what went on between the two of them when they were alone. He'd been honest with her when he told her he could separate business from personal.

No, that wasn't the problem. Something else was.

And he wasn't going to give up until he figured out what it was that kept sending her running out the door every time the two of them got close.

FOURTEEN

GETTING HIS FRUSTRATIONS OUT ON THE FOOTBALL field had always worked well for Cole.

Okay, maybe he also used to take his frustrations out in clubs, and on the media, but he'd been working hard on turning over a new leaf. This year he was going to leave it all on the field. New image and all that.

Preseason was starting this weekend, and he was psyched up and ready for the game. He was secure in his position, though he didn't expect to get as much playing time in this weekend's game against Cleveland as he'd like.

Still, the start of play was always as exciting as the first time he'd walked onto a football field as a professional. It never got old. And this year, on his home team, would be the year that everything was going to change for him.

He hadn't seen Savannah since that night at his condo. She'd laid low, though they'd exchanged a few phone calls. She'd told him she'd be at the game today to help coach him through media interviews, which he'd found laughable, but he'd agreed to meet with her before the game to go over some pointers.

He'd wanted to see her anyway, to gauge her mood and how things were between them. Despite being busy up to his eyeballs with team practice, he'd also been thinking about her a lot. There were times he'd wanted to call her, but he didn't want to push someone who obviously didn't want to be pushed.

Didn't mean the game was over in his mind, though. It was just a temporary retreat.

He still wanted Savannah. They'd just gotten warmed up. Sex with her was great and he liked spending time with her, time that went beyond the image makeover shit she was making him do. He liked the personal time they spent together.

But for some reason what was going on between them kept scaring her into backing away. Maybe she did fear for her job, but it wasn't like he was going to approach the team owner or coach and tell him that he was fucking Savannah. He knew how to be discreet.

He just had a feeling there was something else bothering her, and he didn't know what it was.

"Ready to kick some ass today, stud?"

He was in the team office signing some papers and turned to smile at Elizabeth.

He grinned. "You know it."

She laid her hand on his arm. "I'm expecting you to make me look like a brilliant agent for signing you when no one else would touch you. Don't make me look like a dumbass."

"Don't worry about it. I've got a good feeling about this season. I think it's going to be one of my best yet."

Liz leaned a hip against the conference room table. "That's what Savannah tells me."

He cocked a brow. "Is that right?"

"Yes. Of course that could just be PR on her part, trying to sell the positive aspects about you."

"It's not PR. I'm a changed man."

Liz snorted. "We'll see about that."

"Hey, she's a freakin' miracle worker. You'll see. It'll be like raising Frankenstein's monster from the dead."

"I don't think you were quite that bad. If you were, honey, I'd have never taken you on."

"Thanks for the vote of confidence, as weak as it was."

She laughed. "And how are things going between you and Savannah?"

He arched a brow and leaned back in the chair. "In what way?"

"In that way."

He stayed silent.

"She told me the two of you slept together. And don't bother getting all upset about it. We're good friends and I'm discreet."

"I'm not upset about it. I'm glad she has someone to talk to, since she damn well won't talk to me."

Liz folded her arms. "Hmm."

"Yeah? And what does that mean?"

She pulled up a chair. "Tread lightly with her, Cole. I mean it. She's dealing with some stuff."

"What kind of stuff? Like a bad breakup or something?"

"It's not for me to say. If she wants to open up to you, she will. I just don't want you to hurt her."

"I'm not trying to hurt her, Liz. I'm trying to get her to trust me enough to have a goddamn conversation with me. Or at least stop fucking me and running like hell after."

He couldn't believe he was having this conversation with his agent. With a woman, no less. Men didn't have sex and talk about it. Ever. But he was at a loss as to how to deal with Savannah and needed some insight.

"Do you care about her?"

"If I didn't I wouldn't be so frustrated, and I sure as hell wouldn't be talking to you about it. I've got more important things on my mind, like the start of the season. So yeah, I care about her."

Liz's lips quirked into a smile. "I guess you do. Be patient with her and don't give up. She needs to know you're going to be there for her, that you're not going to abandon her. That's the only advice I can give you."

That would have to be good enough. "Thanks."

"Hey, relationships are tough. And sometimes one side has to do a lot of the work. Just ask Gavin."

He laughed. "How's married life going, by the way?"

"Obscenely romantic. I love it, even though I hardly see my husband since he's knee deep in baseball season. But we carve out time whenever we can. I'm just looking forward to November when we can have our honeymoon."

"Good. I'm glad for you, though why you'd want to be married to my pain-in-the-ass cousin is a mystery to me."

"Somebody had to take him on. I took pity on him." Liz stood and kissed him on the cheek. "Play good today."

"Yes, ma'am."

Liz had walked out the door and Cole saw her run into Savannah outside where the offices were. They stopped and talked for a few minutes. Cole watched the interplay between the two women. There were hugs, a lot of smiling, and some intense conversation. He would have liked to know what they were talking about.

Maybe about him. Or maybe it was just woman talk. For all he knew they were having a conversation about shoes.

They hugged good-bye and Savannah headed into the conference room.

"You talked to Liz?" he asked.

"Just for a minute or two. Nothing significant."

That she had to say that meant they talked about him.

She laid her bag on one of the chairs, then pulled out the one next to his and took a seat. "She told me she expects you to shine today."

"Yeah, I got that order from her."

Savannah smiled. "I have no doubt you'll be successful."

"Me, either." He wanted to drag her into his arms and press a hot kiss to her lips—the ones painted a pretty little shade of dusky pink today. She wore a brown dress and heels, her hair pulled up. He also wanted to kiss her neck, but he could tell she was wearing her professional persona today.

"I need to get down to the locker room," he said. "You wanted to talk?"

"Yes. There will be media interviews after the game today."

"There are always postgame media interviews."

"Yes. And you haven't always handled those well. Especially if your team loses. It tends to put you in a bad place and you take your mood out on the media."

"Not gonna happen today. Have some faith in me. I *have* been listening to you."

"Good. But just in case they come after you, and you know they will, keep your answers relevant to the game and to the Traders. No matter what."

"All right."

She stood. "Promise me?"

She wasn't beating on him. She was worried about him, about how he was going to be perceived by the media and the public on this first game with his new team. He got that. "I promise."

"Okay." She grabbed her bag and headed for the door.

"Peaches."

She paused. Turned. "Yes?"

"Don't you think we should talk about the other night?"

She smiled at him. "Have a wonderful game. I'll be rooting for you."

* * *

SAVANNAH KNEW SHE WAS BEING A COCK-TEASING bitch, and that wasn't in her nature. She'd gone to school with girls like that, girls who gave it out, then withheld it until they got what they wanted.

That wasn't at all what she was doing. What she was doing was losing her ever-loving mind.

"Sorry I'm late. I had to deal with a couple other players, then I had to answer some calls, then email. It never ends." She rolled her eyes.

Savannah looked up and smiled at Liz. Just what she needed, a friendly female who understood.

They were sitting in one of the private boxes, thanks to the team owner who graciously offered up one of his spaces for Elizabeth's use. Liz had invited the Riley family, which included Cole's family as well as Gavin and Mick's family. The box was filled with a horde of Rileys today, except Gavin and Mick, of course, who were busy playing their respective sports. But Mick and Gavin's parents had attended, as well as Cole's parents, and they were all sitting huddled together. Savannah had greeted them when she'd walked in, then settled in at the front of the box so she could watch the game—and Cole's behavior.

It was kickoff. Cleveland had deferred to the second half, so the Traders were going to receive. Savannah leaned forward and watched the return to the thirty-yard line. Good field position as the offense took the field to the raucous applause of the fans.

Savannah's heart was pounding.

"You look like you could use a drink," Liz said as she took a seat next to her.

Savannah laughed. "I might."

"I'm sure you've done a great job with him, but this part is all up to him."

"I know. But I—"

What? Cared about him? Wanted him to win so desperately her heart was in her throat? She had no idea what she felt about Cole. Her emotions were so mixed she didn't know what to do or how to feel. That was the problem with having sex with a client, or at least with *her* having sex with a client.

She could have sex with just some random guy she was dating. If a relationship developed—which it typically didn't—great. There was nothing to hold that back other than her own screwed-up views of love and relationships.

But with Cole, she was entering uncharted territory. Not only was he tangled up in her job, which had always been her one and only true love, she also felt something for him she'd never felt for another man.

She sighed.

"Hey, first play from scrimmage was a good run. Twelve yards. Cole wasn't even on the field. I think you can exhale now, honey," Liz said, rubbing her back.

Savannah looked up. "What?" She looked out at the field, realizing she'd totally missed the first play. "Of course. I guess I'm a little nervous."

"I guess."

Three plays later, Cole ran out on the field. Cassidy went into the shotgun, dipped back, and threw. Cole ran a slant and caught the ball, then sprinted for another fifteen yards and a first down.

The crowd erupted into cheers. Cole calmly threw the ball to the ref and reentered the huddle.

Savannah grinned. So did Liz.

"So far so good," Savannah said.

Cole split his time at wide receiver with Davis and Fields and, depending upon the play called, sometimes occupied the field at the same time as one of them. Savannah made note of the number of plays he was given the ball. By the end of the first half it looked like he was sharing starter responsibility with the other two receivers. And he'd caught two long passes and scored a touchdown.

He was playing very well.

The rookie players got time in the second half, so Cole and the other receivers didn't play.

By the fourth quarter, Savannah was relaxed. The Traders had the lead and were sailing on to preseason victory.

"Our boy looked good, didn't he?" Jack Riley asked.

"He looked very good," Savannah said.

"I think this move to the Traders will be the best thing for his career."

"You can thank our Elizabeth for that," Jimmy said, winding his arm around his daughter-in-law.

Liz grinned. "Just doing my job."

"With a little bit of Gavin's and Mick's urging, I think," Jimmy said with a grin.

"Maybe a little. But I wouldn't have done it if Cole didn't have the talent. Hopefully, this will be a good season for him."

"I've watched a couple of his interviews, Savannah," Cole's mother said. "He seems so much more . . . polished."

A high compliment, coming from one of Cole's parents. "He's learning a lot about the team. He's done his homework."

"He's a little rough around the edges. I have to admit I've cringed a bit during his tussles with the media. I hope you can work with him on that."

She smiled at his mother. "I'll do my best."

"He's just being a guy," Jack said. "They all get mouthy."

Cara frowned. "But that's not always the best way to conduct interviews with the media. That's part of the reason he's gotten such a difficult reputation."

"The media loves bad boys," Jack shot back.

And Savannah was going to steer clear of that argument.

Liz put her arm through Savannah's. "Look, Cole is a dynamite football player, but he's had some issues with his behavior, both on and off the field. With Savannah and me working with him and Cole's natural talent on the field, this is going to be his best year yet. Don't we all agree?"

"It sure will be," Jack said, lifting a beer in toast.

Everyone chimed in, and that was the end of the discussion.

"Nice save," Savannah said as Liz drew her away from the family.

She shrugged. "I'm used to the Rileys. They're a passionate lot. And Jack is always going to defend his son, including his son's failings."

"He's doing better," she said as they took a seat in the corner.

"I'm glad to hear that. I don't think my reputation can take another failure."

"Failure? Please. I think you're one of the best agents in the industry."

Liz batted her lashes. "Oh, compliments. Do go on and on."

Savannah laughed and concentrated on the game, though she spent more time watching Cole on the sidelines. He sat with the other receivers, talked to them, got up and chatted up the line.

He was doing everything right. She couldn't be more pleased.

He'd looked amazing today, not just play-wise, but just . . . amazing wise. He filled out his uniform in a way that made her mouth water. There was something about his arms that made her stomach tumble. It was those lean muscles and hands that were talented in more ways than one.

And she needed to remember her goals with him were professional ones, not personal. She already had two strikes against her in the bad decisions department.

"Got your eye on Cole, I see," Liz said.

"Yes. Observing his behavior with his teammates."

"Looks more like you were observing his fine ass."

Her eyes widened and she craned her head around to see if anyone in Cole's family had heard Liz's comment. Fortunately, they were all absorbed in the game and talking among themselves.

"I was not."

"Oh, please. You think I can't see the way he looks at you?"

"What? No." She paused. "How does he look at me?"

Liz gleamed like a cat facing a full bowl of cream. "Like he wants to eat you all up, honey."

Her body thrilled at the thought. "He does not."

"He does. And you want to take a big bite out of his meaty physique." Liz studied her. "So how's that going?"

Heat spread up her neck. She felt it stain her cheeks.

"So. A repeat performance?"

She laid her head in her hands. There was no point in denying it. "I don't want to talk about it."

"Well, I do." She grabbed Savannah's arm and hauled her out of her seat. "Excuse us. We have some confidential business matters to discuss in the private offices."

Liz took Savannah into the adjacent office suite and shut the door. Savannah fell into the chair and opened one of the bottled waters that was sitting in a cluster on the table.

Liz pulled a chair up next to her and leaned forward. "Okay, spill."

"I swore to myself it was going to be that one time and that was it. But apparently I'm weak, or he's the hottest, most irresistible man I've ever come across. Typically, I'm all business. I've worked with sexy sports players before, and not once has one ever tripped my libido like Cole has."

Liz grinned. "Don't be so hard on yourself. I fell hard for Gavin, and that never happens to me. In this business we're surrounded by hot, sexy athletes. I'm immune to them. Until that one man who does it for you like no one else has before."

"I don't know what happened. I didn't intend for anything to explode between us. It just did. I swear, Liz, it's like an inferno.

After the first time, I thought, okay, big mistake. A wonderful, hot night together, but still, it couldn't happen again."

Liz gave her a knowing smile. "Until it happened again."

"Yes."

"So now what?" she asked.

"Now it definitely can't happen again. I can't jeopardize my job. It's all I have."

"You could have Cole."

"Would you have done that? Early in your relationship with Gavin, would you have sacrificed your career for hot sex with Gavin?"

Liz gave her a knowing look. "Not a chance in hell. And I was already on the cusp after what went down with Mick. Taking up with Gavin was the dumbest thing I ever did."

"So why did you do it?"

"Because I was in love with him."

"Oh."

Liz laughed. "My situation is a little different. I had been in love with Gavin for years before we ever got together. My head and my heart weren't in sync. Logically, I knew that getting involved with him could be a career ender for me, especially right after that debacle with Mick. But my heart wanted him. And once we got together, there was no going back for me."

"So you risked it all for him."

"I guess I did."

"I don't understand that. I guess maybe because I never had a role model to show me that great kind of love."

"Honey, neither did I. Well, that's not true. I had Gavin's family, his parents. I've never known two people who were more in love. They're the best role models for a lasting relationship. Being around them for years showed me that if you want something badly enough, you make it work, no matter the obstacles."

"But you're not using your parents as role models."

Liz snorted. "My parents were the worst role models for any-thing. Love, relationship, parenting. I couldn't get away from them fast enough."

A kindred spirit. "Yet look how you turned out. A smart, strong, capable career woman."

"Thank you. And so are you."

"Despite no role model of my own."

Liz frowned and squeezed her hand. "I'm so sorry. I can't even imagine how much that hurt. I had a shitty childhood and lousy parents, but at least I had parents. No comparison."

Savannah shrugged. "I got through it. Like you, I learned to rely on myself. Put myself through school and everything."

"Then let me return the compliment. Look at you now. A smart, strong, capable career woman. You did that all yourself."

"I appreciate that. Sometimes a woman needs a boost, espe-cially when she's out there all alone."

"But you don't have to do this alone. You have friends like me. And you have Cole—or you can have him, if you allow yourself."

She shook her head. "I can't do that. I can't jeopardize my career for a man—for anyone. My mother gave everything she had for men, drugs, and alcohol, and I watched what they did to her, what she did to herself. She lost herself and she gave up everything that was important. I refuse to ever give up any part of myself. My ca-reer satisfies me."

Liz nodded. "I understand. The past is sometimes hard to let go of. But you do realize that you can't blame Cole for the sins your mother committed. And you're nothing like her."

She nodded. "I know. I'm not weak like she was. I'm strong. But look how easily he distracts me. That scares me."

"Love is a damned frightening thing, Savannah."

Her eyes widened. "Love? Who said anything about love? I'm not in love with him. It's just sex. Mercy, that's frightening enough."

Elizabeth smiled. "Are you sure you're not selling yourself short by not giving you and Cole a chance?"

"A chance at what?"

"At having . . . something."

She looked out over the field, her gaze instantly landing on Cole, her body warming just looking at him.

"It's just physical. It's not love."

"He scares you," Liz said.

"Like you wouldn't believe."

FIFTEEN

TWO GAMES DOWN IN THE PRESEASON AND COLE thought they were doing pretty good. They'd won the first, lost the second by only one point, but Cole hadn't pissed off the media or gotten into a fight with his coach or any of his teammates.

He'd gotten the ball regularly during the first half of the games when the first string played. He was getting plenty of play time, just the way he liked it. Things were syncing with his team.

So far, so good.

He met with Savannah regularly, which he liked, though she was doing a damn good job maintaining her distance on a personal level.

That part he didn't like, but he was laying back and giving her space.

He wasn't about to give up, though. He wanted her, and he saw her looking at him when she didn't think he could see her. She wasn't giving him just business looks, either. When she thought he didn't notice, he caught her looks of hunger, of desire.

So why was she denying herself?

It was midweek and they'd just finished practice. He'd stepped out of the locker room after he'd showered and packed up to find Savannah waiting for him.

"Okay, the party planning is going well," she said.

He frowned.

"Party. Your place. I know we pushed it back a week. But it's on for tonight."

"Oh, yeah. That."

She rolled her eyes. "Yes. That. Invites were sent out. Teammates and wives and girlfriends and coaches."

"Okay."

"I have someone coming over at four to clean your place, and the caterers will be there at five. Can you let them in, or give me a key? Or maybe I can just follow you home. I have my clothes with me."

She was acting so formal, like she needed to ask permission to be at his house. "Peaches. Come home with me. It's fine."

She nodded. "All right."

She followed him to his place. Once there, she was a whirlwind of activity. The cleaning crew came in and suddenly it was all dusting and vacuuming and bathroom cleaning. Once the caterers showed up, he didn't have a spare second to even talk to Savannah, because she was directing setup.

He did his best to stay the hell out of everyone's way while they transformed his place. He decided to go out back with a beer and took a seat, enjoying the quiet. He leaned back in his chair and closed his eyes.

He must have fallen asleep because Savannah poked him.

"What are you doing?"

He looked up at her. "Drinking a beer."

"You need to go inside and get ready."

She had changed into a dress. A pretty sexy one. It was blue. Simple. Sleeveless. Clung to her. She looked hot.

"What time is it?"

"Six. Party starts at seven."

His lips lifted. "It doesn't take me an hour to get ready."

"No, but some people might arrive early. Go."

This was her deal, not his, so he might as well not add to her stress since she already looked like she might start pulling her well-put-together hair out any second. He got up. "Yes, ma'am."

He showered, shaved, and changed clothes, then came back into the living room. Savannah was arranging cups of nuts or something on a table.

It didn't even look like his house anymore. They'd rearranged the furniture, which, according to Savannah, would make for more mingling space and had made room for the caterers to bring in tables to lay out the food. The bar was set up. Everything looked ready to him.

Whatever stress Savannah had seemed to have disappeared. She was relaxed and smiling as she came over to him and tilted her head back.

"You look nice."

"So do you." He took a step forward. She took one back, obviously trying to maintain professional distance. He grasped her wrist, felt the fast thump of her pulse as he rubbed his thumb over her skin.

"Nervous about the party?"

Her gaze met his. "A little. I want it to go well for you."

"It's just the guys from the team, Peaches. Don't sweat it."

"But you don't like entertaining here and I know I forced you into this. I don't want you to be stressed over it."

He laughed. "I'm not the one who's stressed. You're flitting around here like freakin' Tinker Bell. Maybe you need a drink to calm down."

"I'm fine. Not worried at all. This is what I do."

He ran his hand up her arm. "Then maybe it's something else that has your pulse racing."

Her eyes widened and she pulled her arm away. "No, it's nothing else."

"You can't keep running away from me. From us."

The doorbell rang and she offered up a smile. "Yes, I can."

Two of his offensive linemen were at the door along with a girlfriend and a wife. They made a beeline for the snacks, claiming that, after today's workout, they were starving. Savannah played hostess and greeted everyone while Cole held down bartender duties.

Within an hour his place was crowded with people. He was actually surprised that nearly his entire offense showed up. So did the coach, though he assumed Coach showed up to make sure his guys didn't get wasted, since they had practice tomorrow and a game this weekend. The only people drinking hard liquor or mixed drinks were some of the women. A few of the guys had a beer or two, but mostly stuck to water or soda. They all knew what practicing with a hangover was like—it was unpleasant, especially if the coaches knew you were hung over. They'd make your day a living hell.

Cole found himself huddled with Lon and Jamarcus. Kenny had made friends with a couple other rookies, so he hung out with them.

"Your assistant do all this?" Lon asked.

Cole searched the room and found Savannah talking to a few of the women, encouraging them to come to the food table to get something to eat.

"She did."

Savannah caught his gaze and blushed, then smiled.

Jamarcus's girlfriend, Tanya, came up and slid her arm around him. "This is very nice of you, Cole. Thank you for inviting us."

"Thanks for coming."

"And Savannah is so sweet. We're both from Georgia, so we've been catching up. Makes me miss home." She looked at Jamarcus. "We need to go to my mama's house for Christmas."

Jamarcus laughed. "Whatever you want, baby."

Savannah saw them looking her way, so she came over. "How is it going? Can I get you anything?"

"We're great, honey. You should take a break and enjoy some time with your man," Tanya said.

Cole fought a smirk as Savannah cast a worried look in his direction. "Oh, we're not together. I just work for him."

He loved when she blushed like that. He loved seeing her entire body cast in that pretty pink shade when he made her come.

His dick twitched just thinking about getting her naked and making her squirm under his tongue.

When she met his gaze, he knew she knew what he was thinking about. She cast him a warning gaze, then turned to his friends.

"If you're all okay, I'll see if anyone needs anything. Excuse me." She wandered off.

"Wow."

Cole turned to Tanya. "What?"

"I don't mean to be gossipy, because that's not in my nature, but there were some serious fireworks exploding between you and Savannah."

He grinned. "You think so?"

"I know so. Don't you think so, too, Jamarcus?"

Jamarcus looked at Cole, then back at Tanya. "No comment. I'm not getting my ass kicked over that one."

Cole laughed and clapped Jamarcus on the shoulder. "Don't worry, man. Tanya is right. There's something going on. I just don't know what it is yet."

"Well, for what it's worth, she's beautiful. Nice, polite, and friendly. If I were you I'd grab her and never let her go."

"I agree," Tanya said. "If you don't, someone else will snatch her up and you'll regret not taking the chance."

They were probably right. But it was difficult when the object you were chasing was doing her best to avoid getting caught.

* * *

SAVANNAH WAS SO PLEASED. THE PARTY WAS FANTAS-
tic. Cole had spent the majority of the night hanging out with Jamarcus and Lon and mingling with his offensive line. He'd had
some major one-on-one time with Grant Cassidy, the Traders'
quarterback. The two of them had huddled in the corner, having
an intense conversation. When she'd inched over to eavesdrop to
make sure they weren't simply talking about women or sports cars
or something else innocuous, she heard them dissecting plays.

Perfect. It had gone much better than she'd hoped. He was
bonding with his teammates, who all seemed to be having a great
time. Cole was even talking with the coach, who had come up to
her and told her that Cole's performance and behavior was better
than he expected—so far.

She had hope. Of course, it was still only preseason, but she
intended to take this one step at a time. Entrenching him with the
team was a giant first step. Once they all had one another's back,
she'd concentrate on his personal image. Team play was vital,
though, and this was an important night.

Everyone started to filter out by eleven thirty or so, since they
all had practice in the morning, and under the coach's watchful eye,
no one wanted to party too hard. She hadn't intended for this to be
a raucous night of debauchery, anyway. Just a night of food and
drink and a chance for Cole to feel more like part of the team.

After the last player left, the caterers came in and cleaned everything up. Savannah and Cole helped them carry the platters and
tables out to their van, the furniture was restored to its rightful
place, and his condo looked like it had before the party. The van
drove off and she went into the closet for his vacuum.

"What are you doing?" Cole laid his hand on her wrist.

"Finishing the cleanup."

"I have a service that does that."

"I told you I'd take care of everything."

"You're dressed way too nice to act as maid service. Though the mental visual of you in a short little maid's uniform . . ."

She rolled her eyes at him. He laughed, took the vacuum and slid it back into the closet. "Seriously. Sit down. Kick off your shoes and relax."

The last time that happened she'd ended up in his bed. "No, thank you. I think I'll head out and let you get some sleep."

"I'm way too wound up to sleep. Come sit with me and you can tell me what you thought about tonight."

Debriefing was a good idea. She'd like to get his thoughts on his conversations with his teammates. She took a seat on the sofa, but kept her shoes on and her feet on the floor. "I thought it went very well. How did you think it went?"

"It was good. I had fun. You spent the whole night working the room like a pro."

"It's my job. I wanted to make sure you had the time to mingle."

"I did mingle. I talked to everyone. I did what you asked me to do."

She frowned. "I don't recall asking you to do anything. Other than have this party, of course. If you really didn't want to do it, you should have said something."

"I didn't want to do it. But it turned out fine. I had fun. The guys are all great and we needed this. It was a good way to get us all together off the playing field. I haven't really had time to get one-on-one with the offensive linemen, and Cassidy and I went over plays and talked strategy for the season. During practice it's all drills and plays. There's no time to talk."

She relaxed. "So you're saying I made a good call?"

"You made a good call." He stood and held out his hand. "Now come with me."

He pulled her to her feet and led her toward the kitchen.

She frowned. "Where are we going?"

"Outside." He grabbed two beers from the refrigerator and slid open the back door while she stepped outside. The humidity had lifted, so it was—for a change—a nice night. There was a breeze, crickets were chirping, and the sky was clear. They took seats on the chairs, Cole opened the bottles, and they sipped their beers. Savannah enjoyed the quiet after the sheer madness of the party, and Cole seemed content with the silence between them.

This was . . . nice. It was something a married couple would do after a party. Sit outside together and unwind. Or at least she thought that's what they'd do. Since she'd never been married or even part of a couple, she really had no idea. All she knew was that being with Cole was becoming a habit, and it was more personal than professional. Which made her want to bolt.

"You've got that look in your eyes."

She met Cole's gaze. "What look?"

"The one that says in less than five minutes you're going to grab your purse and run out my front door."

She lifted her chin. "I have no such look."

"Actually, you do. It usually appears after we've had sex."

"It does not."

He continued to stare at her, giving her his stoic, unflinching look.

"You think I run away from you."

"I know you run away from me. You've done it more than once. More than twice."

He was right. There was no point in denying it when they both knew it was true. She inhaled and let out an audible sigh. "I can't help it. You scare me."

"Why?"

She didn't want to have this intimate, personal conversation with him. She wasn't ready to talk to him about her feelings. She wasn't the type of person to have open, intimate conversations with anyone about how she felt. Other than Liz, of course. But that was different. Liz knew her story and she understood.

"Peaches. Talk to me."

"You're like a mind reader sometimes. There's one thing that scares me."

He let out a short laugh. "What are you talking about?"

"I was just thinking that I've never told a man how I felt, and then you popped up and asked me to talk to you. It's . . . weird."

"Come here, Savannah."

She did, and he drew her onto his lap. Her nerves danced for a myriad of reasons. Nervousness was one, and the other was excitement, which she always felt being this close to him. How was she supposed to keep a clear head when his body touched hers?

"It's okay to tell me how you feel. You can trust me."

She looked down at him, at his eyes that always compelled her. She'd always thought they were so mysterious, but now they were so clear. "I don't trust many people."

"Neither do I. But you're the one who told me I need to broaden my circle of friends."

"And now who's the pot calling the kettle black?"

"I'm not saying that to throw your words back at you. You were right. I had close friends in school. But not since then. I shut myself off. Getting cut from Arizona—my first team—that hurt. I had started to make friends there. After that, I didn't want to, afraid the same thing would happen again. And then it did happen again. After that, I became my own worst enemy. I didn't trust a team to keep me. And maybe I didn't trust myself to do the right things to stay there, and I didn't do the right things. It was a self-fulfilling prophecy, you know."

"I can see how that could happen," she said. "You got hurt, and you lashed out so no one could hurt you."

"Something like that. So I didn't let myself get close to anyone on any of the teams I played for. If you don't let yourself get close to anyone, when you get dumped, it doesn't hurt."

It was like listening to a version of herself. Only Cole was a lot more honest in how he felt, something she'd never allowed herself to be. He was saying all the things she felt inside but had never given voice to.

"How does it feel?" she asked.

"How does what feel?"

"To be that open and honest with someone."

He shrugged. "I've never done it before. I've never said those things to anyone but you."

Her heart squeezed. "Why me?"

"I guess I just wanted to say it—to someone. Or maybe you needed to hear it. I don't know."

She swept her hand along his jaw, then leaned in to brush her lips across his. He didn't do anything, didn't rise up, didn't even touch her, just let her control the kiss, no doubt afraid she'd pull back or hesitate. Given her propensity for running like hell or pulling away, she couldn't blame him for his hesitation.

But he'd been so kind to her, and he'd opened up to her in a way no man had ever done. She knew how difficult it was for a man to admit his insecurities. That he had with her touched her. It showed her he trusted her, and that meant so much.

She still wasn't ready to tell him all her secrets, but she could trust him with some part of her. She half turned, deepening the kiss, sliding her hand through the lush thickness of his hair. Her breast pressed against his chest, her thigh lay against his stomach, and her heart pounded as she licked against his tongue.

He kissed her back with a fervor that never failed to take her to dizzying heights, but he still hadn't put his hands on her. Was he still unsure about her? She broke the kiss, looked into the smoky depths of his eyes, saw the desire and the hesitancy there.

"Touch me," she said, taking his hand and laying it on her hip.

The sharp intake of his breath was exactly what she needed to hear. When he clenched his fingers around her hip, she dampened with arousal.

"Turn around. Straddle me." He held her hands as she momentarily slid off his lap, then climbed onto his lap, facing him. There was ample room on the oversized cushioned chair to fit her knees on either side of his hips. And since he'd left the lights off outside and in the kitchen, they were shrouded in darkness, affording them plenty of privacy.

He slid his hands up her thighs, skimming his fingertips under her dress, causing goosebumps on her flesh. She laid her hands on his shoulders and lifted.

Mercy, how she craved his touch. Outside like this it felt primitive, catering to this primal hunger she always seemed to feel for Cole—the one she could never seem to satisfy.

He cupped her neck and pulled her toward him for a kiss, though letting her take the lead. She was fine with that, needed the dominance he usually provided. Their lips met in a firestorm of passion that released a whimper from her throat. She inched closer to him, sliding her sex against his jeans. Sensation spread from her pussy and she tightened, clutching on to his shirt.

He pulled his lips from hers and drew the straps of her dress down, then the cups of her bra, drawing her breasts together to tease her nipples with his fingers. She rocked her pussy against him, so caught up in the drugging sensations she moaned out loud. She knew they were outside, that she should be quiet, but she needed an orgasm—she needed him inside her.

The hard ridge of his erection was evident against his jeans. She reached down to rub her hand over it, closing her eyes to revel in his hiss of frustration. Obviously, she wasn't the only one who needed this.

He jerked the button of his jeans open, then drew the zipper down. Savannah eased back only long enough for Cole to drop his jeans and put on the condom he'd retrieved from his pocket. She pulled her panties aside and slid down on his rigid cock, his hands on her hips to help guide her.

She trembled at the feel of him filling her, her pussy quivering and clenching around his thick heat. The painful pleasure made her shiver, and when he was buried deep inside her, she threw her head back and lifted partway, dragging her pussy over his shaft.

"You feel good on me," he whispered, his voice as dark as the night surrounding them.

She dropped her gaze to his and dug her nails into his shoulders. "You feel good inside me."

He thrust, burying himself to the hilt. In return, she pulsed, her pussy tightening around his shaft.

"Just like that," she whispered, moving against him in rhythm.

In answer to their lovemaking, the night went quiet. All she could hear were the sounds of their panting breaths as they moved in unison, both of them seeking climax.

She met his gaze, perfectly visible to her in the slant of moonlight afforded to her. It was enough, capturing her, holding her while she rode him.

He grabbed her hips and lifted her, then drove her onto his cock, rocking her against him. She laid her palms on his chest and slid back and forth over him, grinding her pussy against his shaft.

Buried deep like this, she felt every muscle, every twitch, their connection so deep it was shattering to her senses, to her emotions.

"Kiss me," he whispered. She leaned forward and he grabbed her ass as she met his lips. He squeezed the globes while their tongues tangled.

She wasn't going to last much longer. Cole devastated her emotionally as well as physically, asking her without words to give him everything. And she couldn't deny him.

She lifted, needing the few inches of distance to catch her breath. But when he reached down and strummed his fingers over her clit, applying the perfect amount of pressure, she knew she was lost. And he knew it, too, giving her that wicked smile that never failed to devastate her.

She tightened, her back bowed as he found the spot she needed. She gripped his wrists and held on while she shattered, her pussy clenching around his cock as she burst in orgasm, undulating against him as wave after wave of the sweetest sensations poured through her.

He lifted into her, groaning as he came, pulling her flat on top of him so he could shove his cock deep.

She felt the tremors in his body as he held her, both of them shuddering through the aftereffects.

He was still gripping tightly to her hips, his fingers digging in, long after the pulsing sensations had fled.

"Are you holding on to me because you think I'm going to disappear?"

He let go and she sat up, traced the smile that curved his lips.

"Are you?"

"Not at the moment."

She slid off his lap and they went inside to clean up. He didn't let her go far, and instead, led her to his bed and dragged her close to him. She'd righted her clothes in the bathroom, so they were both still dressed, on top of the comforter, their shoes off, their feet tangled together.

Thunder rumbled outside and a flash of lightning pulled her attention to the door. A storm was rolling in.

"If you're going to bolt, you should do it before that thunderstorm hits."

She laid her head on his shoulder. "Are you trying to get rid of me?"

"I'd prefer you stay the night. I just know you like to leave."

She didn't like to leave. She had to leave, at least at a certain point. There was a difference.

It wasn't something she liked to acknowlede about herself. Indecision plagued her. Staying with him meant more sex, and that was always a good thing. But staying also meant getting close to him. Sleeping with him. Waking up next to him. Opening the door to her heart and her emotions a fraction more.

That definitely scared her.

"I don't like to leave, Cole."

"But you have to. I know."

She burrowed against him and watched lightning arc across the sky. The thunder picked up in intensity.

"I think I'll ride the storm out here tonight, if you don't mind."

"If you stay, I want to fix you breakfast in the morning. No waking up realizing you've made some huge mistake and needing to run out of here like some rabid dog is after you."

He must feel awful every time she did that. She knew how she'd feel if someone did that to her. She laid her hand on his chest. "Breakfast sounds good. I like my eggs scrambled."

He laughed, the rumble as deep as the heavy thunder. "I'll do my best to please you."

She brought her lips to his. "You always do a good job of that."

COLE TOOK A DEEP BREATH, INHALING SAVANNAH'S scent. It meant something to have her here in his bed. He tried not to think about what it meant, because he was tied up and mixed up where she was concerned. It was enough that she was here and had decided to stay tonight.

Her body was soft and pliant as he shifted to his side, drawing her close so that her breasts touched his chest, her thighs resting against his, and their legs mixing it up together.

He'd enjoyed having her outside, watching her breasts rise

and fall in the moonlight as she rode him to one hell of a gut-wrenching orgasm. He'd come so hard he was pretty sure he'd felt it in his hair.

Now, as he brushed his lips over hers, he wanted to take it slow and easy, to love her gently. But the storm outside was throwing slashes of lightning and rocketing deep growls of thunder, and as their kisses deepened, he felt the weather's raw power mixing with his need for Savannah, a hunger for her that never seemed to go away, no matter how many times they were together.

He climbed off the bed and drew his shirt off, undid the button of his jeans and let them fall to the ground. With a sexy grin, Savannah got to her knees and slid the straps of her dress down, letting it fall to her waist. She undid the clasp on her bra and pulled it off, tossing it onto his dresser. She stood on his bed and shimmied out of her dress, then her panties, then fell to the mattress, beautifully naked.

He couldn't get out of his pants and underwear fast enough.

Thunder crashed outside, a strike of lightning that knocked out the power, sending the room into darkness.

He crawled onto the bed, jerking the covers back.

"Are you scared?" he asked as he slid his palm over the soft skin of her belly.

"No. I love storms." She turned on her side, her hand gliding over his shoulder and down his arm, then sliding over to find his hip—and lower. She wrapped her fingers around him.

His cock jerked. He was hard and aching to sink into the wet heat of her pussy. But when she shifted, sliding down his body to put her mouth around him, he decided he could wait.

Her lips surrounded him and he was content to watch her as flashes of lightning bathed her face in a silver glow. Her mouth was magic, her tongue wet and hot as hell as she wound it around the sensitive head, then engulfed him, using just the right amount of pressure when she took him deep.

His balls tightened, threatening to erupt. He held back, enjoying the silkiness of her hair teasing his thighs as she worshiped his cock, dragging her tongue along the underside, then using both her mouth and hands to suck and stroke him.

Enough, or he was going to blow his load down her sweet throat. He pulled her up, laid her on her back, and kissed her, driving his tongue inside her mouth as the storm battered against the door. She whimpered, wrapping her legs around him to imprison him against her.

He reached for a condom. Then he was back, sliding inside her with one deep thrust. She let out a soft cry as thunder hit, the storm raging outside in the same way it raged within him. When Savannah raked her nails down his back and bit at his bottom lip, he knew she felt the same force that boiled inside him. He lifted and powered inside her again, this time dropping down to roll against her, giving her the friction she needed.

"Cole." Her eyes widened and he felt her pulse and tighten. "Make me come."

He loved hearing the ragged edge to her voice. He balanced on the edge, barely holding on. Much as he wanted this surging torment to last, he couldn't keep release back—for her or for himself. This was going to go fast.

He rolled his hips, giving her what she needed, and she came with a soft cry, wrapping her hand around his neck to pull his mouth to hers in a thunderous kiss that tore him apart.

He let go then, releasing at the same time, groaning against her lips as his orgasm tore from him. As powerful as the storm, it ripped through his nerve endings.

Fuck. He shook as it took him over. The things this woman did to him always surprised him.

He rolled to his side, taking Savannah with him, refusing to let her go just yet. Dampened from exertion, she held as tight to him as he did to her.

He was done for. His limbs wouldn't move. He could barely get a breath out, could only feel her heart pounding against his chest, her hand resting limply around his back. He took care of the condom, then drew the covers up, letting exhaustion and the storm lull them both into an exhausted sleep.

SIXTEEN

TRUE TO HER WORD, SAVANNAH STAYED FOR BREAK-fast.

And surprisingly, he'd liked having her in his bed last night. Unlike any other woman he'd ever slept with, he'd always wanted Savannah to stay.

He wasn't about to try to analyze what the hell that meant, or why he enjoyed seeing her sitting across from him at his kitchen table.

It was too weird to even contemplate.

He was a single guy. He liked dating a lot of women. Hell, he rarely even dated them. Yet he'd single-mindedly pursued the hell out of Savannah. Maybe because she didn't want to have anything to do with him.

They even enjoyed doing dishes together.

Too goddamned domestic for his liking. Problem was, he did like it.

Shit.

"I have an event for us to go to tonight," she said as he walked her outside. They'd showered together, and had sex again. He'd definitely liked that part of the morning.

He stopped, realizing what she'd said. "What kind of event?"

"A charity thing."

He paused. "Uh . . . what kind of charity thing?"

"It's an auction. Very snazzy and dressy."

He laughed. "No, thanks."

"What do you mean, 'no, thanks'?"

"I've told you before I write checks to charities. I don't attend fund-raisers."

"Well, you're attending this one. It's good for your image."

"And again, no."

"Why are you being so difficult about this?" She stood with her hands on her hips, tapping her foot.

"I told you. I don't do those events."

"Perhaps you never used to do those events. Now you do."

He started to object, but she held up her hand. "There's no point in continuing to argue. This is part of your image makeover. Charity fund-raisers are a great way to get the media on your side. They make you look good, and frankly they *are* good for you."

"I give plenty to charities. You can ask my accountant."

She shook her head. "Not at all the same thing."

"Charity fund-raisers are boring."

"Suck it up. We're going."

And things had been going so well. "I don't like taking orders."

"Too bad. In this case, I'm the boss."

He moved in. "You didn't seem to mind me being in charge when we had sex."

Her eyes widened as she scanned the parking lot, obviously looking for nosy neighbors. She took a step back.

"That's different," she said. "And if you're going to have a problem working with me because we're . . ."

"Having sex?"

"Yes. If that's going to be an issue, then it'll stop."

"It would be that easy for you?"

"No. Yes. I don't know. My work is important."

"More important than you and me."

She sighed. "You're confusing me, Cole. You know what I mean. I was hired to redo your image. You need to make that your priority. Not us having sex."

"I'd rather have sex with you."

She looked away. "I knew this wasn't a good idea."

He was teasing her, trying to get her to relax. It obviously wasn't working. Her shoulders had practically swallowed her neck. He wasn't ready to give up yet. "Sex is always a good idea, Peaches."

"Not if it interferes with our working together."

"You have to admit the sex is great."

"Yes. It is great. But obviously we're going to have to stop."

He picked up a lock of her hair and rolled it between his thumb and forefinger. "So what you're saying is, you used me."

She laid her hand on his arm. "Cole. No. It wasn't like that. Please. I don't want you to think—"

He laughed and took a step back. "Relax. My feelings aren't hurt. If all you were interested in was a couple romps, that's fine with me. You got your itch scratched. We'll move on."

She looked hurt. He felt the gut punch, but he wasn't going to do anything about it. This was her game to play any way she wanted to. And after everything, she still wasn't sure about him yet. He got that. He could be patient while she did the wary dance. But he didn't think they were done yet. "What time is this thing tonight?"

"Eight o'clock. Do you have a tux?"

"Oh, sure. I keep one in my closet for all those times I go to the opera."

"Okay. No tux. I can take care of that." She pulled out her phone, punched in a number. She held up her hand when he would have said something. "Claud, this is Savannah Brooks. I'm wonderful, thank you for asking. Listen, I need a favor. I need to come over with someone who needs a tux for an event this evening. Do you think you could help me out with this? He's with the Traders."

She swept her gaze over his body. He liked the way she looked at him.

"About six feet tall, two-fifteen or so."

She listened, keeping her gaze on Cole. "I owe you one, Claud. Thanks so much. We'll be right over." She pressed the button and tucked the phone back in her bag.

"You have some tuxedo fairy on speed dial for emergencies?"

She grinned. "Something like that. Claud will fix you up. Let's go."

He wanted to balk. He didn't want to do this, but he needed her to understand that just because they were having sex didn't mean he was going to use that to have his own way. Cooperation was part of the deal, so he followed her to the tux shop, where he met Claud, a very tall, skinny dude who looked more like a mortician than a tailor. He was pale and creepy, with long icy-cold fingers. His monotone sent chills down Cole's spine. And this guy was in the service industry?

Savannah chattered away with him, seemingly unbothered by Lurch. He gave Cole the heebie-jeebies.

Claud, who made Cole stand in front of the mirror and try on different jackets, apparently had a wife and two children, based on the conversation he was having with Savannah. Cole bit back a shudder at the thought of some poor woman having to see Claud's rail-thin, stark-white body naked.

They got through the fitting and left after Claud promised to have the tux delivered to Cole's place by five.

"I can't believe you use that guy," Cole said after they walked outside.

"Why?"

"He's like something out of a horror movie."

Savannah cocked her head to the side. "Really? Claud is one of the finest tailors in town. He's very sweet, though he's a little on the shy side. I like to bring him customers."

"Shy? You think he's shy?"

"Yes. That's why he doesn't talk much. And he has the sweetest wife. Diane has a very bubbly personality. Two adorable little girls, too."

Adorable? They had to take after their mother, then. He walked Savannah to her car. "Do you want me to pick you up tonight?"

"That would be nice. Thank you."

Wasn't she being polite? And distant. "Sure. What time?"

"Six thirty? Cocktail hour is at seven."

"I'll be at your place at six thirty, then."

She got in her car and drove off, leaving Cole standing on the curb.

He didn't like this wall she constantly shoved up between them. Tonight, he was going to work on that.

SEVERAL HOURS LATER COLE AND SAVANNAH HAD entered what would surely be the dullest night of his life.

The event was being held at some fancy schmancy gallery in West County. But the benefit was for the American Cancer Society, so he had no problem chunking out some money.

Maybe Savannah would take pity on him since he was in obvious misery. Sure, the tux fit fine, but the shoes were uncomfortable as hell. He was more of a tennis shoes or boots kind of guy, not shiny black pointy shoes. Maybe he could write a big fat check and they could get out of here early.

Though he had to admit, he could stand to spend a couple hours with Savannah. The silver dress that clung to her curves and sparkled in the overhead chandeliers was as much of a work of art as all the doodads being auctioned off tonight for charity. She'd worn her hair up in some kind of twisty thing, had put diamond studs in her ears, and wore no other jewelry. And she had on sexy silver-and-crystal shoes that made her legs look a mile long. He wanted to be alone with her, have her wear those shoes and nothing else.

He wondered what she wore under the dress. Maybe she could wear the shoes and her underwear.

Yeah, and maybe he needed to get his fantasies under control before his dick got hard.

She threaded her arm through his and pulled him aside, straightening his tie. "Okay, let's go through this."

"I got it. Play nice. Don't insult anyone. Don't hit anyone. Don't cuss. I pretty much have the basic manners thing down. You don't have to worry about me."

She cocked a pretty blonde brow at him. "It's my job to worry. Your image is at stake and this is a very high-profile event. In case you haven't noticed, several sports figures will be at this event tonight, along with the media."

"I already told you I'd be on my best behavior."

"Don't engage the media. If you're asked a question, be benign."

Now it was his turn to raise a brow. "How, exactly, does someone act benign?"

"You can answer football questions, or questions related to being with the Traders this season. Behavioral questions you need to avoid."

"Avoid . . . how?"

"For example—Cole, do you think the reason Green Bay dumped you is because of your behavior?—how are you going to answer that?"

He scratched the side of his nose. "I don't suppose you'd let me tell them to fuck off?"

She looked horrified. "Definitely not. You'll tell them you enjoyed your time with Green Bay, and you think they're a great organization, but it wasn't a good fit for either you or the team. Now your focus is on the upcoming season with St. Louis."

"So you want me to deflect."

She nodded and patted his tie, raising her gaze to his. "Exactly. Don't engage in a pissing match with the media. You'll never come out ahead. Only give them positive, quotable remarks. Never denigrate your former teams."

"But—"

She raised her hand. "It doesn't matter what you really think. State the positive, focus on the Traders and this season. Get the media excited about St. Louis and you. If you're optimistic, they'll be optimistic about you."

"I'll try."

"Good. I'll stick close to you so I can help you out if you need me to."

"Jesus, Savannah. This isn't my first time out in public. I think I can handle this. I've been handling it, in case you haven't noticed."

She gave him a dubious look. And okay, maybe she was right. He hadn't exactly been a champion with interviews over the past couple years. He and the media weren't the best of friends. But he'd give it his best shot because it was clear this was important to Savannah.

"Let's go mingle," she said, plastering on a bright smile.

But as they wandered through the crowd, he could tell she was nervous. He wasn't sure he'd ever seen Savannah nervous. She was always so confident. But she kept glancing his way.

Did she think he was going to pick his nose in public? What kind of backwoods, uncouth redneck did she think he was? He rolled his eyes.

If there was one thing Cole could do, it was work a room. These might not be his type of people, but in the game of conversation he was never lacking.

They stopped at the bar. Savannah got a glass of chardonnay. Cole asked for water.

Grant Cassidy, the Traders' quarterback, was also here tonight. Surrounded by media, he was smiling and charming and always "on." Yeah, he was popular with the media and maybe Cole was just a little bit jealous about that, but if the guys with the microphones and the cameras wanted to give all their attention to pretty-boy Grant tonight, that was fine with him. The less spotlight on Cole, the better.

In fact, he'd be happy to fade into the background. All he wanted to do was play football, play it well, and be left alone to let his performance speak for itself. That's all he'd ever wanted.

Unfortunately, that wasn't Savannah's plan. She grabbed his arm and practically paraded him back and forth in front of the media.

He finally dug in his heels and turned to her. "Really?"

"Really."

It didn't take long for the fish to bite. As soon as they finished with Cassidy, the media swarmed him.

"Riley. How do you feel about being traded? Again?"

"Do you feel like a failure after being dumped by yet another team?"

"What happened with Green Bay? Was it your off-field behavior that cost you the job?"

"Haven't seen you much in the local clubs here. Purposely keeping a low profile, or are we just missing you when we scout out the night life?"

"Maybe you have a girlfriend and are staying in nights? Is she here with you tonight?"

He was going to need a mouth guard to keep from grinding his teeth. He wanted to tell them all to shove it up their asses, his usual response to invasive, moronic questions like the ones they were asking. But he kept his cool and answered them all, maintaining his calm and being as polite as humanly possible.

Despite the irritation prickling up his spine, he put on his best smile. "I feel great about being back home again. I'm jazzed to be with the Traders. They're one of the best football teams in the league and I'm honored to be playing with them."

He gave boring, team-positive answers. He told them he was happy to be with the Traders, that Green Bay was an amazing team and he expected them to have another stellar season, but he intended to look forward, not backward, and all he was doing right now was focusing on football, that's why they couldn't find him partying it up at the clubs.

Surprisingly, Savannah had been right. If he didn't rise to the bait, the media got bored. He ended up fielding questions for about fifteen minutes until they found another sucker to badger and moved off. He turned to look for Savannah, but she had blended into the crowd. He signed a few autographs, fended off a couple frisky women who'd zeroed in on him when they saw him being interviewed, and made his way back to Savannah.

"You handled that well," she said.

"I told you that you don't have to worry about me. I really can handle myself."

"When you want to."

"So tonight I wanted to."

She shook her head, but she was smiling. A genuine smile. That was a good thing. Maybe she was starting to believe in him.

"So what's for sale tonight?" he asked.

"It's a silent auction." She led him over to the items up for bid. "You write your name down, and then someone else tries to out-bid you."

"I know how it works. Let's take a look."

It reminded him of a garage sale, only more expensive. There was a lot of junk, mostly stuff he'd never want to own, like artwork and shit. Though there was other stuff here for the non–art lovers. The trips were nice. Too bad it was the beginning of the season for him. He'd have no time now to take any trips to these exotic locations. He remembered Mick had taken Tara on one of these short tropical vacations. Mick said it had been great. Private and secluded, though he hadn't offered up much in the way of details— not that Cole had expected him to.

Cole looked at Savannah, imagining her in a skimpy bikini swinging on a hammock in some hidden paradise. Yeah, he could definitely get into that.

"What are you doing?"

His gaze met hers. "Huh?"

"Stop looking at me like that."

"Like what?"

"Like . . . you know what."

His lips curved. "Can't help it. I was checking out this private tropical getaway up for auction and imagined you lying naked on a hammock."

Her cheeks went pink. She leaned against him to whisper. "Well, quit imagining that because it isn't going to happen."

"I know it isn't going to happen, but you can't control what I fantasize about, Peaches."

"You have to stop fantasizing about me. About us."

"And you need to quit leaning your sweet little breasts against me or I'm going to get hard."

She pulled back so fast he was sure she was going to topple over on those sexy high heels.

"Look at this state-of-the-art barbecue instead," she said, pointing out some stainless steel grill.

He cocked a brow. "Seriously? I like my grill just fine."

"How about this art piece?"

"It looks like two porcupines mating in Play-Doh." He hoped she didn't fall in love with it.

She gave it a critical eye. "You're right. It's hideous."

"Good. Then I don't have to worry about your taste level after all."

She laughed and moved on. It was more fun watching her examine the different pieces. She wrinkled her nose at some, spent time considering others. So far nothing seemed interesting enough for her to want to bid on anything.

Until she picked up a box. Kind of an ordinary box, actually. It looked old—some kind of antique wood, would be his guess. It was worn, with a scrolled pattern over the top. Savannah opened it up and it started playing music, some song that sounded familiar to him but he couldn't place the tune.

Savannah obviously knew the melody though, because she sucked in her bottom lip and tears sprung to her eyes. She quickly shut the box, put it down, and moved on to the next item.

Something about that song had affected her. He caught up to her and slid his hand in hers. She lifted her gaze to his and smiled.

"See something you like?" she asked.

"No. But you saw something that upset you."

Her smile died. "No, I didn't."

"What song was playing on that music box?"

"Oh. That? I don't remember."

"Peaches. Don't lie to me."

"Beethoven's *Moonlight Sonata*."

"I've heard it before. It's pretty. Kind of sad."

She blinked several times and he could tell there was something about the song that bothered her. He squeezed her hand. "Talk to me."

She shook her hand. "It's nothing. The song reminds me of my mother."

"Is it like one of her favorite songs?"

"Something like that."

"Do you want to talk to me about your mom?"

"Not at all."

She wasn't just upset. She was shaking. "Okay. Hey, let's go back and take a second look at that stainless steel grill."

The tension in her shoulders relaxed and she gave him a smile. "Sure."

But while they were looking over the grill, Savannah's gaze drifted back to the music box. He wasn't sure if what he saw in her eyes was regret or longing, but he did know he couldn't leave it alone. He was going to have to do something about it.

It took a good forty-five minutes to look over every item up for bid. Savannah ended up bidding on a pearl necklace, entering a bidding war with some older woman who claimed she wanted it for her niece.

"She's full of shit," Savannah whispered to Cole as she hovered near the bidding sheet. "She's eyeing it like it's the last piece of prize pecan pie at the county fair and she hasn't eaten in a month. She wants that necklace for herself and I know it."

Cole fought a grin, folded his arms, and nodded. "You're tougher and meaner than she is, Peaches. I know you can take her down."

"I intend to. There are fifteen minutes left in the bidding process and my name is going to be the last one on that sheet if I have to stuff her under the table and stand on her to make it happen."

"If you need backup, let me know. I'll carry her off and lock her in the closet."

She batted her lashes. "You'd do that for me?"

"In a heartbeat, honey."

Laughing, she hovered near the clipboard until old woman bidder hastily wrote her next bid. Then Savannah sauntered over, topped the bid and hurried off, no doubt hoping the woman hadn't seen her.

Unfortunately, she had and the woman hurried back, giving Savannah a glare.

"I want to flip her off so bad."

"Go ahead."

"It would be improper."

"You want me to do it?"

Savannah looked horrified. "Oh, my god, no. I found out who I'm bidding against. That's Helen Sandingham."

"So?"

"She's on the board of directors at the children's hospital. Apparently she's loaded and wields a lot of power in this city."

"Yeah, well, Helen can shove it. I'll make sure you win that necklace."

Savannah laughed. "Leave it to you to be unimpressed."

He kissed her cheek. "Hey, I don't care who she is. You want the necklace, you're going to have it."

With a minute left to go, that Sandingham lady had put in a bid. Savannah wandered over to the table, but didn't write another bid in. Instead, she hovered. So did Helen, pen in hand.

It was on.

This should be entertaining.

Savannah watched the clock and when it was down to fifteen seconds, she hurriedly wrote down a bid. Helen was about to get the last bid in when Cole stepped in.

"Mrs. Sandingham?"

She frowned, looked past Cole, her gaze riveted on the bid board. "Yes?"

"My name is Cole Riley. I heard you're on the board of the children's hospital."

Her chest puffed up. "Why yes, I am."

"I'm one of the new players with the St. Louis Traders. I just wanted you to know if there's anything I can do to help the children's hospital, you can count on me. I just got traded from Green Bay, but St. Louis is my hometown. I like to stay active in charity work, and working with kids is very important to me."

She finally put her attention on Cole. "Oh. Well. Thank you. That's very kind of you."

"I'll be sure to have my agent get in touch with you. Maybe I could arrange a visit to the kids. I could bring along some of the other team members."

Now she was beaming. "That would be wonderful. The children love it when some of the local sports stars come by. I appreciate your dedication to your home city, Mr. Riley."

He'd said it to pull her attention away from bidding on the necklace, but he realized he meant it. From the excited look in her eyes, this would be something he followed through on.

He took her hand in his. "Please. Call me Cole. And I'm happy to help out. I'll have Elizabeth Riley, my agent, get in touch with you and you can direct her to the right people at the hospital to contact."

"Thank you, Cole. It would mean so much to the children. It was such a pleasure to meet you."

"You, too, Mrs. Sandingham."

"Call me, Helen. And welcome home, Cole."

He walked away, giving her a wink. She twiddled her fingers at him.

Cole wasn't sure, but he thought Mrs. Sandingham might have forgotten all about the bidding war she'd been in with Savannah.

Savannah was at the bar sipping a glass of wine. Cole asked for a water.

"You're my hero," she said. "But I think Helen Sandingham might be a little bit in love with you."

Cole took a long swallow of ice water. "I know. We have a hot date later."

"She's out of luck because I'm claiming you for myself. Thank you for distracting her so I could win the auction."

"You're welcome. You got the necklace you wanted?"

"I did. Time ran out so it was way too late for her to write the last bid. And I'm feeling rather smug about it, too. I should feel guilty, but I don't."

"No reason for you to feel guilty. You won it fairly . . . more or less."

She laughed. "With a little interference from you."

"Hey, whatever works. No holds barred in a bidding war."

The head of the auction announced it had officially closed, and for everyone to step up and check out the list of winners. Those who had won needed to pay for their items at the back of the room.

She slipped off the bar stool. "I'll be right back. I need to go settle up and claim my necklace, while simultaneously avoiding Helen Sandingham."

"Sure. I'll go with you. I need to do a little settling up of my own."

Her brows rose. "Did you get that barbecue?"

"I'll go find out."

"Then I'll meet you back at the bar."

He nodded and waited for Savannah to disappear, then went to pay for the items he'd won. He met Savannah back at the bar about twenty minutes later. She had a gleam in her eyes and a velvet box in her hands.

"No fistfight with Mrs. Sandingham?"

"No. It turns out she had bid on a vacation in the Hamptons that she won, so she was too busy clucking about that to all her friends to worry about me and the necklace."

"Good."

"How about you? Did you get what you wanted?"

"I did."

After making a few rounds and more tedious small talk, Savannah said they could leave.

Thank. God.

Though it hadn't been as boring as Cole had thought it would be. At least the bidding war had been entertaining.

He drove Savannah back to her place.

"Would you like to come in for a drink?" she asked as he pulled into the driveway.

"Sure."

He grabbed the bag from the backseat and followed her inside. Savannah laid her purse on the table and strolled into the kitchen while he shut the front door. "I'll go pour some wine."

"Just water for me."

"Fine. I'll be back."

When she came back out, she handed him the water. He handed her the bag.

She frowned. "What's this?"

"I didn't want to upset you, but this seemed to hold your attention at the auction. I wanted you to have it."

She set her glass down on the table next to the sofa and opened the bag. She pulled out the music box. Her hand shook as she laid it over the box.

"Oh." She lifted the lid and the music played. Her bottom lip trembled.

"Shit. I knew I shouldn't have. I'll take it." He reached for it, but she closed the box and laid her hand over his, then lifted her gaze, her eyes filled with tears. "No. Don't. It was so thoughtful of you to buy this for me. I can't believe you did that."

He shrugged. "Like I said, I knew it upset you. But I wasn't sure if it was good memories or bad."

She shuddered out an exhale. "A little of both, actually."

He took the box from her hand and laid it on the coffee table, then pulled her to the sofa, reaching for her glass of wine to hand it to her. "Why don't you tell me about it?"

"I don't like to talk about my past."

"Maybe you should."

She stared at the box and took a sip of wine. "Maybe I shouldn't."

"It obviously bothers you. And you know me, I don't leave anything unsaid, including things I probably should. I'm the best person to unload on."

The corners of her mouth lifted in the hint of a smile. "No, you definitely don't leave things unsaid."

"But the media isn't here. No one's here but you and me. And you can trust me. I'm the last person who's ever going to spill your secrets."

"Why?" she asked.

"Why what?"

"Why are you being so nice to me?"

He swept a curl that had escaped behind her ear. "Because something in that box opened up memories, and those memories are hurting you. And like the music in that box, it's obviously something you're shutting away instead of dealing with. You should talk about it—exorcise the ghost and make it go away."

She cocked her head to the side and looked at him. "You're a pretty smart guy."

"And that surprises you?"

"Not at all."

"Okay, then. Start talking."

SEVENTEEN

SAVANNAH DIDN'T KNOW WHERE TO BEGIN, OR IF SHE should even talk about everything she'd bottled up inside.

It had been brewing for a while now. Maybe since that day she'd gone for dinner at Cole's family's house. It had been nice to spend time with his family, but also unsettling, seeing what he had and dislodging memories of what she'd never had. Then the conversation with Elizabeth and now the music box.

She was shocked Cole had bought the music box for her. Such a sweet gesture. Even more gallant was his willingness to sit here and listen to her problems.

What man voluntarily did that? No man she'd ever dated. Not that she and Cole were dating. They certainly weren't. Having sex, yes. Dating . . . no.

He was being kind. Something that wasn't typically attributed to him.

She was learning so many things about him.

"So? Are you going to talk?"

She shifted her focus back to him. He stared at her intently, held her hand, his thumb brushing lightly over hers. "This isn't part of my job."

"Consider yourself off duty, Miss Brooks. Now unload on me. Tell me about the music."

She took a deep breath, then let it out, realizing maybe it was time to talk about it. "I mentioned it was a song my mother liked."

"You did. You miss your mom?"

She let out a quiet laugh. "No. Yes and no. I don't know. Not really." She paused. "Sometimes. It's hard to miss what you never really had."

"Okay, that was a mouthful. Talk to me about your mom. You told me a while back it was just the two of you. Were you close?"

"No."

That one word said a lot. Cole heard the pain and bitterness in that word. And loneliness.

"Did she have to work a lot to support the two of you?"

"Support? No, she didn't work to support us. Mostly she was on welfare, food stamps, whatever she could do to get by. She'd work occasionally, but only when she absolutely had to, when the system made her. When I was old enough to stay alone, she'd go out at night and work—sometimes."

He didn't like the direction this was going. "Work where? Like as a waitress?"

She took a hard swallow of wine. "No. Not as a waitress. She'd get jobs at nightclubs as a stripper. When she got too worn down and haggard-looking from the drugs to do that, she'd just whore herself out on the streets."

His stomach dropped. "Jesus, Savannah."

She wouldn't meet his gaze, instead stared at her hands. "Yeah."

"How did you survive?"

"I stayed out of her way. She was mostly stoned all the time, so she didn't bother with me. She'd get high and play classical music. She loved classical. And she'd play Beethoven, especially that music—the one in the music box—over and over again. She'd dance around the house—sometimes she was even fun. She'd grab me and we'd dance together. When I was little, I never knew she was high. I just thought she was fun. Until I got older and realized there was something terribly wrong about her."

That's why the song triggered the memories tonight. That's why it was both a sweet and awful memory for her.

"The welfare and food stamps brought in enough food—when she remembered to go buy it. When I was old enough, I'd go get it, but I had to steal enough money from her purse to get groceries. She didn't like to part with the cash because that was her drug money."

"The state—"

"Did nothing. She made sure the state couldn't take me away. I was a meal ticket for her."

He frowned. "In what way?"

"Not the way you think. I mean I was a dependent, so the state paid her for me. She might have been a lot of things, but she never used me other than to get money from the state. She never brought guys to the apartment. She always did her . . . 'work' on the streets. She kept men away from me. Always told me to never be like her. She told me to make sure to go to school every day and stay away from boys. She wanted better for me than she had."

She paused, caught her breath. "I guess, in her own way, she tried her best."

Cole couldn't imagine what it must have been like for Savannah as a child, to grow up with a drug-addicted whore of a mother who was likely too addled to care for her daughter. He wasn't big on emotion, but Christ, his heart hurt for her.

"So what happened to her?"

"She left when I was thirteen."

"What do you mean . . . left?"

"I mean she left. Decided she didn't want to be a mother anymore. Or maybe she was so high she simply forgot she was a mother. I have no idea. When she didn't come home for a week I finally ran out of food and there was no money to buy more. I got hungry, so I had to tell the school. Social services took me in after that."

Cole was stunned. A child of that age left all alone. He couldn't fathom the loneliness and fear, what that must have been like for her, wondering when or if her mother would be back. "Did they look for her?"

"So they told me. I'm sure they didn't look hard. Where were they going to look? They knew her history. I figure she hooked up with someone and left town. Or maybe she figured I was better off without her. That's what I'd like to think, anyway. They never told me she was dead, so . . ."

He was sure she wanted to think her mother was still out there somewhere. Still alive. Better than the alternative of dying of a drug overdose in an alley somewhere.

"So you ended up in foster care."

"Yes."

She was so calm. He wanted her to rage or cry, or hit something, to let out the emotion he knew she held in. But this was her story and she had the right to tell it—and to feel it—however she wanted to.

"How were the families you lived with?"

She lifted her gaze to his and offered a smile, but it wasn't her normal, happy one. "Pretty good, actually. I got shifted in and out of a few at first, then ended up with a solid family. I had siblings— two younger sisters, which was nice, and attentive parents, which was even better. I had always loved school, and without having to worry or care for my mother, I could finally focus more on my studies. I wasn't a problem child, so my foster parents didn't have issues with me. We all got along great, I was an A student, and I ended up getting a scholarship to the University of Georgia."

Yeah, just one big fucking happy family. Only she left out the love part. He bet she wouldn't have done anything to make waves just so she wouldn't be abandoned again.

"Did you miss your mom?"

"She dumped me," she said with a shrug. "No point in missing her."

"But you did miss her."

She frowned. "Don't push this, Cole."

She tried to jerk her hand away, but he held firm, refusing to let her run this time. "Why hold it inside, Peaches? Isn't it better to get all the hurt and anger out?"

She shifted to face him. "It was a long time ago."

"Doesn't make it hurt any less. Hell, I hurt after being abandoned by a goddamned football team. But I have a strong, tight-knit family who loves me. I don't know what I'd do if I didn't have them. And look at you—you're smart, you're successful, and look at the person you've become. You did this all on your own."

She looked down, then back up at him. "I didn't do it alone. I had a very nice foster family, I was lucky to land a really great scholarship, and I had mentors to help me along the way."

"But not a family—not your mother. The person who should have been there for you, cheering for you and supporting you."

"Not everyone has the traditional nuclear family, Cole. Some of us actually survive that."

"I know." He leaned in and brushed his knuckles across her cheek. "And you can try and pretend it's okay. That you're strong and tough and you don't need anyone. That you didn't need her. But that's all bullshit. I know it, and you know it."

Savannah stared at Cole.

"You're so pushy. I told you my story. Why can't you leave it alone?"

"Have you ever dealt with it?"

She'd spent so many years holding it all inside.

"I'm here right now, aren't I? I obviously dealt with my past."

"I'm not talking about surviving it. Yeah, you survived it. But you haven't let go of it." He rubbed her arm. "What she did to you mattered. It wasn't fair."

He was wrong. She was fine. It didn't matter. She had always shown everyone how strong she was.

"Show me how you feel, Peaches."

Damn him. In a matter of a few weeks, he'd seen right through her. One music box, and he'd known.

Her bottom lip trembled. She got up, walked to the window to look outside, staring at the darkness, not really seeing anything but the years falling away, stripping away the cool, confident woman she was now, revealing the scared little girl she once was. She'd vowed to never go back to that place, to never revisit those feelings again, yet here she stood.

Cole wrapped his arms around her. She stiffened.

"It's okay to be vulnerable, Savannah, to let someone see you scared."

"I'm not scared. Not anymore."

He tightened his hold on her. "She hurt you, abandoned you. What kind of mother does that?"

"She was sick."

"Stop making excuses for her." He turned her around to face him. "Did you ever get mad at her? Did you ever lash out, even in a room by yourself, and voice how you feel?"

She looked past him, to all those nights she'd waited in the foster home. "Every time the phone or doorbell rang, I was sure it was her. That the reason she'd left was so she could get clean, and then she was going to come back for me.

"But every time the phone or doorbell rang, it wasn't her. She didn't get clean. She didn't come back. She wasn't thinking about me, only about herself. Like always, it was about her and what she needed, never about what I needed."

He swept his hand down her arm, his touch light. He wasn't pulling her in, wasn't trying to hug her, just giving her comfort. "What did *you* need?"

Anger and hurt finally won. She slumped against him. "I needed my mother. I needed her to take care of me." Tears spilled from her eyes and she didn't try to hold them back. The floodgates had burst and pain wrenched from every part of her. "Why did she do that to me? Why didn't she take care of me?"

Her legs wobbled and she started to sink to the floor. Cole was there to catch her, to wrap his strong arms around her. He dropped down and pulled her onto his lap.

She leaned her head against him and sobbed, so hard that for a while she felt like she couldn't breathe. And through it all, Cole held her, stroking her hair and her back while she cried out the misery, loneliness, and abandonment she'd felt as a child and all through her adulthood.

For the first time in all these years, she let the memories come through, remembered the good times she'd had with her mother, and all the bad times, wrenching fresh tears and agony so painful she wasn't sure she'd survive it.

And still, Cole held her, murmuring words of comfort, a solid presence while she let go of it all.

When she had nothing left to cry, she leaned her head against his shoulder, so spent she couldn't even talk. Cole picked her up and carried her into the bedroom. He sat her on the bed and went into the bathroom, came back with a warm washcloth to wipe her face. He took down her hair, slipped off her shoes, and unzipped her dress, making her stand so he could slip it off her, then he moved her onto the bed and put her under the covers.

Exhaustion took over and she crawled in. He undressed and climbed in the bed with her, shut off the light and pulled her tight against him.

There was so much more she wanted to say to him, but she didn't have it in her to have that conversation.

Not now. She needed to regroup.

She closed her eyes and snuggled against his warmth.

COLE LAY IN BED FOR A LONG TIME, LISTENING TO THE sounds of Savannah's breathing.

She'd fallen asleep right away, but it wasn't an easy sleep.

He figured he'd hold her until she drifted off, then he'd get up and watch some TV. It was still early, after all.

But the way she held on to him—clutching him like she was lost at sea and he was her goddamn lifeline—made him rethink his strategy.

She'd gone it alone. Her entire life, she'd had no one. The success and position she held now had been her own doing. She'd had no parents along the way to help her, to cook her meals and make sure she did her homework, no one to kick her ass when she needed it, no one to kiss her boo-boos when she failed and tell her everything was going to be all right.

How tough did someone have to be to survive a childhood like that?

Pretty fucking tough.

Yet she was so sweet. She wasn't a hard-ass, wasn't jaded after all that had been done to her. In bed, she was giving and generous. And she smiled a lot. She seemed to enjoy life.

Whereas he'd been nothing but a giant pain in the ass, taking for granted everything that had been given to him. He'd had it so easy, while his parents had struggled to give him a good life so all he had to do was go out and live his dream.

He and Savannah were as different as night and day. How could she tolerate being around him? He was nothing but a spoiled football player who craved the spotlight. He didn't deserve to be sharing a bed with her. She needed someone who cared for her, who thought of nothing but her, who'd give up everything just to give her the kind of life she deserved.

He sucked in a breath and realized it was time he made some serious life changes. It was time to go all in and stop hesitating about the things he really wanted in his career. In his life.

It was time to start taking some chances.

EIGHTEEN

SAVANNAH WOKE ALONE IN HER BED, FEELING A LITTLE disoriented and with a wicked headache, but fully aware of what had happened last night.

She sat up, drew her knees to her chest, and laid her head in her hands.

She'd been making a lot of boneheaded moves since she'd met Cole.

Having sex with him, of course, topped the list. But falling apart in front of him last night came in a close second.

What had she been thinking, unloading all her personal history like that?

He'd made it too easy, asking all those leading questions, and giving her the music box that had started the rush of memories. Not that it should have made a difference. She'd always been good at keeping her past right where it belonged—in the past. She was supposed to be helping him exorcise all his demons, not the other way around.

Instead, she'd wilted like some frail Southern flower that crumpled at the first sign of frost.

She gave herself credit for having more backbone and fortitude than that.

"Ugh. You're becoming a marshmallow, Savannah."

"Hey, I like marshmallows."

Savannah's head shot up as Cole walked in carrying two cups of coffee. Despite her irritation with her behavior last night, she couldn't fault the company this morning. His hair was sleep rumpled, his jaw darkened with a day's growth of stubble, his chest bare, and he looked utterly delicious wearing nothing but the tuxedo pants from last night, unbottoned and slung low on his hips.

"I didn't know you were still here."

"Obviously." He handed her a cup and took a seat on the edge of the bed, sipping his coffee. "So what about you and marshmallows?"

Her coffee had been made perfectly, with a teaspoon of sugar and a dollop of cream. He'd been paying attention.

"Thank you. And nothing about marshmallows."

He set his cup on the nightstand. "I'm a big fan of marshmallows, you know."

"Is that right?"

"Yeah." He took her cup and put it down, then leaned in and pressed his lips to her neck, sliding his tongue along the side of her throat.

She shuddered out a sigh.

"Marshmallows taste sweet." He nipped at her ear, then pushed her back against the pillows and drew her camisole strap down her arms, baring her breasts. He took a nipple between his lips, flicking his tongue over the quickly hardening bud. When he sucked, sensation shot right to her pussy, making her writhe in anticipation.

He popped the nipple out of his mouth and grinned up at her. "Sweet and sugary, just the way I like my marshmallows."

When he moved down her body, lifting her camisole to lick his way across her stomach, she sighed and relaxed against the pillows, knowing where this was going.

This was exactly what she needed. The tension she felt when she woke dissolved, but when his teeth grazed her hip bone and he drew her panties down, a new tautness took its place, a delicious, anticipation of what was to come.

And when he swiped his fingers across her pussy lips, she shuddered.

"Yeah, you're a juicy little marshmallow, all right," he said, then put his mouth on her sex.

"Cole." His name fell from her lips in a moan. Her legs fell open and she gave him whatever he wanted, because when the warm wetness of his tongue was in command, she was his slave.

He slipped his hands under her and took his time pleasuring her, pressing his tongue against her clit, covering her with his lips, only to take her right to the brink and then back away to press kisses to her thigh. She hovered on the edge several times and he knew it, brought her there, and right when she thought she would come, he'd take the prize away, building her anticipation to a screaming level.

She dug her heels into the mattress, lifted her butt and all but shoved her pussy in his face, demanding he give her what she needed. He gently pressed her hips down, held her there, and put his mouth on her clit, giving her the orgasm she so desperately craved.

It was an epic climax, a tidal wave of heat and sensation that tore a scream from her throat. She was still riding the wave of it when he put on a condom and slid inside her, taking her mouth in a hot kiss that made her pussy clench around his cock.

He groaned against her lips and thrust deep. She wrapped her legs around him, the spirals of orgasm still with her as he rocked against her.

He lifted, braced his hands on either side of her to look down at her, his face drawn with intensity as he moved inside her. She reached up for him and he dropped down, then rolled to his side, drawing her leg over his hip.

"I want you close to me, like this," he said as he pushed deep, rolling his hips to rub against her clit. He swept her hair behind her ear and kissed her neck while he continued to move inside her.

She sighed at the magic of his mouth, the delicious things he did to her as he made love to her. Everything about him turned her upside down. Being with Cole brought out emotions she'd tried so hard to bury, feelings she'd never wanted to experience.

He kissed her jaw, brushed his lips against hers, then met her gaze again as he gently thrust in and out, taking her ever closer to another orgasm, this time doing it slow and deliberate, brushing his body over her clit, tasting every inch of available skin he could, and running his hands over her as if this were the first time he'd ever touched her. He was so tender in the way he moved over her, pushing her back against the mattress so he could thrust deeper inside her. It brought tears to her eyes and she had no idea why. The way he looked at her tightened her chest and made her want to hold on to him and never let go.

The feelings inside her wanted to erupt, made her want to say things to him she shouldn't say. It was emotion welling, coupled with the intense feelings of their lovemaking. She held the words back, but not the sensations as he drew the orgasm out and she burst, holding tight to him as she catapulted over the edge, this time with him. He groaned and gathered her close, powering hard into her with repeated thrusts, which only heightened her pleasure.

Spent, perspiring, she held on to him and fought back the ridiculous tears that sprang to her eyes. She had no idea what was wrong with her.

Residual emotion from last night, no doubt. What else could it be?

Cole stroked her hair, kissed her neck, and lifted his head.

"I'm starving. How about you?"

She managed a bright smile. "Totally."

He climbed off the bed, pulling her with him. "How about a quick shower, then I'll take you to breakfast."

Part of her wanted to beg off so she could be alone with her thoughts and emotions, but she knew he wouldn't let her hide anymore. "That sounds like a great idea."

COLE KNEW THERE WAS SOMETHING ON SAVANNAH'S mind. She'd been quiet during their morning lovemaking, and at breakfast.

Maybe she was still thinking about last night. Breaking through her stone walls had been monumental, and not something she'd wanted to do. So she likely had some regret. He of all people understood that. Telling people about yourself—especially the unpleasant parts—wasn't a fun thing. Personally, he hated it, yet he'd forced her to do it. What did that say about him that he'd done it to someone he claimed to care about?

But maybe it had helped her?

He dragged his fingers through his wet hair, then grabbed a brush, throwing off thoughts of Savannah. She was a grown woman capable of making decisions for herself. She was confident and capable and smart, and he was the last person who should be able to influence her. If she hadn't wanted to talk about her crapload of unpleasant memories from the past, she wouldn't have opened up to him about it.

He finished dressing and left the locker room. Surprisingly, Savannah was waiting outside for him. He fully expected to have to chase her down, that she'd run and hide from him after all they'd been through.

Yet there she was, fresh and beautiful in her summer dress

and high heels with her hair pulled into a ponytail. She'd become such an integral part of his life he couldn't imagine not seeing her every day.

He smiled and walked over to her and they headed down the hall to the exit.

"You had a good practice today."

"Thanks. It's coming together."

"I think you're a good fit for this team. It also helps that you're working with the players and the coaches and not against them."

"That probably does help."

She stopped and turned to him. "So you're admitting I might know what I'm talking about."

"You have certain skills that might be useful."

She rolled her eyes and continued walking. "I have some other suggestions."

He held the door for her. The blast of heat nearly took his breath away. "Can it wait until we get someplace air-conditioned? I'm dying. And hungry."

"Wimp. We'll go to my place. I'll fix you something to eat."

"Sounds good."

He followed her to her house. Once inside, she threw her purse down. "Let me go change. Help yourself to something to drink."

He went into the kitchen and grabbed a glass of ice water. Thirsty after today's practice, he finished it in about four swallows and refilled his glass. Savannah came in wearing a pair of capris and a sleeveless top, then leaned against the center island.

"What are you hungry for?" she asked.

He leaned across the other side and brushed his lips across hers. "You."

She kissed him back, her lips warm and eager. But then his stomach grumbled and she pulled back, laughing.

"As much as I like that suggestion, let's feed you first."

She made grilled turkey sandwiches with salad. He ate two sandwiches, drank two more glasses of water, and ate three cookies for dessert.

"Are you sure you've had enough?" she asked, arching a brow.

"Hey, I worked hard today."

"I pity the poor woman who marries you and has to feed you."

His stomach twisted at that comment, but he left it alone. "My mom said the same thing when I was a teenager."

"I'm sure she did."

They cleaned up the dishes and went into the living room. He stretched out on the sofa and slung his arm over the back. Savannah curled up next to him. He liked that she was comfortable enough, even when they were about to discuss business, to sit by him.

"So what did you want to talk about?"

She shifted to face him. "We've talked about your contributions to charity in the past."

"Yeah."

"A lot of players start their own charities. I think this would be a good idea for you, not only from an image standpoint, but more important, from a humanitarian one."

"I've never done it before because I wasn't in a place that felt like home to me. Now that I am home, this is a good place to begin one."

She half turned to face him, a look of surprise on her face. "What? No arguing?"

"I know. Surprise, huh?"

She grinned. "Totally shocked, actually."

"Smart-ass."

"But seriously, I'm glad you agree with me. Is there anything that comes to mind?"

It was something he'd already been thinking about, so he already had a half-formed idea in his head. "When I was a kid, I lived at the local parks. My friends and I would hang out on the equipment, or play basketball or football. A lot of the playgrounds around here need refurbishing. Cities don't have the money in their budgets to spend on parks and recreation anymore, and kids don't have places to go. When they don't have a place to hang out and have fun, they get in trouble."

"That's very true. So what's your idea?"

"I want to refurbish some existing playgrounds and build some community centers where kids have a safe place to hang out and play sports."

"You're talking a lot of money."

He shrugged. "I have a lot of money. I've been in the league for a while now. I'm single and I've been investing. I've got money to put into this."

She laid her hand on his arm and gave him a smile that warmed him from the inside out. "I love this idea. This is a such a worthwhile investment, Cole."

"For my image, you mean."

"No. For you. For the kids of the communities you're going to help."

"Good. Let's get it started. I want to be as hands-on with it as I can. I know with the season about to start I'll be busy a lot, but I don't want to staff all of it out."

"You don't have to. A lot of it will be hands-on building and rebuilding. You can be involved in that, and get your family and friends to participate. The more volunteers we have on these projects, the better."

"I know my family would love to get involved. Some of the guys on the team will, too."

"I'll get in touch with an attorney who'll help start the foundation paperwork so you can get the money funneled into it. In the meantime, we can go search for parks and locations."

He stood. "Let's go."

"Where?"

"To look at locations."

"Now?"

"Yeah."

She laughed. "You're excited about this."

"Shouldn't I be?"

She stood and slipped her hand in his. "Yes, you should be. You should be very excited about it. But the Cole Riley I met the first day wouldn't have been."

He pulled his keys out of his pocket. "That guy doesn't exist anymore."

SAVANNAH STOOD IN A FORMER PLAYGROUND IN South City overgrown with weeds and debris. Equipment—at least the equipment that still stood—was broken and long ago rusted.

Kids ran up and down the neighborhood, and some ran through the playground, but none stopped to play. Then again, why should they? There was nothing to play on. No swing sets, no basketball nets, and the grass had long ago stopped growing.

It made her sad, but also hopeful, because she saw the potential. Put in new sod, resurface the asphalt, put up some nets and new equipment and the myriad kids she saw running around here would have a place to come play.

"We used to live a couple blocks from here," Cole said as he spun the rickety old merry-go-round, which let out a pathetic, rust-induced squeak.

"Some of the equipment that's still standing is dangerous."

He grinned. "Yeah. We'd spin around on this thing with our heads hanging off, going faster and faster until we got sick. Or we'd stand up and spin, then go flying off."

She shook her head. "They make safer equipment these days."

"So I've heard." He looked at her. "What fun is that?"

"I'm sure kids find enough danger without playground equipment doing that for them."

"If you say so. It's more fun to live life on the edge."

"You're such a boy. I hope if I ever get married and have kids, I have all girls."

He laughed. "There were plenty of girls taking that merry-go-round ride with us. Girls can be daredevils, too."

She lifted her chin. "Mine won't be."

"Famous last words, Peaches. You'll probably have six boys. All holy terrors."

Her eyes widened. "That is not funny."

"I have no doubt you could handle them. You handled me."

Savannah's heart twisted at the thought of six boys, and then her mind filled with visions of dark hair and stormy gray eyes—all little versions of Cole, with the two of them running roughshod over a herd of sons.

No. She had to get *that* thought out of her head. He wasn't the marrying type and she'd already sworn she was never getting married and absolutely never having children. Double heartache wrapped in a messy, ugly black bow.

No, thank you.

So why was she suddenly thinking of kids and playgrounds and houses and families and Cole?

She met his gaze and he was giving her a look. "What?"

"You have this sappy, contented smile on your face."

"I do not."

"Thinking about those six little boys you're going to have, no doubt."

She narrowed her gaze at him. "Stop it. I'm not having kids."

"Really. And why is that?"

"I don't want to talk about this." She started toward the car.

He opened the door for her and she slid in. As they drove, she was aware of the silence but didn't know what to say to change that.

The second playground was much the same as the first—in dire need of repair. At least she had something to talk about now as she envisioned bright playground equipment and a swarm of kids enjoying the renewal of the park.

"This is such a great idea, Cole."

He nodded. "I'm eager to get started. How long do you think it'll take to do the paperwork?"

"Not long. Setting up the foundation is merely a formality. I'll be sure to have Don make it a priority."

"Thanks."

They looked at a few other locations where there were no parks, but it was obvious they were needed.

"So, are you afraid of kids?"

She jerked her head in his direction. "What? No, I'm not afraid of kids. What gave you that idea?"

"The horrified look on your face when I teased you about having six boys?"

She disguised her discomfort at his bringing the topic up again with a laugh. "Oh, that. I think it was more the idea of having six sons. I love children."

"Good to know." He turned and headed back to the car.

"Why?" she asked after they'd gotten in.

"Why what?"

"You said it was good to know that I liked children."

"Oh. I want you to work on this foundation with me. If you hate kids, it wouldn't be much fun for you."

"I'd love to work on this with you. I want to see these parks completed and filled with children playing."

"Great."

There was something he wasn't saying. She wished she knew what it was. But she really wanted that topic closed, so she wasn't going to ask.

"Since there's a home game Sunday, we're going to my aunt and uncle's bar after the game," he said. "There's a party there to watch Mick's game that night."

"That sounds fun. Are you saying I'm invited?"

"Yes. Will you come?"

He was acting so strange. She shifted to face him. "I'd love to be there. Thank you for inviting me."

"You're welcome. I'll pick you up after the game."

"Cole, I'll be at your game on Sunday. I can just follow you."

"No. I'll pick you up at your house after the game."

"O-o-ka-ay. Whatever works best for you."

"That works best for me."

Now he was acting really odd. Eager and excited and also . . . shifting kind of uncomfortably, giving her these expectant looks. She didn't know what to make of it.

"Is something wrong?"

He gave her a quick glance, then returned his focus to the road. "No. Why?"

"Nothing. Nothing at all."

She was reading too much into it. Her own discomfort, likely.

It was the whole kids thing. And her feelings about Cole, which were growing more intense every day. She didn't know what to do about them—about him, or how she felt for him.

She'd always prided herself on being able to handle any situation, but this was new territory for her. She'd never planned to get involved with Cole at all, let alone fall in love with him. Not that she had an inkling of what love was all about.

Or what she was going to do about it now that she realized she was in love with him.

The mere thought of it scared her to death.

NINETEEN

IT WAS THE FIRST GAME OF THE SEASON. COLE WAS NO rookie, so this should be business as usual, but his stomach was tied up in knots as he and the rest of the team took the field.

New team jitters, probably. And the chance to do this all over like it was the first time for him.

Maybe it was a first time. Clean slate and all that shit. New image, fresh start, and a chance to show everyone he'd changed. He intended to focus on football, and keep the dramatics off the field this season.

The stadium was packed. It was a sellout and the fans roared when the Traders came out. Cole didn't even try to block the sounds of the fans. He soaked it all in, drawing the energy of the crowd as he did his warm-ups, then took his spot on the sidelines with his teammates.

Kenny Lawton looked wide-eyed and a little sick. Cole grinned, remembering his own rookie year. He'd been so damn scared during that first game. He knew exactly how the kid felt, so he walked over to him to give him a pep talk.

"You're going to see some action today, Lawton."

"You think so? I know I did in preseason, but this is an actual game. They're not gonna play me."

"Coach Tallarino is known for getting his rookies in the game right out of the gate. You'll take at least a pass or two. Best way to get over those jitters."

"I'm not jittery."

Yeah, not much. The kid was dancing around from foot to foot, and it was August and they were in a domed stadium, so he wasn't moving around to keep warm. Kenny looked like he might pee his pants any second. Cole slapped him on the back of the helmet. "You're going to kick some serious ass, Lawton."

"Thanks. I just hope I don't drop the ball."

"There's a secret to that."

The kid looked up at him with serious brown eyes. "What's the secret?"

"Don't drop the ball." Cole winked and Kenny laughed, then blew out a breath and dropped his shoulders.

"Okay, man, I'll try to relax."

"You do that." He put his arm around Kenny's shoulder. "Take this all in. It's your rookie year, your first game. This is only going to happen once. Enjoy it."

They watched the kickoff. Miami returned it twelve yards, and it was game on. Defense was solid, so Miami punted after their first possession, and it was time for the Traders to take the field. First two plays had the running backs in, and they gained a first down. Davis and Fields went in on the first pass play on second down and short yardage. Fields caught the ball on a slant and picked up an additional four yards, gaining them another first down. After a couple runs and a successful shovel pass that netted fourteen yards, they were at midfield and Cole was in.

He took his position to the left, mindful of the Miami defenders. When the ball was hiked, he ran a post pattern, pushing past the

cornerback. He turned and the ball hit him right in the numbers—
he loved Grant Cassidy's throwing accuracy. But he went down
when the safety slammed into him, so he only gained ten yards. If
he'd managed to break free, there would have been nothing but the
goal line ahead of him.

But at least they'd gotten another first down.

He was pulled out for another couple running plays. The team
was in the zone, moving the ball consistently and incurring no
penalties. Cassidy threw a bullet to Jay Martin, their tight end, who
pulled it in twelve yards out and dashed into the end zone, scoring
their first touchdown of the game. The entire sideline broke into
wild cheers. And the crowd went crazy. Cole just soaked up the
adrenaline rush.

By the end of the first half they were up ten to nothing. Cole
had been given several plays, and was two for three. Coach gave
them the requisite pep talk in the locker room, but the team was
doing a good job. Defense was kicking ass; they just needed to put
more points up on the board.

Fortunately, they received the kickoff to start the second half.
They got the ball on the thirty-yard line after a great return by
special teams. Cole went out for the first play, but only as a decoy.
He blocked for the running back, who took it twelve yards for a
first down. He stayed in for the next play and took a pass sixteen
yards for another first down. The offensive line was opening up
holes like crazy. When he ran a post, he blew through an opening
and saw nothing but the end zone ahead of him, two defenders hard
on his heels. He dug in and ran for all he had and hit the end zone
for a touchdown.

His teammates caught up and mobbed him. He couldn't remember ever being this happy, or more a part of a team.

Coach pulled him out for the next offensive series, and Davis
and Fields took some passes for yardage. By the fourth quarter they

were up by twenty-four points and the offensive coordinator signaled for Kenny Lawton to go in on the next offensive series.

"You're going to do great," Cole told him. "We've got this game
in the bag, so no pressure. Just read the signals of the defense. And
don't forget to catch the damn ball."

Lawton nodded and ran out when the offense took the field. He
lined up, ran his route at the snap, and dropped the pass.

Damn.

Lawton was left in for another shot at it, and this time he caught
the ball on a play-action pass for an eight-yard gain.

Hell yeah. Kenny grinned so wide you'd have thought he'd just
caught a touchdown pass in the Super Bowl.

Cole remembered what it was like to catch your first pass in a
regular season game. It was monumental and something you never
forgot. When Kenny came back to the sidelines, he, Davis, and
Fields all slapped him on the back.

"Good job, kid," Cole said.

"Thanks. I mucked up the first one, though."

He looked pained about it, too.

"Don't worry about it," Jamarcus said. "It sure as hell won't be
the last pass you drop. We all do it."

"More than we want to," Lon admitted.

Cole liked these guys. He liked playing for this team. And when
the whistle sounded to end the game and they'd won, the team
gathered around to celebrate, hooting and hollering and slapping
one another, celebrating with the fans as their way of thanking
them for their support. Cole was dragged around the stadium and
shoved around in the locker room.

For the first time since he'd started playing professional football, he actually felt like he was part of a team.

Things were changing. He'd done a lot of the changing, and he
had Savannah to thank for that.

When the media came in to interview him, he answered their questions—even the tough ones—honestly.

"I have a lot to prove this season. I'm with a great team, and I'm lucky to be here. I've been given another chance, and I'm going to work my butt off to prove to the team and to the fans that I deserve to be here."

He left it at that, and the media seemed satisfied. Maybe because it was the truth, and he'd finally left his attitude behind.

Now it was time to look forward.

SAVANNAH COULDN'T BE MORE PLEASED FOR COLE. IT had been such a great game. His performance on the field had been nearly perfect. And off the field? She couldn't have asked for more. She'd listened to his after-game interview, and he'd done everything right, had answered the media's questions honestly, and had even added touches of humor. He'd had a complete turnaround, and she wouldn't be surprised if he continued playing well. The media hounded him for interviews now, but more for the positive than the negative.

She hoped his family celebrated his success today.

She went home and waited for him to pick her up, knowing he had those interviews and a team meeting. It took him an hour and a half, and she nearly ran to the door when he rang the doorbell. She opened it and threw her arms around him.

"Congratulations," she said when he scooped her into his arms. "I'm so proud of you."

He brushed his lips across hers, then grinned. "Thanks. But it's only the first game. I don't want to get my hopes up."

"I think you should definitely get your hopes up. It's going to be a great season and you *should* be positive and hopeful about it."

He kissed her again, this time wrapping his arms around her and giving her a deep kiss that curled her toes and made her hotter than the weather outside. When he pulled back, she licked her lips and tried to calm her rapid pulse.

"You're good for me. And my ego."

She laughed and laid her hand on his chest. "I don't think your ego has ever needed any boosting."

His lips curled. "You ready to go?"

"Yes. Is there anything I should bring?"

"No. There will be a ton of food and drink at the bar. And family, too. It should be pretty crazy, especially since Mick's game is tonight."

"I can't wait."

Riley's Sports Bar was an amazing place and, as Cole had warned, absolutely packed with people, a mix of both customers and Cole's family. His parents were there, along with his sister, Alicia, as well as his aunt Kathleen and uncle Jimmy, who owned the bar. His cousin Jenna was bartending, Jenna's fiancé Tyler was helping her. Tara was there, too, surrounded by the family in protective mode. They grabbed seats at a huge table reserved for the family.

Savannah met Tara's son, Nathan, a very handsome teenager who smiled at her, shook her hand, stayed long enough to be polite and exchange a few sentences, then ran off with his cousins to play games in the back room.

Cole got her a seat, then went off to get them drinks. She figured she likely wouldn't see him for a while since he was being congratulated by his family and several of the patrons.

"Come sit by us," Alicia said.

"Thank you." She changed tables, since Cole had found them a cozy table for two. They had plenty of time to be alone later. She'd much rather sit with his family.

"It's a madhouse, isn't it?"

She grinned at Tara. "It's amazing. You must love it."

Tara laid a hand on her belly, which had expanded some since she'd met her the night of Elizabeth's wedding. "I do love it. I unashamedly adore this family. My own left a lot to be desired, so I was always sad not to be able to give Nathan a big extended family."

Tara looked around. "Now we have all this. Nathan loves the Rileys. They've accepted him as their own and have since the beginning."

Savannah could imagine they would. The Rileys seemed to have an unending capacity for love and acceptance.

"And with the new baby coming, I feel like the luckiest woman alive. He or she will never lack for love."

Savannah saw Cole sandwiched between his father and uncle, talking with Ty at the bar. Their gazes were glued to the action on the TV. "I can see why."

"Do you have a big family, Savannah?" Alicia asked.

Savannah pulled her attention away from Cole and back to the women. "No. It was just me and my mom."

"So this might be overwhelming to you."

"Not really. I find it all just a little bit wonderful."

Tara laughed. "So did I when I first met them. I have to admit it wasn't just Mick I fell in love with, it was his entire family. And when Mick and I decided to get married, we figured it would be best to relocate here—for Nathan's sake and for mine."

"Mick plays for San Francisco, right?"

"Yes. And that's where my business was. But he knew how much his family meant to me, and to Nathan. And his season is only a few months out of the year. With only half of his games being at home, it made sense to make our home here, where the family was. Now that I'm pregnant, I'm so glad we're in St. Louis. Otherwise I'm pretty sure his mother would have packed up and moved in with us."

Savannah laughed. "I take it she's excited."

"Beyond thrilled. Which in turn thrills me." Tara's eyes filled with tears and she blinked. "Sorry. Damn hormones."

Alicia put her arm around Tara. "I think it's normal to be like this when you're pregnant, honey."

"Oh, god, you're not getting weepy again, are you?" Liz pulled up a seat at their table and kissed Tara on the cheek. "I swear to god, woman, you're like a walking faucet."

"I know. I can't help it. Everything makes me happy lately, and when I'm happy, I cry." Tara looked across the table at Savannah, then shrugged. "I'm sorry."

"I don't think you should ever apologize for being happy. Or for being pregnant and hormonal."

"Thank you."

"Don't encourage her. She'll cry more." Liz shifted her gaze to Tara and winked.

Tara stuck her tongue out at Liz. "It's going to be like this for at least four and a half more months. Suck it up and deal."

"If I must. The things an aunt-to-be must tolerate."

Savannah's stomach tightened. She'd pay all the money she had to be a part of a large family like this, to be able to celebrate triumphs, get together and talk babies and husbands and just about anything.

To have sisters, even by marriage.

To have a family. Her foster families had all been temporary. Nice at the time, but not permanent. When she'd left, there had been no ties, no one to come back to. Just like always, she'd been alone.

She took a deep breath and shrugged it off. This wasn't her family and wasn't going to be. She smiled when Jenna came over and fell into a chair.

"Oh. My. God. This place is a nightmare tonight."

"Why are you even working?" Liz asked. "Shouldn't you be turning the reins over to your new manager and getting your sweet ass over to the new place?"

She shrugged. "It's Mick's first game and I wanted to be here. The new place is coming along fine, and Dave needed help so I just stepped in to assist behind the bar, then I got sucked into chatting with the regulars. Old habits die hard, ya know."

"What new place?" Savannah asked.

Jenna turned to her. "Hi, Savannah. I'm so used to just launching myself into the middle of a family conversation I forget you might not be used to it."

"It's no problem," Savannah said with a laugh.

"Good. You kind of have to get used to that with this family. Anyway, I'm so glad you could make it tonight. Cole told me he'd be bringing you."

"He did?"

"He did," Jenna said with a waggle of her brows. "In answer to your question, I'm opening a new club. A music club. Well, kind of a music club. More of an open-mike kind of place, where people can come in and show their stuff."

Savannah caught the excitement in Jenna's eyes, the way she wriggled in her chair when she talked about the club. "How thrilling for you. It sounds like a unique place, and a lot of fun. I can't wait to check it out when it opens."

Jenna grinned. "Thank you. I'm pretty stoked about it. Of course at the same time I'm also planning my wedding. Nothing like a little massive juggling."

"Hey, that's why you have family. So we can help you," Tara said.

"Please. You're busy being pregnant."

Tara rolled her eyes. "And that makes me, what? Incapacitated? Brain-dead? Incapable of doing what I do best? For your information, I can be pregnant and plan your wedding at the same time. The baby is due in January and your wedding isn't until late next year. By the time this little one arrives, I'll be up on my feet again and ready to take care of the final details."

Liz looked over at Savannah. "She thinks she's some kind of superhero. We all think she's insane."

"I don't know," Savannah said. "She looks pretty capable to me. I'll bet she can handle it."

Tara nodded. "See? Savannah believes in me."

"Oh, I believe in you, honey," Jenna said, patting Tara's hand. "I just don't want you to overdo it. Isn't it enough to have a new baby to take care of?"

"Mom and Liz and you will help. I'll have plenty of people to help with the baby, and God knows Mick will be all over that baby when he or she arrives. So, see? I'll have plenty of time to deal with the wedding."

By the time Cole came back to drag her out of the chair, she was immersed in wedding and baby talk and reluctant to leave.

"Hey," Jenna said. "Where are you going with Savannah?"

"It's halftime, Miss None-of-your-business. I'm taking her outside for a walk."

"Sure you are," Liz said. "Will we see her again tonight?"

Cole laughed. "Yes. I promise to bring her back."

He directed her toward the back of the room, his lips near her ear. "The women will suck you into their vortex of female talk and soon I'll lose you forever. Next thing you know, Jenna will hook you into to helping her with the music club."

"I am very good at PR and image building, you know. I could offer her some assistance."

"Don't tell her that. She'll sink her claws into you and never let you go."

She laughed as he led her out the back door and into the garden. There were tables set up, places for people to eat and drink overlooking a lovely garden with trees and flowers. Of course no one was out here tonight since there was a game going on. Inside it was raucous. Out here, it was peaceful and quiet. Such a night-and-day difference.

"This is nice."

"It's still hot outside, which is why no one is out here. Well, that and the game, of course."

"Of course. And I see Mick's team is doing well."

"They are. Up by fourteen points at the half."

She turned to face him. "And did you lead me out here to give me a score update?"

He laughed. "No. I wanted you all to myself for a minute or two."

"Really? And why is that?"

He gave a quick glance at the door, then pushed her up against the wall. "For this."

His lips met hers and she wound her fingers into his hair. They hadn't touched tonight and she missed the contact. Now, as his tongue touched hers, her body ignited in passion. Maybe it was because his family was only a few feet away—crowds of people who could walk outside any moment. The thrill of the forbidden, per-haps, or maybe it was because she craved his mouth on hers and his hands on her body, but she swept her hands over his shoulders and down his arms, wishing they were at her place or his so she could have him right now.

When he pulled away, the half-lidded look of his eyes and the hard breaths he expelled told her he felt the same way.

"Damn, I wish we were alone right now," he said as he gripped her hips and pulled her against him. His erection made her clit throb.

"Me, too." She lifted her gaze to his. "I want you, Cole."

He looked around, then took her hand and led her around the side of the building, casting them in darkness.

"How about here?" He wound his arm around her and squeezed her butt, drawing her against the hot, hard part of him that made her bite down on her lower lip.

She knew what he was suggesting, and a couple months ago she'd have never gone for it. Outside, no. A bar filled with people just a short distance away? Not a chance. Anyone could walk outside for some air or a cigarette or to make a phone call.

But her body pulsed for him, and she trusted him to take care of her.

She raised up and pressed her lips to his throat. "Yes. Here."

Cole didn't think Savannah would actually go for it. But as soon as she said yes, he popped the button on her jeans and slid his hands inside, dipping his fingers into her moist heat. He kept his focus on her face, watching her eyes widen, her lips part as he found her center and rubbed it with the heel of his hand as he coaxed his fingers into her pussy.

She reached for his wrist—he thought she was going to be too reserved to do this out here. He should have known better. She held him steady and rocked her pelvis toward his fingers, panting as he thrust deeper.

She laid her head on his chest while he pumped inside her.

"Cole. Oh, god, that's going to make me come."

His dick felt as hard as the bricks behind them, and if he didn't get inside her soon he was going to come, too—right in his goddamn pants. His balls quivered every time she let out one of her sexy little moans and gasps.

She was whispering to him, clutching his shirt like a lifeline and riding his fingers hard, spilling hot juices over him as she tightened and shuddered. She tilted her head back and he kissed her when she cried out with her climax, absorbing her cries, sliding his tongue in her mouth while she jerked and trembled with the force of her orgasm.

Damn, that was good. He withdrew his fingers and let her watch as he licked them.

"I like the way you taste, Peaches. I wish I could pull your jeans down and lick your pussy and make you come again."

She shivered against him. "I'd like you to do that to me out here."

He liked her wicked little thoughts and wished he could follow through with them. But they had a limited amount of time and he needed to be inside her. So he jerked her pants down, unzipped his own and grabbed a condom out of his pocket. He put it on and pushed her up against the building, spread her legs as far he could and thrust into her slick heat.

"Oh," she said, digging her nails into his arms as her pussy clenched around his shaft. He slid his hand under her shirt, pulling her bra aside to flick her nipple with his fingers.

"Cole. Yes. Oh, yes."

Their coupling was fast and furious. He swept his hand around her butt, shielding her skin from the brick while he tunneled hard into her, his balls filling fast with come. He ground against her, releasing his hold on her breast so he could grab her hair and pull her head back for a punishing kiss. She gave exactly what she got, whimpering against him and making him crazy. He felt her tighten, knew she was coming again from the sounds she made. He couldn't hold on and let go, his climax so hard and fast it made his legs buckle. He leaned against her and gave her all he had, powering up into her with one last, hard thrust, emptying himself with a loud groan.

He needed a minute to catch his breath. They were both panting. Savannah raised her gaze to his, hers so trusting and open and filled with an emotion he couldn't name.

"Wow," she whispered, her lips lifting in a sexy smile.

"Yeah." They adjusted their clothes.

"My hair's a mess. And I'm sure I'm blushing a hundred shades of pink," she said.

He pulled her to him and kissed her again, this time slow and easy, which was all he'd meant to do when he took her outside. "You look beautiful, like you always do."

"You always know just what to say." Her lips curled in a warm smile that never failed to punch him in the gut.

He grabbed his phone. "Halftime's over. We should go back inside before someone comes looking for us."

He slipped his hand in hers and led her back around toward the back door. But what he really wanted to do was take her home and make love to her again, this time slowly, without clothes on, so he could love every inch of her body.

He'd do that later.

TWENTY

FOUR GAMES INTO THE SEASON, AND THE TRADERS remained unbeaten.

It was still early, but Cole was filled with a sense of destiny. The team was firing on all cylinders. Defense was a beast, holding teams to few or no points. Recorded sacks were off the charts, their best season so far. Offense was hot everywhere, from the running to the passing game. The offensive line was blowing open holes everywhere and giving Cassidy plenty of time to stay in the pocket and get the passes off. It was a perfect storm.

They'd even won on the road. Coming off two road games in a row, the team was confident there was no one they couldn't beat. And Cole knew after playing in the NFL for a lot of years that confidence was everything in this game. You had to believe you could win.

They all believed they could win.

While he'd been playing, Savannah had been working on setting up his foundation. The paperwork had been set up and they were ready to get started on the first playground and community center. He'd been advised to wait until the off-season to begin work, but once the idea had formed, he didn't want to put it off. He might not be able to be as hands-on during the season as he would be when he wasn't playing, but there was no sense in delaying. The faster the playgrounds were completed, the sooner the kids would have somewhere to go.

After practice today he was meeting Savannah, the contractors, and family, friends, and teammates at the playground site. They were going to get their hands dirty. He was anxious to dig in.

Concrete had already been poured and construction started on the community center, but in the meantime they were going to work on clearing out the area for the playground. That meant mowing and weeding and clearing out trash.

That his teammates had offered to help meant more to him than he could say. Savannah had been the one to mention it to them. He never would have thought to say anything to them, but they'd all gone out for dinner one night after a home game, and she'd brought it up and said they could use some volunteers to clear the field.

His entire offensive line had spoken up and said they'd help. So had Grant Cassidy, the quarterback. So had Kenny, Jamarcus, and Lon.

He'd been surprised. Savannah had laid her hand on his arm and told him this was what it was like to have friends.

He was realizing that. People had his back now, both on and off the field.

Another thing he had her to thank for.

He picked up Savannah and they arrived at the field early enough to go over the plans with the contractor. Everything was on time and in order. The community center would take about six weeks to build. The foundation was already in the process of hiring staff for the center. Everything was falling into place.

His teammates and family arrived, and everyone dug in right away clearing debris and rocks.

"Some of this stuff is heavy," he told Savannah as she bent to try to pick up a rock. It wouldn't budge.

"You're right. There's no way anyone can pick this up. We'll need a loader."

Kaman, one of their linemen, nudged Savannah out of the way. "I got this." He picked up the rock like it weighed nothing and toted it over to the trash bin.

Savannah looked to Cole, who shrugged and grinned.

Savannah was having the time of her life. So much of what she did involved sitting at a computer, challenging her mind. It was nice to get out and work with her hands. Even with gloves on it ruined her manicure, but she could get that fixed later. Just being with Cole's family and friends was always a plus.

Not only had his team members shown up, but Cole's family was here as well. Tara, Jenna, and Elizabeth had all said hello to Savannah when they arrived, and Savannah had noticed Cole's sister, Alicia, his parents, and even his aunt and uncle.

Savannah went over on her break to grab some water. Alicia was there chatting with Tara, who was in charge of the drink tent, since she'd been given strict instructions by Mick to do no heavy lifting.

"How's it going out there?" Tara asked.

"Good. Everyone's doing such a great job."

Tara sighed. "And here I stand, handing out bottles of water."

Alicia laughed and shoved an errant hair away from her sweat-soaked face. "You can hardly move boulders in your condition."

"I know, but it's frustrating. I'm not incapacitated. I'm pregnant. I'm healthy. I do yoga. I work out all the time."

"But you can't lift heavy objects. And what if someone whacks you with one of those old rusty metal pipes or a board?" Savannah asked.

"I know. You're right. I'm safer here. I'm just whining." Tara handed out a couple waters to a few of the players who stopped at the tent.

Pizza was brought in for lunch. The guys came in, grabbed several pieces, then ran off to chat and eat, leaving the women to sit under the tent together. Savannah was more than happy to take a few minutes to sit down. She was in good physical shape, but all that bending and lifting was hard. Her back was going to be killing her by tonight.

"I'm exhausted already," Liz said as she swiped the napkin across her lips. "I won't need to work out for a week."

Alicia laughed. "I know the feeling. Pilates was never this hard."

"I was just thinking how nice a hot bath is going to feel tonight," Jenna said.

"So maybe I'm not jealous of you all anymore," Tara said, biting into a slice of cheese pizza. "The baby makes my back hurt enough."

Jenna stretched her back and let out a loud groan. "Between this and the work we're doing over at the new club, I'm ready to throw the white flag. I'll end up in great shape when we're done, though."

Liz rolled her eyes. "Bitch, please. You're a stick."

Jenna flexed her biceps. "Yeah, but I'm a stick with hard-core muscles now."

Savannah laughed.

"Isn't it fun being around us, Savannah?" Alicia asked. "All the bickering and bitch-slapping?"

"Yeah, but she doesn't mind, because she's having hot sex with your brother."

Savannah gaped at Liz. "I can't believe you just said that."

Alicia's lips quivered as she fought a smile.

"She can't believe it, but she's not denying it, is she?" Tara asked.

"I noticed that," Jenna said. "So, come on. Spill. But not in too much detail. Cole is my cousin. I get enough of that from Liz who likes to go on and on about her sex life with my brother."

"Hey," Liz said. "I have to talk to someone about Gavin."

Tara let out a soft snicker. "You can talk to me, you know."

"And I do. But I like to annoy Jenna."

"Bitch."

"Jenna does have a point, though. We're all curious, but since Cole is my brother, hold the sex detail to a minimum," Alicia said, leaning forward in her chair. "How long has this been going on?"

Four sets of eyes were focused intently on her.

She hadn't planned to say anything at all about her and Cole. Until Liz had to blab.

"So, come on, Savannah, spill," Tara said. "I want to know the details about Cole putting that dreamy, I'm-getting-a-lot-of-sex look on your face."

Alicia laid her head in her hands. "Oh, crap. I do not want to think about my brother having sex."

"Exactly what I always say to Liz. She ignores me and goes right on with the gory details," Jenna complained. "At least Tara tones it down and just sticks to the mushy love stuff."

"I save the intense sex details for my conversations with Liz," Tara said.

"Yeah, like how she got knocked up. That one was good. They were alone in the house one night. Nathan had spent the night with a friend and Mick suggested they get naked. They didn't even make it upstairs, so—"

"Oh. My. God. I don't want to know about how my future niece or nephew was conceived." Jenna closed her eyes and shook her head.

Savannah burst out laughing as Jenna plugged her fingers in her ears and started singing.

"You all crack me up."

"And we're keeping you from giving us your own juicy details," Tara reminded her. "So spill."

"Oh. Well, nothing to tell, really. We're . . . seeing each other."

Liz gave her a look. "That's a broad concept."

Alicia cocked a brow. "Which means what, exactly?"

"I don't know, exactly. Other than we're seeing each other. For now."

"Does that mean it's only temporary?"

She shifted her gaze to Tara. "I can't answer that, because I don't know. He has his career and I have mine."

"Well, honey, we all have careers," Liz said, giving her the kind of patient look one would give a child who didn't understand the topic of conversation. "What does that have to do with you screwing his brains out or falling eyeballs-deep in love?"

"Love? Who said anything about love? We're just having sex."

Tara snickered. "And how is the sex?"

Alicia pushed back her chair and stood. "That's my cue to get back to work."

"Right behind you," Jenna said.

"Cowards," Liz called after them.

Jenna flipped her off.

Liz laughed, then turned back to Savannah. "So, about that sex . . ."

"I'm not telling you about my sex life with Cole."

"Why not? We all talk about ours."

She looked to Tara, who said, "It's true. We're like sisters, and when we're troubled or need advice about our men, we go to each other."

"I'm not troubled. Nor do I need advice. Not at the moment. But thank you very much for the offer."

Liz looked over at Tara. "I don't think she's going to give us the gory sex details."

Tara sighed, leaned back in her chair, and laid her hands over her stomach. "It doesn't look that way. I'm very disappointed."

Savannah gave them a blank look. But then Tara laughed, and so did Liz. Liz swatted her on the leg.

"We're kidding."

"Oh."

"Really, woman, you need to lighten up."

She blew out a breath. "I do, don't I?"

Tara stood and stretched. "You'd think all that sex you're having would ease some of the tension."

Savannah let out a snort, cupped her hand over her mouth, then broke out in a full laugh. "Oh, god. It does. It really does."

"Obviously you need a lot more of it, then. Maybe more public sex, like the kind you had behind the bar the other night?"

Savannah's eyes widened. "What?"

Tara came over and put her arm around Savannah. "We all try to sneak away during family gatherings, honey, but this family is too filled with eagle eyes. The swollen lips, messed-up hair, and I-just-got-screwed-within-an-inch-of-my-life look on your face was a dead giveaway."

She felt the telltale blush creep up her neck and cheeks. "I knew that cold splash of water on my face and quick fix of my hair in the bathroom wasn't going to fool anyone."

"Oh, it probably fooled some," Liz said. "But not us. We've been there, done that. We all knew you had a hot quickie in the garden."

"I was jealous, since my man had an away game," Tara said. "I hope it was good."

Savannah sighed. "It was."

Tara nodded. "Thank god someone's getting great sex, then. Mick has two road games before he gets home. And before long I'll be as big as a house."

"And he'll still be jumping your bones until you're ready to pop that baby out," Liz said.

Tara grinned. "Probably."

Savannah loved these women more and more every minute she spent with them.

But when she felt strong, warm, very masculine hands on her shoulders, she shivered and tilted her head back, already knowing whose hands those were.

"Hey there."

"Hey, yourself. Done with the girl chat?"

Her gaze met Liz's and Tara's, who both gave her a knowing smile. "I think we're done."

"Good. I want to show you something."

"Sure. See you both later."

They waved her off and she walked through the playground with Cole. A lot of the larger debris had been cleared away by the guys and by the loader they'd brought in, leaving the site nearly bare.

"Wow. Huge accomplishment today."

He slanted a smile at her. "It has been. They're coming to dig this up, then grade the area to even the ground out." He laid out the blueprints for her, and though she'd already been through them, she loved hearing the excitement in his voice as he talked about all the equipment that would be put into place.

He was so different now, so focused on doing things for others. And his teammates—his friends—kept interrupting them, giving him good-natured teasing as well as asking him questions about what to do next.

She stayed out of his way and let him work.

By the time they finished up for the day, it was getting dark.

Because his uncle and aunt extended the invitation, Cole invited everyone to Riley's bar for dinner and drinks. Most of the guys came along. Tara was tired, so she went home.

Jenna was happy to not be working at the bar, and instead be a customer. They gathered at a table, ate burgers, and visited with Cole's parents and aunt and uncle.

"You two are getting to be a familiar couple together," Cole's mother said as they finished their meal. "I'm getting a hint that there's more than just a business relationship there."

Savannah didn't answer, just looked at Cole, who shrugged and said, "You know, Mom, you might be right about that. But that's between me and Savannah."

"Yeah, good luck with that one," Jenna said. "Have you ever known the family to butt out of a relationship?"

"I beg your pardon," Cole's aunt Kathleen said. "I have never interfered. I only offered advice a couple times."

Jenna snorted. "Sure, Mom. Whatever you say."

Ty slung an arm around Jenna. "Your family is awesome. And helpful in the relationship department when a nudge is needed."

Jenna arched a brow at Ty. "Are you insinuating I needed a nudge?"

"More like a kick in the behind," Jenna's mother said.

Ty snorted and Jenna glared then said, "Okay, you might be right about that."

"Babe, I'm always right."

Jenna rolled her eyes.

"The Rileys never butt in where they're not welcome," Cole's mom said. "I only asked if Cole and Savannah were dating."

Cole put his arm around Savannah. "We're dating. Subject's closed."

"I think we've just been asked to mind our own business, Cara," Kathleen said.

Cara laughed. "I think you're right." Cara turned to Savannah and squeezed her hand. "But I will say you've been very good for my son, so I hope this lasts a very long time."

She could think of nothing to say to his mother other than, "Thank you, Mrs. Riley."

Her stomach tightened. This all felt so good, so natural. Being around his family made her want more than she had ever thought to hope for.

But this wasn't her family, so she needed to stop hoping. As she well knew, things could change fast, and all her hopes could disappear. It was always best to be realistic.

After dinner everyone left. The guys had early practice tomorrow, and it had been a long day. Cole drove her home.

"Do you want to come in?" she asked as he walked her to her front door.

"You know I do."

She closed the door behind him.

"Something to drink?"

"No." He headed into her bedroom.

Curious, she followed him in there. He pulled off his shirt, kicked off his shoes and went into her bathroom, where he turned on her shower.

"By all means, make yourself at home."

He paused midway through pulling off his shirt. "I'm dirty and sweaty after today. I need a shower. Do I need to ask permission?"

Her lips quirked. "No. I could use one myself."

"Then get naked and get in here."

He dropped his pants and slipped into the shower.

It took her less than thirty seconds to divest herself of her clothes. When she opened the shower door, he held out his hand and helped her step in.

The shower was warm and steamy, and his body was hot and smelled of sweat. She loved the scent of a man who'd worked hard. He pulled her under the water to wet her body down. She grabbed the shampoo.

"Don't be in such a hurry. Let me do that," he said, taking the shampoo from her hand and pouring some into his hand.

She closed her eyes and immersed herself in this. No man had washed her hair before. Her beautician did, of course, but this was a decidedly different experience. His hands were bigger, and a little rougher, but she liked the feel of him rubbing her scalp. His movements were more sensual, as if he were enjoying the experience instead of it just being his job.

He tilted her head back under the spray, rinsed her hair, then applied conditioner, sliding his fingers through the strands of her hair. He rinsed again, then lathered his hands with body wash and turned her around so he could wash her back.

Again, he took his time, rubbing her back, using his strong hands to massage the soreness out of her shoulder muscles. She leaned into him and every knot melted away under the hard pressure of his fingers. And when he rolled his fist down the center of her back, she laid her palms against the shower wall, certain her knees were going to buckle.

"That feels so good. Were you a massage therapist in another life?"

"No. I just like touching you."

He grasped the globes of her butt and squeezed them gently, massaging them as well. Her nipples hardened.

"Do I have to pay extra for that?" she asked.

"You can give me a tip later."

She wriggled her butt against his erection. "I think you're the one who has a tip for me."

He turned her around and poured more body wash into his hands, rubbed them together, then lathered them over her breasts. "I think you're getting a little saucy with me."

She raised her arms, gasping at the sensation as he washed her breasts. Her nipples, so sensitive to his touch, ached. He grabbed the spray handle and rinsed her, then bent and took one peak in his mouth, sucking hard until she moaned with delight.

Then he took the spray and aimed it between her legs. Her eyes widened and she gasped.

"Do you get yourself off this way? I've heard women do."

She offered a wicked smile. "Of course I do. It's very handy when I'm in a hurry and need an orgasm." She took the spray handle and put it back in its cradle. "But why would I want to do that when I have you here to make me come?"

He wrapped an arm around her waist and kissed her, his tongue dipping inside to wrap around hers. She could think of nothing but the beat of his heart, the heat of his skin, and the firmness of his body, which always drove her a little bit crazy. She laid her palms on his shoulders and held on while he slid his hand between her legs, teasing her with light strokes that revved up her need to fever pitch.

And when he dropped to his knees and shouldered her legs apart, she leaned against the shower wall and watched. Water sluiced down the front of her and over Cole. He raised his head to give her a devilish smile before putting his mouth on her sex.

Oh, god, yes. This is just what she'd wanted. His tongue lapping at her clit, slick and hot and taking her right to the edge so fast it made her head spin. Steam rose all around them as he slid two fingers inside her and finger fucked her while he sucked her clit.

"Cole. I won't last long."

He didn't answer, just sucked her and continued to fuck her with his fingers, relentless in his pursuit of the orgasm she couldn't hope to hold back. She arched against him and let go, releasing a hoarse cry as she came. He held her as she rode the waves that went on and on, sending pulses of sweet pleasure throughout her core. When he rose, he kissed her, letting her taste herself on his mouth. She licked his lips and dove in for a deeper kiss, then wrapped her fingers around his rigid shaft, stroking him until he let out a harsh groan.

She loved the sounds he made, loved giving him pleasure as much as she loved receiving it. She squatted down, water raining down over her back as she took his cock in both her hands and wound her fingers around the shaft, then lifted the soft head to her mouth, tilting her head back to look at him.

He was staring down at her, his expression fierce as she put the crest between her lips and closed her mouth over it. She kneeled on the shower floor and pushed forward, taking his cock into her mouth as she did.

"Christ," he whispered, then laid his hand on the top of her head.

She focused on his cock, flicking her tongue over the different textures as she pulled the shaft deeper into her mouth. Pulses of salty flavor spilled onto her tongue when she withdrew and she lapped them up, teasing the crest by rolling her tongue over it.

"You're killing me, Peaches," he said, and she hummed as she took him deep into her mouth again, then reached underneath to cradle his ball sac, giving them a gentle squeeze as she began to move her mouth back and forth over him.

"Yeah, like that," he said, using his hand to guide her movements. "Suck me harder."

She loved when his voice got rough, when he gave her those commands that told her what he liked. It made her pussy quiver, her nipples tighten, just as his balls tightened into hard knots in her hand. She squeezed them again, and took his cock deep into the back of her throat, using her other hand to stroke him as she sucked him.

"Oh, fuck, that's going to make me come. Harder," he said.

She did, giving him the suction he needed. And when he thrust deep into her mouth and came, she milked him, swallowing his come and holding on to him while he rocked against her lips, shaking with the force of his climax.

He leaned against the wall for support and she licked the last of his come from the tip of his cock, then rose and kissed him as he had kissed her. He pushed her against the wall and devoured her lips, licking at her tongue until her legs were weak and her clit trembled with need.

They both washed, and Cole turned the shower off. They climbed out and towel dried, then Cole took her to bed.

"I hope you're not too tired, because I'm not finished with you yet."

She smiled at him and rolled over, spreading her legs. "I'm not too tired."

"Good. But you're facing the wrong way." He threw a pillow in

the middle of the bed. "Get on top of that. I want you from behind."

Swells of desire and anticipation filled her as she positioned herself on her belly on top of the pillow. She heard Cole tear open the
condom wrapper, and then he was on top of her, inside her, and she
raised up, pushing back against him as her pussy latched on to his
cock.

"Fuck. That's good," he said, settling on top of her to lick the
side of her neck.

He reached underneath her to rub her clit.

"I'm going to make you come again, Peaches. Then I'm going
to come inside you. Hard."

She shivered as he thrust deep, then pulled out only to power
inside her again, each time strumming her clit with unbearable
sweetness. She was rolling toward another orgasm, he was slam-
ming her deep into the mattress, and she wanted it to last.

"Harder," she said, pushing his hand away to rub her own clit.
"Grab my hips and give it to me harder."

He pulled her up onto her knees so she'd have better access to
make herself come, and so he could hold on to her and push deeper
inside her. And when he thrust, she cried out, chills breaking out
on her body. This connection between them was intense, nearly
unbearable. And when he grabbed her hair and jerked her head
back, it only intensified her pleasure.

"You're mine, Savannah." He plunged deep.

Oh, God. "Yes."

"Mine." Harder this time.

"Yes."

When she shattered, she screamed. Cole dug his fingers into
her hips and buried himself inside her, yelling as he came with a
series of quick thrusts.

She collapsed onto the bed and he went with her, falling next
to her.

She was certain she couldn't breathe, at least not for a full minute. When she could, she rolled to her side and swiped her hair away from her face so she could look at Cole.

His eyes were open—or at least partially open.

"I'm convinced you're trying to kill me."

She laughed. "I'm not sure who's trying to kill who."

He left only long enough to get rid of the condom, then came back, pulled the covers down and pushed the pillows up on the bed, dragging her against his chest.

"You're like no one I've ever known, Peaches."

She drew circles over his chest. "I suppose that's a compliment."

He pressed a soft kiss to her lips. "It means you're the most amazing woman I've ever met. You're special to me in ways I can't explain."

She shuddered, so pleased by the compliment.

The two of them lay there quietly for a while. She was content to listen to the sound of his heart beating. Just being there with him was enough for her.

"What would you think about the two of us moving in together?"

She shot up in bed. "What?"

His lips lifted. "You heard me."

"Where did this come from?"

"It's something I've been thinking about."

She grinned. "Really?"

"Yeah."

"And why have you been thinking about it?"

He shrugged. "We spend a lot of time together. We obviously . . . like each other a lot. We're compatible."

Her stomach fell. No declaration of love. They *liked* each other. They were compatible. For all he'd just said, he could have been advertising for a roommate. Or a pet. "I see."

He shifted to face her. "What's wrong?"

She slid out of bed and grabbed her robe. "Nothing. I'm just tired. And I've got a lot to do tomorrow. You should probably go."

He got out of bed, too, and came over to her. He put his hands on her shoulders. "Peaches."

She backed away. "Really, Cole. I'm tired and I need to get some sleep."

"It's what I said. About us moving in together. You're freaked out."

"No. I'm tired. Really, you need to go."

"I want to stay tonight."

"No."

He studied her for a minute, then nodded. "Okay."

He grabbed his clothes and got dressed. She followed him out to the living room and walked him to the door. He turned to her.

"You want to talk about this? If you don't like the idea of us moving in together, that's fine. We can keep things as they were."

Right. Where they were friends and compatible. She fought back the tears. "I really need to get some sleep."

"So we'll talk tomorrow."

"Sure."

He leaned in to give her a kiss, and she turned away. His lips brushed her jaw.

She saw the confusion and hurt on his face, but she couldn't deal with his issues right now. Not when she was minutes away from falling apart.

"I'll talk to you tomorrow."

She nodded and held the door. "Sure. Good night."

The tears began to spill before she had the door completely shut.

Stupid. She was never girlie, never cried over stuff like this. She'd never cried over a man, because no man had ever meant anything to her.

Until now.

He'd asked her to move in with him. That was a huge step. So he hadn't gotten all romantic and said he loved her. Big deal.

But it was a big deal.

Maybe to someone else the words didn't mean anything. But she was in love with him. And if he didn't feel the same way, there was no point in taking this any further. Otherwise she'd only end up feeling more hurt than she felt right now.

And this hurt a whole hell of a lot.

TWENTY-ONE

SAVANNAH WOULD HAVE MUCH PREFERRED AVOID-
ance. Avoidance of any personal problem was always her best so-
lution.

Unfortunately, she had a meeting with the GM of the Traders
that morning, and of course the team had practice.

Which didn't mean she'd have to run into Cole. In fact, she was
adept at not running into people she didn't want to run into. So
after her meeting, she was on her way out and the team was still on
the field.

"Hey, girl, what are you doing here?"

Elizabeth. Damn.

She pasted on her brightest smile.

"Hi. I had a meeting with McNee."

"Oh. Fun for you, I'll bet."

"Always. Well, I've got to go."

Liz frowned. "Do you have another meeting?"

"Uh, actually, no I don't."

"Great. Let's go get some coffee. And maybe a muffin or a scone. I'm starving. I had an early meeting this morning and didn't have a chance to have breakfast." She linked her arm with Savannah's and led her down the hall. "Gavin's in town for a stretch of home games and I traded food for sex. Can you blame me?"

"Not in the least." Maybe some breakfast and conversation would take her mind off Cole. And at least she could get out of this building and away from him.

They went to a nearby coffeehouse. Savannah ordered a cup of coffee and a blueberry muffin. Liz decided on a scone.

"I'm sure you're happy to have Gavin in town," Savannah said.

Liz popped a piece of scone in her mouth, chewed, moaned, then swallowed. "I'm just glad to *have* Gavin." She grinned. "I don't get him often enough during the season, which, by the way, lasts too damn long. A hundred and sixty-two games? What fucking idiot thought that one up?"

Savannah laughed. "Either someone without a wife or someone with a wife he couldn't stand."

"Amen to that. Poor Gavin. He probably hates home stretches. I wear him out."

"I seriously doubt he hates that part."

"Okay, you're right. He doesn't hate it. And speaking of sex, how are things with you and my oh-so-hot client?"

Her heart clenched. She shrugged. "Okay, I guess."

Liz frowned. "Uh-oh. What's wrong?"

"Nothing's wrong." She picked at her muffin. "Things are great."

"Did I ever mention I have an excellent bullshit meter? Tell me what happened."

She could hedge, make something up, but Liz would push until she gave in, so she might as well avoid the battle now. "He asked me if I wanted to move in with him."

Liz's brows lifted. "And that's a bad thing?"

"No. But he said it's because we like each other and we're compatible."

Liz laid her coffee cup down. "Fuck a donut sideways. He did not."

"He did."

"What the hell does he think you are? A cocker spaniel?"

Leave it to Liz to make her feel better. "I don't know. I don't think I reacted well. I asked him to leave."

"Hell, I'd have kicked his ass. What is wrong with that man?"

She lifted her gaze to Liz. "He's probably afraid to tell me how he feels. Or maybe he doesn't feel the same way I feel."

"And how do you feel?"

She sighed. "I'm crazy in love with him. And it scares me."

"Why does that scare you?"

"You know why. I've purposely set up my life to be alone so I won't be hurt."

Liz waved her hand. "Yeah, yeah. And how's that working for you?"

"Not very well. I didn't set out to fall in love with Cole, you know. It happened purely by accident."

Liz snorted. "It usually does. Honey, you can't control love. It blindsides you. It's what you do about it when it does happen that counts. Have you told him how you feel?"

Savannah's eyes widened. "Oh, god no."

"So he's supposed to be psychic. Maybe he's afraid to tell you how he feels because he thinks you don't feel the same way."

She laid her hands on the table and looked at Liz straight on. "Mercy. I never thought about it like that."

"I'd like to knock both your heads together. But especially his. Men are such dickheads sometimes. Most of the time, actually."

"Please don't say anything to him. I'll handle this."

Liz shrugged and picked up her coffee. "Whatever you want. My lips are sealed."

* * *

COLE HAD A TERRIBLE FEW DAYS OF PRACTICE, AND an even lousier game on Sunday. It didn't help that it was an away game today, even though they weren't that far away since they'd played Kansas City. It still wasn't the home crowd.

Not that it had made a difference.

The whole team had played like shit, so he couldn't even chalk it up to it just being him.

And they'd lost. By two fucking points. A blowout you just accept and move on. But to lose when the game was that close sucked.

Coupled with that, he hadn't talked to Savannah in five days. He hadn't seen her at practice, or at the game. They had even talked earlier about her making the drive over to see the game in Kansas City.

He'd tried to call her a few times but she wouldn't return his calls or his text messages. And when he'd gone by her place, her car wasn't there and she didn't answer her door.

She was doing a damn good job of avoiding him, which made it hard to figure out what the fuck he'd done wrong.

So he was in a piss-poor mood when it came to media interviews after the game.

"Cole, does it feel like old times again to be on the losing end of a game?"

"Hey, Cole, do you take personal responsibility for losing this game today?"

"Riley, do you feel like the jinx is back again since you lost the game?"

"How about those three dropped passes today?"

He wanted to tell them all to fuck off, eat shit, and die. Instead, he bit his lip and answered their questions with honesty. He'd played a bad game and he felt like he'd let his team down, but he was going to work harder and do better next week. When they figured out he wasn't going to take the bait, they moved on to pick on some other poor sucker who'd also had a lousy day.

At least he found a friendly face waiting for him outside the locker room.

Liz didn't look very friendly, though.

"Yeah, I know," he said as she walked with him down the tunnel. "I played like shit today."

"It was one bad game. You'll do better next week."

"I will."

She stopped, turned to him. "I want to talk to you about Savannah."

"What about her? Is she okay?"

"She's fine. But you're an asshole."

Okay, maybe she'd talked to Savannah and he could gain some insight into what the fuck was going on. "What did I do?"

"Come on. Let's go get a drink. You have a couple hours before you have to leave."

She took him to her car and drove him a couple blocks to a restaurant. They got a booth in the bar and ordered drinks.

"So you've talked to her?" he asked as soon as they got their drinks.

"What the hell's the mater with you?" she asked.

"I have no idea what you're talking about."

"I'm not supposed to be talking to you at all. I promised Savannah I wouldn't. But it's obvious you need some coaching in how to talk to women."

He rolled his eyes. "Seems to me I was doing just fine without your help."

"You asked her to move in with you."

"She told you that?"

"Yes. And how did you ask her?"

He frowned. "What?"

"Did you tell her how you felt about her?"

"What? I don't remember exactly what I said."

"From what I gathered, it was like inviting one of your fraternity brothers to be your roomie."

He stared at her. "It wasn't like that at all."

"Wasn't it?" She stirred her drink. "Maybe you should think on it and reevaluate how you feel about her."

"I know how I feel about her."

"Really? How?"

"I—" He frowned again. "None of your goddamned business. That's between me and Savannah."

"Have you told *her* how you feel?"

"Well . . ." He thought on it, thought about what he'd said that night. About how they were compatible. How he liked her. He hadn't been able to get the words out. Not about how he really felt about her. They'd stuck in his throat.

How that must have sounded to her. "Shit."

"Exactly."

"I thought she knew how I felt."

"And she would know this, how?"

He dragged his fingers through his hair. "Fuck."

"She told you about her childhood, didn't she?"

"Yeah. And the thing that scares her the most is someone not being there for her. Someone not loving her."

"Now you're beginning to see the light. There may be hope for you yet, dumbass."

He paid the bill and they got up to leave.

He went over to Liz and took her hand.

"Thanks. I needed to hear this. Now I have to find her and tell her how I feel. I love her, Liz."

"Oh, you prick. You're going to make me all teary-eyed, and I'm not wearing waterproof mascara."

He laughed. "Sorry."

"I'll drive you back. Now go make it all better for your girl."

TWENTY-TWO

SAVANNAH HAD PUT IT OFF LONG ENOUGH. SHE HAD never been a coward and she wasn't going to be one now. She had to talk to Cole and tell him how she felt. He'd made the first move and had suggested they move in together. So he hadn't given her the whole I-love-you hearts-and-flowers spiel. So what?

And what had she done? She'd focused on what he hadn't done, instead of what he had done. He'd made an amazing step toward a committed relationship. She'd been the one to fumble the ball. She was supposed to be the one with the amazing communication skills. Instead of opening up and talking about things, she'd gotten all emotional, closed up, and thrown him out.

Now she had to fix it.

If he didn't want to move forward with her after that, so be it. At least she would have put her cards on the table. She could walk away with a clear heart then.

She was going to invite him over tonight. She knew he had

practice earlier today, but as far as she knew he had nothing on his schedule tonight.

She'd lain low for a week now, not answering his calls, too afraid to talk to him or see him, too afraid he might not feel the same way she did.

But she missed him. And she had to know. One way or the other, she had to know.

She picked up her phone, stared at it, formulated in her mind what she would say.

Failure wasn't something she had much experience with, except on the other side, where she coached her clients. She'd coached many of them through failure, taught them to come out stronger because of it. To be on this side of it was humbling. It hurt to fail, made her want to curl up in a ball and not try again. She'd worked so hard her entire life to be a success, and she had been. She hadn't stumbled—not even once. She'd set goals for herself and she'd met every one of them, because she was determined to go it on her own and never have to depend on anyone again.

But she *had* depended on someone—Cole. She'd put her heart in his hands and he'd disappointed her.

That's what humans did. They tried, but they often disappointed those they loved the most. She'd learned that with her mother, which was why she'd spent her entire life avoiding putting her heart out there.

Cole would probably disappoint her again. Was she willing to take that risk? Could she live with the potential for heartbreak?

Or was she searching for a perfect man in her mind that simply didn't exist?

That was too much pressure for any guy. Maybe it was time she accept him for who he was—an amazing man with flaws, just like she had flaws.

She took a deep breath. "You're not a child anymore, Savannah. It's time to grow up and take a chance on love."

She raised her fingers to punch the buttons on her phone, then jumped when it buzzed in her hand.

It was Cole calling. She clicked the button. "Hello?"

"Hey. You answered."

Guilt washed over her. "Yes. I'm sorry I didn't before."

"Are you home?"

Her stomach tightened. "Yes. Can you come over? I'd like to talk to you."

"Actually, I'm right outside your door."

"You are?" She hurried to the door and opened it. He was there, on her doorstep, looking so gorgeous and warm and human she wanted to throw herself into his arms and beg him to forget the conversation they'd had last week. Instead, she clicked off her phone. "So you are."

"I've been here almost every day I was in town. Multiple times. You weren't here. You didn't answer the door."

"I was out a lot at meetings. They're assigning me a new client."

"And you were avoiding me."

That, too. "Come in."

She shut the door behind him. He stood just inside, didn't go into the living room, as if waiting for an invitation.

Well, this was awkward and uncomfortable.

"Have a seat, Cole."

"Only if you sit with me."

"Would you like something to drink?"

"No, I just want to talk to you."

"All right." She sat on the sofa, and he came over and sat next to her.

She swallowed, her throat dry. There were so many thoughts whirling through her mind, so many things she wanted to say, but they were jumbled up in her head. She should have written them down, made an outline so she could go through them step by step.

He took her hand. "I was a jerk."

She lifted her head. "What?"

"Let me back up. When you first met me, I was a jerk. You changed me. You made me think differently, to learn to pause before I blurted out the first thing that came into my head, which was usually something that was all about me and how I felt and what I wanted. I learned from that, you know?"

She smiled at him. "Yes, I know. I've seen evidence of that over the past few months. You've done a wonderful job."

"Thanks. But that's not what I'm here to talk about, other than to thank you for being patient with me when I know I wasn't easy to be around."

"You weren't as difficult as you'd like to think you were."

"I took those lessons to heart. And along the way, I got used to having you in my life. You were the backbone of the person I became, the person I always wanted to be. And I guess I became complacent, always assuming you'd just be there, that you'd want to be with me."

She did want to be with him. But this was his moment to talk, so she'd let him finish.

"What I said to you that night I asked you to move in with me—it was thoughtless. I wasn't prepared to tell you how I really felt about you, and it came out all wrong. I knew I wanted you with me, but I choked."

"I don't understand."

"I know. You've worked with me on being clear in what I say, so the media doesn't misinterpret me. And when it came down to the most important conversation I've ever had, I fucked it all up." He rubbed his finger over her thumb, distracting her. The sensation sent shivers up her arm. She fought hard to concentrate on what he was saying, but all she could think about was how much she'd missed his touch, being near him, and how much it hurt to be apart, to have this distance between them. And she needed him to know that.

"I love you, Savannah."

That got her attention. Her gaze shot to his. "You do?"

"Yeah. Do you think I'd ask someone I wasn't in love with to move in with me?"

"I don't know. I didn't know how you felt about me. You said you liked me, that we were compatible."

He rubbed his temple. "Yeah, that. Like I said, I was being an asshole. I was scared. I've never told a woman I loved her before. And when it came time to say it, I dropped the ball. I'm sorry."

She scooted closer to him and swept her hand across his jaw. "It's okay. I didn't handle it any better than you. I doubted how you felt about me and I got scared, too. So instead of telling you how I felt, I kicked you out. Instead of opening a dialogue between us, I ran and hid from you."

He took her hand in his. "I'm in love with you. I don't take those words lightly, Peaches. And with love comes commitment. I'll always be here for you. I'm not going anywhere. I'm never going to leave you."

The words sunk in. Her heart blossomed with such an outpouring of emotion she thought she might burst with it. And she realized he needed to hear it from her, too. "I love you, too, Cole. I've loved you for a while now. I'm ashamed to admit I was too afraid to tell you, because I didn't know how you felt about me."

His lips lifted. "Well, now you know. Can I say I'm damn happy to hear you say it? I was afraid you didn't feel the same way, that I was going to tell you I loved you and you were going to pat me on the shoulder and say 'that's nice' and that we'd always be friends."

She laughed, then climbed on his lap. "I was hoping you knew how I felt."

"I was hoping you knew how I felt." Now it was his turn to laugh. "Christ, we're such a mess. I think we need to work on our communication skills."

"I think you're right."

"You've always been a good teacher. I'll trust you to help me work on mine. I promise to tell you I love you every day."

"And I'll try harder to always tell you what I'm feeling. I admit I'm pretty good at telling others how to live their lives, but not so good at dealing with my own. I've made a lot of mistakes, so I'm going to need your help."

"I'll always be here to help you."

She loved hearing that from him. And even better, she believed him, because he had always been there for her.

She bent and kissed him. He wrapped his arms around her and laid her on the sofa, deepening the kiss until her head was filled with love and her body was filled with desire. When he reached for her breast, she covered his hand with hers, holding it there, letting him feel the rapid beat of her heart.

When he lifted his hand, she was out of breath. "Want me to tell you what I'm feeling right now?"

He raised her skirt and rested his hand on her panties, teasing her sex. "You're wet. I'm not psychic, but I have a pretty good idea what you're feeling."

She gazed at his face, unable to fathom that this extraordinary man loved her. "What are you going to do about it?"

He slipped his fingers beneath the silk and rubbed her aching flesh, teasing her until she was panting. "I'm going to make you come, Peaches. And then I'm going to slide my dick in you and make love to you and make you come again."

She grinned. "I like this idea." She arched against his hand. He removed her panties, slid his fingers inside her, and rubbed her clit with his thumb.

He dropped off the couch and onto his knees, drawing her legs over his shoulders. He put his mouth on her pussy and licked her, the heat and wetness of his tongue taking her right to the edge of madness. She lifted up on her elbows, watching him as he lapped at her with his tongue and sucked her clit. Sensation spiraled within her until she couldn't hold back. And when she came, their eyes met and she let him watch her release, arching against him as wave after wave washed over her.

When the pulses subsided, he stood, licked his lips and smiled down at her, then kicked off his shoes and dropped his pants to the floor. He grabbed a condom and took a seat on the sofa, pulling her on top of him.

"You are the sexiest woman I've ever known," he said as he lifted her skirt over her hips.

She rocked her sex against his erection. "You've always made me feel sexy." She took the condom wrapper from his hands and tore it open, then fit the condom onto his rigid cock. "You make me want to do things I've never done before."

"Like having sex outside my family's bar?"

She laughed, then raised up and slid down over his shaft, gasping as he filled her. "Yes, like that."

He grabbed her buttocks and spread them as he speared his cock into her, burying himself deep. She unbuttoned her blouse and undid the clasp of her bra, releasing her breasts. His eyes went half-lidded as she grabbed her breasts and teased her nipples while he surged into her.

"You have no idea how much I like seeing you play with your nipples like that."

"We have a lot to explore with each other, don't we?" she said, moaning as he rocked back and forth. With his cock buried deep inside her, she pulsed, her clit rubbing against him. She plucked at her nipples, sending sensation coursing through her nerve endings.

He wrapped his hand around the nape of her neck and brought her toward him for a blistering kiss that made her tingle all over. With the other hand, he held tight to her ass, grinding against her until she felt the stirrings of orgasm. She whimpered against his lips.

"Come on, Peaches. Come on my cock so I can let go."

His words never failed to rock her world, to encourage her to soar. And as he gripped her butt and lifted against her, she broke, crying out against his mouth with her orgasm. He went with her, groaning out her name as he thrust upward in several bursts, both of them shuddering and gripping each other as their worlds collided.

He swept his arm over her back, divesting her of her blouse and bra. She much preferred his caresses on her bare skin.

"See how much easier this will be when we're living together?" he said later as they climbed into her bed. "One of us always has to get up and go home the next day. I'd much rather already be home."

"Which of our places do you want to live in?"

"Well, there's your house, which would make more sense than my condo."

"That's true."

"But I actually thought we might want to buy a bigger house."

She arched a brow. "Really? Why?"

"Well, because eventually we'll want to get married and have kids . . ."

She gaped at him.

He paused. "I'm rushing you. Or scaring the hell out of you. I should propose or something first, shouldn't I? I never get this shit right. Or would you rather we take this slow?"

She shook her head, no longer afraid. "No. You're doing it all right. And I'm fine with taking it one slow step at a time. A bigger house it is."

She leaned against him, listening to his strong heartbeat as they cuddled together.

Maybe he didn't say all the right things, and maybe he didn't do it all in the right way, but he was hers, and she was his, and they'd figure it all out together. Because she knew now that both of them were in this for the long haul, and that he'd be there for her no matter what.

And that's what counted the most.

KEEP READING FOR AN EXCERPT FROM THE NEXT
PLAY-BY-PLAY NOVEL BY JACI BURTON

THROWN BY A CURVE

AVAILABLE SOON FROM BERKLEY BOOKS

GARRETT SCOTT SAT IN THE ST. LOUIS RIVERS THER-
apy room facing an entire team of sports medicine specialists, all
wearing looks of doom on their faces.

From the team doctor to the therapists who'd been working on
his shoulder for the past nine months, their faces said it all—he
wasn't ready to pitch yet.

He was tired of it. Tired of being molded and manipulated and
poked and prodded like some kind of experiment. His shoulder
wasn't getting any better and he still couldn't throw a pitch. He was
done. His career was over, and no amount of fake, hopeful expres-
sions would make him believe any different.

"Let's go over to the pulleys," Max said. "If we increase the
weight . . ."

"No. It's not going to help. I can't get my full range of motion
and no pulleys, no weighted balls, no water therapy, and no amount
of stretching is going to get it back."

"You don't know that, Garrett," Max said. As head of the therapy team, when Max had a plan, everyone always listened. "We haven't finished with the therapy and the season hasn't started yet. There's plenty of time."

Phil, the team doctor, nodded. "Max is right. You just haven't given it enough time."

Garrett glared at them both. "I said no. This has been going nowhere and we all know it."

Everyone started talking at once, but it was all white noise to him. They were blowing smoke up his ass about how he was going to pitch come April.

He'd heard it before, all the pats on the back and the encouragement that didn't mean anything if you couldn't get a fastball across the plate. They were just words. Empty promises.

The only one who didn't say anything was the woman hovering in the background. Dark hair pulled back into a ponytail, she wore the same team-color polo shirt and khaki pants as the other specialists and held a digital notebook. And she was giving him a look. A pissed-off one.

"You haven't said anything," he said, focusing his gaze on her. "What do you think?"

She blinked and held her notebook close to her chest. "Me?"

"Yeah."

"I'm not in charge of your recovery. There are people here with much more experience than me."

"You've watched my therapy, haven't you?"

"Yes."

"What do you think?"

They all turned to her, waiting. She finally shrugged. "I think your team is right. You'll pitch."

"My arm is stiff."

She moved forward and he got a good look at her. Despite the ugly uniform, she was pretty. Really dark hair and stunning blue eyes and a mouth that he was definitely noticing now that she'd opened it.

"Because you're babying it, because you won't give it your all. Your therapists know what they're doing, but you fight them at every turn."

As soon as she said it, her eyes widened. Max crossed his arms and Garrett could tell he was irritated.

Garrett wasn't. His lips quirked. "Go on."

"Look, I didn't mean to insult you."

"Yeah, you did. You've sat back quiet for all these months and you obviously have something on your mind. Spill it."

She looked up at Max, who shook his head.

"Don't look at him," Garrett said. "Tell me what I'm doing wrong."

She sat next to him on the bench and laid her notebook down, her gaze lifting to his.

"Fine. You're argumentative, confrontational, and a general pain in the ass to deal with. Honestly, no one wants to work with you because you fight your recovery. Half of healing is mental and your head is the biggest obstacle to getting back on the mound."

Huh. He looked up at the rest of the group, who all did their best to avoid his gaze. "I see."

But when he looked back at—he had no idea what her name was. "What's your name?"

"Alicia."

"Okay, Alicia. You think you can make me a pitcher again?"

She gave him a confident smirk. "I know I can, if you pull your head out of your ass and work with me."

He liked her confidence. He liked her. She sure as hell was better looking than the rest of the sports medicine group. And she smelled good.

"Alicia," Max warned. "Why don't you head up to the office and I'll finish up here with Garrett?"

Alicia nodded, then stood and left the room.

Garrett laughed, the first time he'd laughed in a long damn time. "It's okay, Max. I like her. She's honest."

He'd never noticed her much before because she'd either been an observer or working with another player. As soon as the door closed, he turned to Max.

"I want her in charge of my therapy."

"No," Phil said, interjecting himself into the conversation. "As your doctor, I'm advising against it. Max is the head of sports medicine for the team. He's the best. Alicia doesn't have the experience he has."

"I don't give a shit if she's the water girl. She's confident. She's a sports medicine specialist, isn't she?"

"Well, yes," Max said.

"Then I want to work with her."

"You have a multimillion-dollar arm, Garrett. I'm not entrusting it to her."

Garrett stood and stretched, then looked at Manny Magee, the St. Louis Rivers coach, who'd been sitting in the corner of the room, silently taking it all in. "These guys have all been working on me for months and I haven't seen the results needed to throw a single goddamn pitch. I want her to work with me."

Manny stood and ambled over. He was tough, and always honest, so he knew Manny would give it to him straight. "That's because she's right. Physically, you're healing fine from the injury. A lot of your problem is you're resisting the treatment."

Maybe Manny was right, but he doubted it. What he needed was a new therapist. If Alicia and her smart mouth could get the job done, then maybe his career wasn't over.

He looked at Manny—at all of them.

"I need a change. What we're doing isn't working. And maybe someone new can help with that."

"I don't give a damn if a circus clown works on your therapy, as long as you're on the mound opening day," Manny said. "Just be ready for the season. We need your arm."

SHIT. SHIT. SHIT. ALICIA MASSAGED THE GIANT HEAD-ache that had taken refuge between her eyes and counted down the minutes until her boss entered the office and fired her.

She'd always had a smart mouth, always spoke first and thought later. But to insult the entire St. Louis Rivers medical team in one sentence had been a serious, colossal fuck-up. She'd had some success as a therapist and had been getting great feedback from her boss in the time she'd been here. This was the job of her dreams, and to make matters worse, her cousin played for this team. Gavin was going to kill her.

The worst part was, she knew she was right. Garrett Scott was a seriously amazing pitcher. His injury had been bad, but there was no reason to think he wouldn't come back and be a great pitcher again, provided he cooperated with his rehabilitation. The problem was, he was the worst patient she'd ever seen in terms of coopera-tion. He resisted therapy, he argued with the treatment plan, and she knew damn well he wasn't doing his at-home exercises. He was one of those athletes who thought of himself as some kind of super-hero. Get injured, do rehab, and be fine in a few weeks.

Unfortunately, serious injuries didn't work that way, no matter how young or virile you were. You had to work at your own recovery. The team had done a fine job on their part. He just hadn't done any of his part. He blew off his therapists with jokes and promises to do better the next time. And they all liked him so they placated him.

Ugh.

What he really needed was a fulltime babysitter. Which she didn't want to be.

She lifted her head as Phil and Max came through the door, along with the Rivers' coach and general manager, Manny Magee.

Great. They brought the coach with them. She was definitely fired. Manny had a reputation for being fiery and loud. She might even get screamed at before they canned her ass.

She sat up straight and lifted her chin, determined to take it like the professional she was.

Correction. If she was a professional, she probably shouldn't have told the Rivers' star pitcher to pull his head out of his ass.

"Alicia," Phil said. "What you said to Garrett downstairs . . ."

"Yes, sir. I know. I was out of line. I'm sorry."

"Actually," Manny said, "it was exactly what he needed to hear."

She frowned and shifted her gaze to the coach. "Excuse me?"

"Garrett has been the perfect specimen of a pitcher for five seasons," Manny said. "We plucked him out of college ball, he spent six months in AAA before we brought him up, and he's been in our starting rotation ever since, with one of the lowest ERAs of any pitcher in the league. He's won the Cy Young Award twice, pitched a near-perfect game last year, and held the strike-out record the past two seasons. He's the golden boy."

She'd reviewed his file. She knew his record. But hearing it from Manny gave her an understanding. "He's never failed."

Manny nodded. "At anything. He doesn't know how. So having this injury threw him for a loop, ya know? The kid is one of the nicest people I've ever worked with, so don't take his black moods to heart. He'll get that kindness back once he finds his footing."

She looked from Manny to Phil to Max. "Wait. I'm not fired?"

Max laughed. "No, Alicia. You're not fired. Instead, we're putting you in charge of Garrett Scott's rehab."

Again—oh, shit. That's what she got for opening her mouth.

Phil and Max went over her new assignment. After they had left and Garrett came in a few minutes later, she stood, suddenly nervous. She'd always been a fan. The Rivers were, after all, her hometown team. And Garrett was nothing short of the most gorgeous man she'd ever laid eyes on. Six-feet-four inches of dark-haired, dark-eyed intensity, with a leanly honed body that was a work of art.

She'd spent her adult life studying body mechanics. She loved sports and sports players, and Garrett was one of the best.

And now he was all hers. Talk about a huge responsibility.

"They told you?"

She swallowed. "Yes. My question is . . . why me?"

He shrugged. "Because you stood up to me. I need to work with someone who isn't going to take shit from me. The rest of them tell me what they think I want to hear. They pacify me. I don't think you'll do that."

She needed to relax. Think of him as a patient, not a hot man standing only inches away.

"No, I definitely won't do that. I'm not going to take shit from you. And I'm going to work you until you beg me to stop. And when you beg me to stop, I'm not going to. I'm going to make you pitch again, Garrett. But it's not going to be easy."

"Okay. I cleared your schedule so you're only working with me."

She arched a brow. "You know, I can work with more than one player at a time."

"Probably. But you're only going to work with me."

A little ego there. Understandable. She'd deal with it. "Fine."

"Then let's get started."

"We will. On Monday. I'll take a few days to familiarize myself with your treatment plan, then develop one of my own. Since today's Friday, the weekend will give me the time I need."

"Fine." He whipped out his phone. "What's your number?"

She gave it to him.

"Okay, good. I'll call you on Sunday and we can get stuff set up. Does that work for you?"

"Sure." He gave her his number and she pulled her phone out of her pocket to add it in.

He was punching info into his phone, then lifted his gaze to hers. "What's your last name?"

"Riley."

His lips lifted. "Any relation to Gavin?"

"Actually, he's my cousin."

He looked up. "No shit. Is that how you got this job?"

He wasn't the first person to ask that question, and it always annoyed her. "No. I got this job because I'm good at sports medicine. I'm so good at sports medicine that you'll be pitching opening day, Garrett. Which has nothing to do with my cousin, and everything to do with me."

He laughed. "I like you, Alicia."

She wasn't sure how she felt about him. Jury was still out. She headed to the door. "You won't like me when I start kicking your ass, Garrett."